THE BASKERVILLE CAPER

FRANK NORMAN

THE
BASKERVILLE
CAPER

MACDONALD & CO
LONDON & SYDNEY

A Macdonald Book

First published in Great Britain in 1981 by
Macdonald & Co (Publishers) Ltd
London & Sydney

Copyright © Frank Norman 1981

ISBN 0 356 08530 9

Photoset by
Rowland Phototypesetting Ltd
Bury St Edmunds, Suffolk
Printed in Great Britain by
Redwood Burn Ltd
Trowbridge, Wiltshire
Bound at The Dorstel Press

Macdonald & Co
London & Sydney
Holywell House
Worship Street
London EC2 2EN

The last time I saw that early movie of *The Hound of the Basker-villes* on the box – the one starring Basil Rathbone as Sherlock Holmes – it crossed my mind that it might be a lovely caper for my own private eye, Ed Nelson, to reinvestigate. My thanks are also due to my wife, Geraldine, who, with not inconsiderable assistance from Sir Arthur Conan Doyle, provided me with a plot.

CHAPTER ONE

Down in the Hide Away club Willy Paradis's team of desperadoes were enjoying their lunch-hour booze-up and boastful conversation. Drummer Bill, Willy's first lieutenant, was telling me a bloodthirsty anecdote about the time he got himself togged up in a policeman's uniform and went down the East End to sort out the MacAllister firm single-handed. He'd told me the story at least sixteen times before and it never failed to make the hair at the nape of my neck stand on end. But then, as is widely known around the manor, I am a man who is prepared to listen to anyone so long as he is paying for the drinks.

'Bowled dahn there in my dirty great Yanky motor wiv a tommy-gun on the passenger seat,' he was saying. 'Drummed up on the knocker of Charlie MacAllister's gaff and shouted, "Open up in the name of the law". Ole Charlie comes to the door, in his dressin' gown and 'jarmers, and says, "Wotcha want copper?" an' I put fourteen slugs in 'im before 'e could say anuvva dicky bird. Then the rest of 'is team come beltin' aht from all over the gaff, abaht ten of 'em there was . . .' The last time he told me it was eight and the time before that six – the next time it would probably be a dozen. 'I sprayed the bleedin' lot of 'em wiv 'ot lead, soon as they put 'emselves on offer an' I left the soddin' gaff fulla dead men – there ain't been a team worth a light in the East End since.'

'Saint Valentine's day, wasn't it, Drummer?' I put in.

'Yeah,' he agreed eagerly, 'Saint Valentine's day nineteen forty-seven.'

'I saw the movie,' I said and polished off the dregs of my whisky.

Drummer tilted his eyes at me and a worried expression

passed over his face. He was trying to make up his mind whether or not I was taking the piss. But Drummer was as thick as two planks and deep thought came hard to him, so he let it go and told the barmaid to put up another round.

Then a heavy hand fell on my shoulder. I turned to find Willy Paradis leering at me. There was, in his ice blue eyes, the menacing glint that gangsters specialize in.

'Still boozin', are yah?' he rasped. 'Can't keep away, can yah, Ed?'

I said: 'I'm crazy about your decor, Willy,' and mustered a boyish smile. 'Not to mention the stimulating company.'

'Well, don't frow up on me carpet like yah did last Fursday night, uvvawise I'm gonna get the dead needle to yah, son.' He adopted a more affable tone of voice. ''Opin' ter meet up wiv that pound note geezer agin wotcha was 'avin' a cosy little rabbit wiv last night, are yah?'

'Pound note geezer? – down here?' I gasped incredulously. 'There hasn't been any class down here since the day they made shpielers legal and you moved in your first crooked roulette wheel.'

'Less of yah lip, son,' he warned. 'I'm talkin' abaht the geezer Ruby Bull brung dahn 'ere an' yah was chattin' up double-confidentchal like over at the corner table. Do yahself a bit of good, did yah?'

I thumped my forehead with the heel of my left hand.

'Hang on a sec,' I said. 'I think it's coming back to me. Little finger in tweeds and a shifty look in his eye, wasn't he?'

'It ain't fer nothing they reckon yah the shrewdest private eye on the manor,' sneered Willy. 'Wot wus yah rabbitin' abaht?'

'Do leave off, Willy,' I cried. 'I haven't been able to remember what happened yesterday for the past two and a half years. I suffer from what the medics call alcoholic amnesia. That's why people tell me things they wouldn't tell a priest – talking to me when I'm sloshed is like confiding in a brick wall, right?'

Willy nodded his agreement, but I could tell from the look in his eyes that he wasn't prepared to leave it at that.

'Try!' he snapped.

I gazed at him reproachfully. I couldn't work out what he was so interested for.

'What's it all about?' I asked craftily. 'As far as I can remember he was a dopey little bloke. Feeling a bit nervous in the company of underworld talent, I reckon. Can't think what he was doing down here – slumming around Soho dives went out of style in the early fifties. He seemed to be on the legit, although I know it's dangerous to go by appearances. He shelled out for doubles all evening and a mug punter who does that gets a licence to give me an ear bashing.'

'So 'e didn't lay no job on yah?' Willy wanted to know.

'I didn't wake up this morning with a pocketful of readies I couldn't account for,' I assured him. 'So the answer to that has got to be "no".'

'Yah sure?'

'Sure as the Pope is that he's going to Heaven when he kicks the bucket.' I lit another fag and slugged some more whisky. 'How come you're so interested in the little geezer, anyway?'

A smile rippled over Willy's ugly mug, like a man who's gone through the card at Catford dog-track, and his eyes began to sparkle.

'I've bin doin' a bit of figurin', know wot I mean?' he said.

I gazed at him mystified. 'What about?'

'That little bloke.' Willy preened himself. 'It was Ruby Bull wot brung 'im dahn 'ere, right?'

'Right,' I nodded. 'So what?'

'So wot I asked meself is a posh geezer in a 'airy 'ackin' jacket doin' in the company of a diabolical villain like Ruby Bull?' He underlined the point with a pregnant pause.

'Maybe he's Ruby's father?' I suggested.

9

Drummer, who had kept shtoom throughout the discussion said: 'Ruby's ole man is in Park'urst nick doin' a fifteen stretch, ain't 'e?'

''Course he is,' I agreed apologetically. 'He's been on the missing list so long I forget what happened to him.'

'Shutcha mouth an' pay attention,' snarled Willy. 'The reason why that sweed knows Ruby is because they're partners on some kind of tickle. Ruby's bin fencin' a lot of tomfoolery ter 'im more'n likely, that's 'ow come they're thick as thieves. Bizness associates, know wot I mean?'

I shrugged non-committally and looked for the meaning of life at the bottom of my empty glass.

'I'm not saying I remember anything much about the little twerp,' I admitted. 'But he certainly didn't come on like a bloke who fenced hot sparklers. Now I come to think about it, he kept on telling me about his business – I can't remember what the sodding hell it was, but it sounded straight enough to keep the income tax men chuckling all the way to the bank. If he'd been talking bent I reckon I'd've sussed him out, even pissed.'

Willy waved that aside with a flourish of the diamond ring on his pinky and said: 'E said 'is name was Reg Mortimer an' I tumbled right away that 'e was a bent antique dealer. Probably got a junkshop somwhere aht in the sticks.'

I beckoned to the barmaid and pointed at my empty glass, then turned to Willy and gave him another of my boyish smiles.

'How did you work that out, maestro?' I asked.

'A right doddle, Ed,' he replied enthusiastically. 'First off 'e looked a right berk in that tweed whistle and them brown boots caked with red mud – "never trust a bloke who wears brown boots" 'as always bin my motto, son. But the fing wot really got me thinkin' was the mud wot 'e 'ad all over 'em. There ain't no ploughed fields around So'o, right? So it stands ter reason that 'e'd've 'ad ter've brung it up wiv 'im from somewhere in the sticks, don't it?'

'You can't find enough earth in Soho, nowadays, to fill a

window-box,' I conceded. 'But you can swim in it in Hyde Park and Hampstead Heath?'

'Dead right there, son,' he replied thoughtfully. 'But any mud wotcha liable ter get on yer boots in 'Yde Park or 'Ampstead 'Eaf 'as gotta be the colour of dog shit on account of that's the only shade of mud we got in London, see?'

Not being a man who has made a close study of the colour of London mud I was unconvinced and found myself asking him how come he was so sure about the mud on Reg Mortimer's boots originating in the sticks. Drummer Bill gave me an evil glare and came up with the answer.

'The colour of poxy mud in the bleedin' Smoke is wotever fuckin' colour the guv'nor says it is.'

That kind of simple logic can be very dangerous to split hairs with, particularly when it is mouthed by a gangster. I gulped some whisky from my replenished glass and kept my trap shut.

'Fing is,' Willy explained doggedly. 'I 'ad a read of this book abaht geology when I was doin' a laggin' in Wandsworth just after the war.'

'The slammer is as good a place as any to catch up on your education,' I smiled. 'Clancy Murphy did a correspondence course on medieval English history while he was doing life for bumping off Dingo Sparrow, the Australian shoplifter. When Clancy got out on parole after eighteen years he had a PhD and got a job teaching Irish navvies at the Ruskin Workingmen's College in Camden Town.'

'Wot's a PhD?' Drummer demanded to know.

'I dunno,' I said. 'A kind of diploma you get when you've had a right old study up of something and pass an exam, I think.'

'Like the form yah get stacked up against yah dahn the Yard when yah done plenty of villainy?' he asked.

'Very similar,' I said.

'Fing abaht Clancy,' Willy put in, 'is all that stuff 'e studied up abaht suits of armour drove 'im right rahnd the twist. 'E now don't know nuffink abaht nuffink wot 'appened after ten sixty-six when King 'Arold got that arrow in 'is mince-pie when we 'ad that spot of bovva at 'Astings.'

Tearaways normally confine their topics of conversation to illegal transgressions they have successfully pulled off in the past, further transgressions they hope to pull off in the future, scrubbers they have caught clap off and time they have proudly served. Willy's utterances had his team agog and they gathered around to listen to what he might say next.

'Any old 'ow,' he continued. 'Like I was sayin', there's all kindsa different coloured mud in different parts of the country on account of the earf's crust ain't the same all over, right?'

'Right,' chorused the tearaways.

'So the full strengf of the situation is it's dahn to where yah are wot shade of dirtcha got. An' the dirtcha got in the Smoke is brown or black dahn ter yah differenchal fermal analysis, right?'

'Right,' they chorused again.

'Okay,' I sighed, 'so where did this bloke Mortimer get the red mud on his boots?'

'Devon,' said the tzar of Soho, without a moment's hesitation. 'Any ole lag wot's done bird on the Moor will tell yah that the rock-breakin' work party always comes back ter the nick, at bangin' up time, wiv a load of *red* mud on their boots.'

The hounds gazed at the governor in open-mouthed amazement for a moment or two, then gave him a round of applause.

'So you reckon he's an escaped convict?' I concluded when the boys had quietened down a bit.

'No, Ed, I ain't sayin' that,' snapped Willy. 'All I reckon is 'e comes from somewhere dahn in Devon and 'e's more'n likely got a junkshop.'

It was no skin off my nose who Reg Mortimer was or where the hell he came from. Why the cunning gangster was asking me a load of dopey questions about him was a complete mystery but then, of course, everything Willy Paradis does is shrouded in mystery.

I turned to the bar and reached for my drink. One of the lads had got in another round and the glass was full to the brim. It looked like the lunch-time session was going to take care of the rest of the day again. I'd just about got the glass gingerly to my lips when Willy jogged my elbow. Whisky splashed down my shirt front and soaked through to the skin.

'Thanks a bunch, mate,' I groaned. 'You're not satisfied I should pickle my kidneys in this stuff, you reckon I should take a bath in it as well?'

'There 'e is,' muttered Willy. 'The geezer I was on abaht.'

'Who?'

'The right sweed wiv the pound note accent.' He jabbed a thumb over his shoulder. 'The bloke in the 'Arris tweed whistle comin' in the door.'

I glanced over Willy's shoulder. Reg Mortimer, if that's who it was, was a little studious-looking bloke of about fifty. I seemed foggily to recall having had a drink or two with him the night before. He glanced about nervously, then headed in our direction.

'Good morning, Ed,' he beamed as he came up to the bar. 'I was hoping that I would find you here.'

With Willy earholing at my elbow I wasn't sure how to play it.

'How's it all going on?' I inquired cautiously. 'We met last night, did we?'

'We most certainly did, old boy. Don't say you've forgotten?' His voice had social climbing smeared all over it as thickly as treacle on a boarding-school suet pudding.

'Yeah,' I replied off-handedly, 'I remember you all right.'

'Good,' he said. 'What are you drinking?'

'Whisky, soda and ice,' I told him quick as a flash. 'Make it a large one.'

A guttural chuckle came out of Willy. I didn't look at him but kept a fixed smile on the tweed-clad country gent who was making a production over ordering a couple of drinks.

'I'm so pleased that you remember me, Ed,' he said, as I raised my glass to him. 'You will recall, no doubt, that we were introduced by our mutual friend, Ruby Bull, and I believe you said you were a private investigator.'

'Did I really?' I laughed. 'I try to keep quiet about that out of office hours.'

'Yes. I do realize that you may have been just a shade the better for drink.' He smirked and offered me his hand a second time. 'Reginald Mortimer is my name – I'm an antique dealer from North Devon.'

'There yah are,' Willy congratulated himself. 'Told yah so, didn't I?'

CHAPTER TWO

The next morning, hunched over a tabloid, at my usual corner table in the coffee shop across the road from the office, I nursed a monumental hangover. A small headline tucked away in the middle pages of the paper said: DRINK CAN DAMAGE THE BRAIN. It was no news to me. I lit another cigarette and ordered a third cup of black coffee. It was bucketing with rain outside. That and the galloping inertia that accompanies hangovers had not put me in the mood to scout around town for Lady Leach's emerald necklace.

It was an insurance company job, plain and simple, and my only current source of income. Acme Alliance had put me on the payroll – £25 a day plus expenses and mileage – last week. Bert Fagley, the 'small claims' manager, had got me on the blower and laid out the caper. A cat-burglar had turned over Lady Leach's swank Belgravia gaff while she was spending the evening at the opera and her emerald necklace had gone on the missing list. It was insured with the company for seventy-five grand. (Anything worth less than a hundred thousand comes under the jurisdiction of the 'small claims' department nowadays.) There was the usual ten per cent reward for its recovery, subject to the usual conditions: the return of the tomfoolery to its rightful owner and the arrest and conviction of the tea-leaf. It had Second Thoughts Steegmuller's MO written all over it, but I hadn't got around to having a cosy little bunny with him yet. Second Thoughts can get downright obstreperous with people who ask embarrassing questions about his chosen field of endeavour. So I wasn't exactly falling over myself to make a meet with him.

I reckoned it would be another day or two before Bert

Fagley started ringing me up with whining complaints about my lack of progress. Acme Alliance were a tight-fisted old Victorian firm who demanded results for their lolly. But they didn't have any details about my bottle-a-day drinking problem salted away in their computer so far as I knew. In which case a spot of beautifully phrased old moody would probably buy me another week on their pay-roll, maybe two if I added a dash of low cunning to the old moody. Upstarts like Bert Fagley are always selling me short – they are far too preoccupied with their own self-importance to realize what a clapped out jolthead I really am.

I gulped the last of my coffee, paid my bill at the cash desk and shambled back across the street to my office in Regent Chambers. I'd just got myself nicely curled up on the sofa and almost akip when some inconsiderate bleeder roused me with knuckles on the door.

'Who the hell is it?' I groaned.

'Reginald Mortimer.' He sounded determined to disturb my slumber.

'The office is closed today,' I shouted back. 'There's been a death in the family.'

'It's about a death in *my* family that I wish to speak to you,' cried Mortimer. 'Please let me in.'

I was tempted to tell him to 'bugger off', but my kindly nature got the better of me and I staggered across the room and opened the door.

'I'm sorry about your bereavement,' said Mortimer as he brushed by me. 'But I must talk to you.'

'I'm mourning the demise of my liver,' I said. 'Who's died in your family?'

He sat down in the clients' leather-upholstered chair. I went around the desk and slumped into the swivel.

'Well, it's not exactly a member of my family,' he explained sombrely. 'It's my very close and dear friend, Sir Charles Baskerville.'

I lit a snout and wondered if I ought to get out the Hankey Bannister's.

'What did he die of?' I asked absent-mindedly.

Mortimer braced himself and said: 'I'm not certain, Ed, but I think he may have been murdered.'

The decision about the Hankey Bannister's was taken for me. I yanked open the bottom drawer of the desk and reached for the bottle.

'Fancy a snort?' I asked.

'No thank you,' Mortimer sniffed reprovingly. 'It's far too early in the day to be drinking whisky. Even a fine old brand like Hankey Bannister's.'

'You know it?' I cried warming to him a little. 'I'm addicted to it, but there's only one pub I know of in Soho where they have it on the optic.'

'Yes I'm very partial to Hankey Bannister's,' Mortimer mused. 'Only wish it were more widely available. In the West Country it's difficult to find, even at better class wine merchants.'

'Sure you won't have a nip?' I asked him again.

'Well, perhaps just a small one to keep you company.'

I went over to the corner wash-basin and rinsed my tooth-glass under the cold tap.

'Say when,' I said, tilting the bottle over the glass.

'Just a light one with lots of water,' he said. 'Yes, yes that's plenty. No, no, no more. That's absolutely ample, thank you so much.'

I handed him the glass and gave myself a hefty belt in the cracked earthenware mug I usually used for instant coffee.

'Cheers, Reg,' I toasted him, tossed off half the drink and returned to the swivel. 'Hope you don't mind me calling you by your Christian name, mate. We Hankey Bannister connoisseurs are a rare breed and it'd be wrong of us to stand on ceremony, right?'

'Quite so, Ed,' he replied cautiously.

He sipped his whisky with his little finger sticking out like a dog's dick. People who drink with their little finger sticking out get up my nose. He was pushing our slender acquaintance to the limit – Hankey Bannister's or no Hankey Bannister's.

17

'I'd hoped to have a word with you in the Hide Away club yesterday,' he started out earnestly. 'But you seemed rather preoccupied.'

'I usually have a lot of elbow bending to do when I'm out and about around the manor,' I grinned.

Reg gave me the kind of disparaging look that schoolmasters reserve for badly behaved prep-school boys.

'There can be few private investigators who have managed to achieve such a close working-relationship with the underworld,' he told me. 'I was very impressed.'

'What do you mean "working"?' I growled, uncertain about what kind of a go it was he might be having at me.

'I take it you'd only go down a low dive like that when you were on a case. I trust you're not going to sit there and tell me you drink as heavily as that for pleasure?'

He let out an uneasy laugh and crossed his baggy tweed legs the other way round to how he'd had them before.

What I could have told him about going out on the booze with tearaways, bent CID filth and coppers' narks would make a riveting leader in *The Times*. But I was still unsure whether he was taking the piss. The losing battle I was fighting with my monumental hangover had left the old grey matter too fogged to work out anything as difficult as that. I gazed at him mournfully, wishing he'd just go away and leave me in peace.

'Let's just scrub round the introductory chatter,' I sighed. 'Why did you come to see me? Who was this Baskerville bloke and what d'you want me to do about it? But I'd better tell you right at the off, I don't touch murder cases.'

'Surely you could make an exception?' he urged. 'I'm not even certain this was a case of murder, it's just that I can't get the suspicion out of my mind and I have to find out.'

'Not a chance, mate,' I came back at him adamantly. 'The last time I made an *exception* and took on a murder case, I wound up in dead schtook and nearly got bumped off in a dark back alley by a dirty great hairy gorilla armed with a meat-axe. Now you wouldn't want a terrible thing like that to happen to me again, would you?'

He went a bit pink in the boatrace and started clucking with annoyance. At least I took it to be annoyance – with the notable exception of retired major-generals you can hardly ever tell when a bloke from the upper-classes is doing his nut.

He crossed his legs round the other way again and said: 'Ruby Bull gave you the strongest possible recommendation and I've spent two days trying to have a word with you.'

I began to feel a bit sorry for him. It can't have been much fun for a country bumpkin like him to drag around drinking dens in my wake.

'Tell you what I'll do,' I said guardedly. 'If you're prepared to lay a consultation fee on me, I'll listen to your story and maybe tell you where to find the kind of help you need.'

He produced a thin wad of tenners from the inside pocket of his hacking-jacket as quick as a flash. It appeared he'd come prepared for any eventuality – I wondered idly if he had a shiv up his sleeve or was packing a gun.

I trousered the lolly and shrugged slightly.

'I'm all yours, Reg,' I said. 'Let's have it.'

He reached into his inside pocket again and produced several newspaper cuttings.

'It's an extraordinary story, Ed,' he said, as he handed them over to me. 'These are cuttings from the *Western Morning News* and I think you should read them for a start.'

'Most of the yarns I get paid to listen to are pretty ropey,' I replied unenthusiastically and gave the clippings the once over.

The first was headlined TOURISTS SIGHT UFOs OVER GRIMPEN MIRE. The story beneath told about how several holiday-makers, from the Great Sourton caravan site, had seen a saucer-shaped, luminous object hovering over Grimpen Mire late at night. One eye witness, a

Mr Tom Tucker from Stepney Green, East London, said: 'Me and my old woman come out of the boozer at closing time and was walking back to the caravan site when all of a sudden we seen this dirty great thing up in the sky. All glowing it was, like it was on fire or something. To start with I thought it was the beer making me see things, know what I mean? See, they don't have the same beer down this neck of the woods as they do down the East End of London. But my old woman was on port and lemon and she seen it and all, so it must've been a flying saucer on account of port and lemon is the same all over, ain't it?' I glanced at the 'by line'. The hack's name was Fletcher Robinson. His racy style was wasted on a provincial daily. I guessed that he must be a cub reporter with his eyes on Fleet Street.

He went on to say that the local constabulary at the nearby village of Coombe Tracey had been unable to come up with any reasonable explanation for the sightings. But they had strongly denied the rumours, now rife in the neighbourhood, that Dartmoor was being invaded by Martian hordes. This, however, was not the view of Ivor Frankland of Lafter Hall. A keen amateur astronomer and well known locally for his somewhat eccentric behaviour, he had assured our intrepid *Morning News* reporter that he personally, through the powerful telescope in his attic, had observed the luminous flying object hovering over Grimpen Mire on no less than three occasions during the past month. There was not the slightest doubt in Frankland's mind that it could possibly be anything other than a space-craft from another planet – very likely Mars.

The second cutting, also carrying Fletcher Robinson's 'by line', said that a troop of boy scouts, rambling on the moor, had taken to their heels in disarray upon sighting a 'big silver, cigar-shaped object' darting about over their heads.

I glanced up at Reg and said: 'You going to tell me that your friend Sir Charles got bumped off by little green geezers from outer space?'

'I'm not entirely sure, Ed,' he replied. 'But it is certainly a possibility that we shouldn't rule out.'

'Outer space investigations are out of my orbit,' I smirked.

He rebuked me with his eyes and said: 'This is very far from a laughing matter, Ed, I assure you.'

'Sorry, mate,' I shrugged. 'Okay, let's hear the rest of it.'

'You can see from the cuttings how seriously these flying saucer stories are being taken in the neighbourhood. People are getting panicky. Even highly intelligent people are taking it seriously, like Frankland, for instance – he writes for the *Spectator*, you know.'

'What's that?' I asked.

'One of the most highly respected and influential weekly magazines in the country,' he cried, obviously surprised by my ignorance.

'That probably accounts for the fact that I've never heard of it,' I came back at him.

'Never mind,' he said. 'I only mentioned it so that you won't run away with the idea that Sir Charles was a complete ass for taking the UFOs so seriously. He was a very, very frightened man.'

I leaned back in the swivel, lit a fag and said: 'Fill me in on this Sir Charles geezer. Where did he get his handle from? What was he doing in the West Country? You know, that kind of stuff.'

'The Baskervilles are an old Devon family,' he explained. 'There've been baronets at Muddicoombe since the fourteenth century. But Sir Charles inherited the title alone. He didn't inherit any money but he made a large fortune, out of property speculation in the late sixties, and sold out just before the market slumped. He also made a number of successful investments in other areas and ended up a very wealthy man.'

'You've either got it or you ain't,' I murmured. 'Making lolly the easy way is a talent that a skint merchant like me knows nothing about.'

Reg scowled a little, but let it go and pressed on.

'Baskerville Hall had fallen into decay, through several decades of neglect, and Sir Charles decided to buy it back from the Rural District Council. I believe the old place had been used as a retreat for unmarried mothers for a time, and later as a boys' borstal. But for the past fifteen or twenty years it had been left to rot. It had been Sir Charles' life's ambition to buy back the property and restore it to its former grandeur.

'The council was only too thankful to get it off their hands again. Muddicoombe is pretty remote, you see, and they had no possible use for a large house there.'

'Sounds like the kind of tumbled-down dump that crooked estate agents unload on starry-eyed townies who are longing to have a little place, away from it all.'

He let that go too and continued: 'Sir Charles really put his heart and soul into doing it up. He got a top firm of builders over from Plymouth, had them go over the whole structure and strengthen it, put on a new roof of genuine old tiles – very difficult to find nowadays – and once the building was well under way, he started to put his mind to the furnishings. That's where I came in. He wanted everything in period, you know, which is no easy matter with a house that started life around 1450 and has been built on to by every generation since.'

'Sounds like a job for Oliver Messel,' I smiled. 'I was once up in the penthouse suite he did at the Dorchester Hotel, very tasteful. Got invited up there by a movie actress who wanted me to sort out some kind of love triangle her husband had got tied up in with a couple of rough trade sailors – never did get to the *bottom* of it.'

'Please hear me out, Ed.' He was getting testy about the interruptions.

'Sorry,' I said and shtoomed up.

'When you see the house you'll understand the problem,' he continued earnestly. 'But I think you'll be impressed by what we achieved.'

I decided not to argue about the way he was taking it for granted that I was going down there.

'A man can do anything once he sets his mind to it,' I remarked kindly. 'Particularly if he's got plenty of gelt to back the project.'

'Quite so,' he agreed. 'From what I've told you, I'm sure you'll understand why Sir Charles was such a happy, thoroughly fulfilled man. That's what made it so awful when he started to fall apart over the UFO business. It was frightful to watch a man one really admired crack up like that.' He let out a long heavy sigh.

'How about a spot more whisky?' I suggested sympathetically.

'Well, perhaps just a little,' he said. 'I find it rather upsetting to talk about this ghastly business, I must confess.'

I replenished his glass and my earthenware mug, then returned to the swivel and gazed at him attentively across the desk.

'I remember vividly the day that Sir Charles saw the mysterious flying object for the first time,' Reg continued. 'It was quite late at night on the fourteenth of April this year.'

I made a note of the date on my ink blotter and said: 'That would be a little over six months ago?'

'Quite so, quite so,' he agreed. 'I was relaxing in the living accommodation above my shop in Coombe Tracey when suddenly I heard a car screech to a halt outside. I went over to the window and peeped through the curtains expecting to see one of those beastly unwashed caravan dwellers from London being breathalysed by the police. Drunken driving has become quite a problem in the area in recent times and there is usually a police car parked outside the Devil's Stone Inn at closing time. But to my complete surprise it was Sir Charles' Rolls parked untidily at the kerb so I hurried downstairs to let him in.' He lifted his glass to his lips with trembling fingers and quaffed his whisky. 'He was absolutely ashen-faced, Ed, and shaking from head to toe. I helped him upstairs to my little sitting-room and when I'd got him into an armchair and poured him a large brandy I asked him what on earth had happened. For a time he seemed unable to speak, but eventually he blurted out that he had just been pursued across Baskerville Park by a flying saucer full of "little green demons".'

Reg let out a little laugh. 'Well, to begin with, as you may well imagine, I thought that he was pulling my leg or had had a little too much to drink. But he was in such an agitated frame of mind that I was compelled to take him seriously. I put him up in my spare room that night and the following morning he seemed to have completely recovered from the ordeal. We returned to Baskerville Hall to investigate the matter. But a full day spent tramping on the moor revealed no trace of the flying object and no clue to its whereabouts – if indeed it existed at all. Reluctant though I was to suggest to Sir Charles that he had been imagining things, I did point out that the mist over the moorland can often be strangely deceptive. But he dismissed my suggestion angrily.

'During the next few weeks Sir Charles' general demeanour went from bad to worse as his sightings of the UFOs became more and more frequent until eventually, I must confess, I feared for his sanity.'

'Sounds like the kind of stuff that could easily drive a bloke bonkers,' I conceded.

'Finally I suggested to him that he got right away from Muddicoombe for a while and went to the villa he was building in Tenerife. His doctor had apparently been suggesting just the same. Sir Charles had a heart condition and the state he was in over the UFOs was putting an intolerable strain on it. It was obviously a sensible plan and Sir Charles was to leave on July the 14th. On July the 12th we had a farewell dinner together; Mrs Barrymore, the housekeeper, is a marvellous cook and really excelled herself. That was the last time I saw him alive.'

Reg bowed his head and drew a hand across his eyes with a deep sigh.

'Cheer up,' I said. 'You'd better let me in on the final act of the drama or I shan't be able to advise you.' I looked at my watch. 'Pubs will be open soon, you know,' I warned him.

'Well, it just so happened that the following night, at a little after eleven, I was driving along the main road that passes the drive of Baskerville Hall when suddenly a man leapt into the road right in front of me waving his hands above his head. I braked violently and pulled into the hedgerow and there in my headlights, to my utter astonishment, stood Mr Barrymore, the butler. He seemed to be in an extremely agitated state and when I got out of the car and went up to him he was trembling and dumb with fear. I managed with some difficulty to get him into the car. Halfway along the drive to Baskerville Hall he had recovered sufficiently to blurt out: "Sir Charles is dead, sir. Sir Charles is dead." "Where is he?" I asked him. "How did it happen?" But Barrymore was in such an overwrought state that I could get no sense out of him until we had arrived at the house and he pointed a trembling finger down the yew alley.'

'What's a yew alley?' I put in.

'An avenue of yew trees with a path down the middle.'

I lit a cigarette and nodded to him to continue.

'Well, I parked the car at the end of the yew alley, left the headlights full on, and went to investigate. I found Sir Charles' body crumpled on the grass verge quite close to the far end. The yew alley is about fifty yards long; there is an old summer-house at the end and a gate that leads out on to the moor halfway down. Sir Charles was lying face down and when I turned him over the car headlights lit up his face.' He paused and shivered at the memory. 'The sheer terror etched on it was the most ghastly sight I have ever seen. It has haunted me ever since, Ed – it was as though he had been possessed by demons. I formed the opinion that he had been literally terrified to death. I sent Barrymore back to the house to phone for the police and I scouted around, as best I could by the light of my car's headlamps, to see if I could find some clue to how Sir Charles could have met such a hideous end.'

I gazed at him soberly, then looked down at the glowing end of my cigarette.

'Did you find any clues?'

'I'm not sure,' he replied candidly. 'But there were one or two things that I thought decidedly odd.'

'Such as?'

'Well, firstly there were the footprints. It had rained quite heavily earlier in the day and Sir Charles' footprints were clearly visible on the muddy path down the yew alley. The peculiar thing was that those coming down the path after the gate changed suddenly as though Sir Charles had begun to creep along on tiptoe.'

'Sounds like he was having it away on his toes a bit lively,' I volunteered.

'That is exactly the conclusion that I came to, Ed,' cried Mortimer. 'He was running away from something.'

'Aren't we all,' I sighed. 'What else did you discover?'

'Sir Charles' footprints were not the only ones that I saw in the yew alley.'

'Well, if Barrymore found the body there would be his as well.'

'Yes, of course, but there were others.'

'A man's or a woman's?'

Reg gave me a dodgy look and his voice sank almost to a whisper as he answered:

'Ed, they were the footprints of a gigantic hound!'

CHAPTER THREE

It crossed my mind to tell the geezer that you don't normally find dogs in flying saucers – but I decided that it was a grey area not worth getting into. Then the phone rang – the jangling bell cut through my aching head like a rusty knife. I made a grab for it and almost fell on the floor.

'Go away,' I grated into the receiver.

'Feelin' knackered are yah, Ed?' a familiar voice rasped in my ear.

'No more than usual, Willy,' I said. 'What can I do for you?'

'It's more like wot I can do fer you, son,' grunted the crafty old gangster. 'Yah got that little shmock from the sticks wiv yah, ain'tcha?'

'How did you know that?' I asked.

'Yah ain't finkin', Ed,' he chuckled. 'Ain't nuffink buzzin' on my manor I don't know abaht, is there, son?'

'Yeah, yeah,' I sighed and started thinking. Willy Paradis had had Reg followed, that much was clear. What for, was another matter. 'So what d'you want?' I inquired.

'Tell the geezer I know Dartmoor like the back of me German an' if sumink dodgy 'as come orf dahn there I'm definitely the bloke wot can sort it aht, right?'

'You've got a one-track mind, Willy,' I clipped. 'What makes you so sure it's villainy he's on about?'

A deafening roar of laughter split my eardrum.

'Do me a favour, son!' he bellowed. 'When was the last time someone knocked on yah door 'oo wasn't up ter their ear'oles in skullduggery?'

I delved about in my empty head for a decent wisecrack.

'I won't dignify that remark with an answer, mate,' was the best I could come up with. 'So what if he's laid a few quid on me for a bit of advice? – It doesn't mean I'm taking the case . . .'

'Since when 'ave yah bin in a position to pick an' choose?' he put in.

'Since I picked this bleedin' phone up,' I told him. 'If a diabolical tearaway like you starts sticking his hooter in a case of mine before it's even got off the ground I'd need my brains tested if I didn't back off, right?'

'Watch yah mouf, son,' Willy warned, 'or yah might find yahself wivaht no brains left ter get tested.'

'Okay,' I said, in a more affable voice. 'But do you mind declaring your interest?'

'Not on the blower,' he snapped. 'Just tell the little geezer that Willy Paradis 'as put 'imself on offer. I'll tell yah the full strengf later. Just fetch 'im dahn the club an' we'll 'ave a little drink and a rabbit.'

I was pretty sure that it would end in a lot more bother than I could handle, but I found myself agreeing.

'When?'

'Right nah,' he said. 'I'm goin' ter the races this arternoon.'

I said: 'See what I can do,' and hung up.

The next thought that popped into my head was that it was no skin off my nose if Willy wanted to get in on the act. In fact, it was double handy and would probably give me a very good reason for walking away from the case before the off. But I'd lifted a consultation fee off poor old Reg, so the least I could do was advise him where to turn to for help. And if it did turn out to be a murder investigation, Willy was welcome to it.

Reg wasn't exactly delighted at the idea of seeking help from a racketeer. In fact, he took more persuading to pay a return visit to the Hide Away club than it takes to induce an Irish colleen to part with her virginity. He caved in at last, but only when I'd promised to stick around and see he came to no harm. It was an idle promise, but then, my craggy dependable face always has belied my chicken liver.

'Who's next in line for the baronetcy?' I asked him as we dodged along the crowded pavement on our way to our meet with Willy.

'Henry Baskerville,' he replied. 'He's a cousin of Sir Charles and has, for the past three years, been third secretary at the British Embassy in Kuwait. As executor of Sir Charles' will I can tell you that, as well as the title and the Baskerville estate, Sir Henry will inherit the vast fortune that Sir Charles accumulated over the years from his various speculations in the property market.'

'How much is that likely to come to?' I asked.

'Something in excess of two million, even after death duties,' he confided.

'Much as that?' I gasped. 'I wouldn't put that about if I was you, Reg. Especially around this manor. A rumour, in the Soho underworld, about someone coming into that kind of spondulicks is liable to get the natives over-excited – Willy Paradis, in particular, has been known to lose control of himself completely at the prospect of getting his grubby mitts on large amounts of money that don't belong to him.'

'I will bear that in mind, Ed,' Reg replied shakily.

'So what happens next?' I asked. 'Has the baronet shown up yet to claim his inheritance, or is he still playing Lawrence of Arabia in the desert?'

'Sir Henry has now resigned from the Foreign Office,' he told me. 'He has decided to live at Baskerville Hall and run the estate. I had a cable from him a day or two ago requesting me to meet him off the five-thirty flight from Kuwait this evening.'

'Heathrow?' I asked.

'Yes, I have arranged for a limousine to pick me up at the Savoy at four-thirty. Perhaps you'd like to come?'

I declined just a little too snappily and when he showed no signs of taking offence, I quickly asked him if there were any more clues on how Sir Charles might have snuffed it.

'There is one thing,' he said hesitantly. 'I'm afraid Sir

29

Charles had taken to smoking Cannabis. Some friends in the pop music world had got him into the habit of smoking it. And in an effort to keep the guilty secret from the domestic staff at Baskerville Hall – Mr and Mrs Barrymore, who serve as butler and housekeeper – he only smoked the stuff out of doors. Every evening he would amble up the yew alley puffing away at a hand rolled cigarette or two.

'On the night he died he had leaned on the wicket gate halfway down the alley that gave on to the moor while he inhaled his drugged smoke for the last time. As it so happened I found the stub or roach, as I believe it is known in the drug world, of the cigarette lying there beside the path. I pocketed it before the police arrived. There seemed no point in letting the authorities in on Sir Charles' little secret after he had passed on.'

'I see,' I replied thoughtfully. 'I take it that means you think that whatever frightened him to death appeared while he was leaning on the gate finishing his joint?'

'Quite so, Ed.'

'Then he ran away down the yew alley and his ticker packed up?'

'Yes.'

'And you found him lying there about an hour or so later with his face horribly contorted with terror?'

'Yes.'

'Why didn't he make for the house?' I wondered aloud. 'From what you've told me I get the impression he was running in the opposite direction.'

'Quite so,' he agreed. 'The way I see it, he was being chased.'

I said: 'I see,' and left it at that.

We'd reached the Hide Away and I led the way down the filthy old stairs into the gangster's parlour.

Willy was grinning all over his cunning kisser as he welcomed us. He ushered us to a quiet corner table and ordered double Scotches all round. For some mystifying reason Reg still hadn't got the message that I ran on whisky and that the more of it I drank the better I worked. But the disapproving look that took possession of his face soon evaporated when Willy pressed a vintage bottle of champagne on him. The wily old villain knew what kind of juice appeals to social climbers.

Then we got down to business. Reg ran through the flying saucer stuff again and Willy studied the news clippings with a twinkle of amused disbelief in his mince-pies. Under the influence of vintage Bollinger the story of Sir Charles' demise was even more sinister and chilling than first time round.

Willy laid a number of pertinent questions on him and rocked back in his chair eyeing us speculatively.

Then without any mucking about he told Reg what he'd better do about it: take Ed Nelson down to Devon with him to sort out the mystery.

'Thanks a lot,' I groaned and took a hefty slug out of my third double whisky.

'That is exactly what I want to do,' Reg cried enthusiastically. 'I only wish I could persuade him.'

'Yah can leave that ter me, Reg,' Willy grinned wickedly. He stood up and jerked a thumb over his shoulder. 'Come over the bar, Ed, I wanna little bunny wiv yah in private.'

I scraped back my chair and followed him, clutching my drink and thinking about making a dash for the door.

I am not a bloke who takes kindly to being ordered about even by geezers who are liable to fill me in if I refuse to bend to their wishes. But I'd known Willy long enough to realize that he wasn't the kind of chap it was wise to argue with – the time had come for a spot of low cunning.

'What's your interest in this caper, Willy?' I asked him straight out.

He glanced about to make sure that we would not be overheard. His team of scallywags were at the far end of the bar, deeply immersed in a six-handed game of spoof. The top-heavy barmaid was watching them.

'Fing is, Ed, I wantcha ter keep an eye on 'im for me,' he said out of the corner of his mouth.

'Who?'

He flicked his eyes in Reg Mortimer's direction, ''Im.'

'Why?'

'Got me reasons.'

'Listen, guv,' I snapped. 'If you reckon I'm going to belt two and a half hundred miles down the motorway on a blind date, you've got another think coming. If you want me and Drummer to have a knuckle about it on the cobbles that's fine by me, OK?'

'Awright, awright, son.' He passed a hand wearily over his pudding face. 'I don't want no bloodshed dahn ter larkin', but if I blow dahn yah ear'ole yah gotta stay shtoom, right?'

I nodded and reminded him of the motto printed on my business card: STRICT SECRECY OBSERVED. I'd cribbed it from the back page of my Post Office saving account book – no private eye can hope to reign long without a few quid in the Post Office because he never knows where he's going to be the next time he runs out of readies. The few confidences of my clients that I actually remember were as safe with me as they would be in a bank vault.

'It's like this 'ere,' he told me in a barely audible voice. 'As it 'appens it's double 'andy that little finger comin' in 'ere wiv that potty story abaht that Baskerville geezer gettin' bumped orf. It so 'appens there's a nice little tickle building up wiv containerisation of bent merchandise wot's bin 'arf inched outa stately 'omes aht in the sticks, see? Me an' the lads 'ave got the London end nailed dahn tight as a coffin and we sees ter it that no uvva firm gets a look in. It's set up right as ninepence, son, and we guarantees ter get all the stuff that comes our way aht of the country wivin twenty-four 'ours, geddit?'

'I get it,' I chuckled. 'Big time fencing with our partners in the Common Market. It had to come sooner or later, but I don't see what it's got to do with the Baskerville caper and all that old nonsense about UFOs on Dartmoor.'

'It ain't got nuffink ter do wiv it at all, mate,' he agreed. 'Leastways I don't fink it 'as. Wot I've got the dead needle abaht is that some crafty bleeder is creamin' orf big jobs west of Taunton and sneakin' dirty great containers ahter Plymouff, see?'

'My, my,' I grinned. 'I do believe I'm beginning to cotton on. Some enterprising fella is showing a bit of initiative and taking you to the cleaners.'

'Yeah,' Willy growled, 'an' when I get me mitts on 'im 'e's gonna be double sorry abaht it. I sent one a me team dahn ter Plymouff ter suss fings aht and froo 'avin' a right study up of the ordnance survey maps, every time the scream goes up abaht anuvva country 'ouse gettin' turned over, we've narrared the centre of operation dahn ter wivin ten miles of this Muddicoombe dump. That's 'ow me lug'oles started flappin' even more when I tumbled 'e was an antique dealer.'

'And right away you jump to the conclusion that he's the brains behind it?' I asked in astonishment.

'Yah know me meffods,' he replied cautiously. 'I'm prepared ter admit 'e don't look like a geezer wiv 'is nut screwed on right. But it don't do ter underestimate a sweed, even if 'e do come on like 'e don't know wot time of day it is.'

I glanced across the room at Reg, he was beginning to look pretty lonely sitting at the corner table all on his tod.

'All that's as may be,' I said. 'But what if it *does* turn out to be a murder case? – And what if the flying saucer turns out to be real?'

'In that case,' laughed Willy, 'you'll be able ter clean up all rahnd. I mean ter say if yah manage ter capture a little green geezer from Mars single 'anded just fink of all the publicity yah bound to get in the linens – probably wind up on TV even.'

'I'm not going,' I gulped, 'and that's final.'

'Suitcha self, son,' he replied easily. 'But if yah don't yah might as well shut up shop. Yah all washed up on this manor an' one a these dark nights yah got a right kickin' comin' from me an' the chaps.'

'You're a wonderful human being, Willy,' I sneered. 'All heart, know what I mean?'

'Yeah,' he beamed. 'It means yah got the message an' yah goin', right?'

'Only if I'm on wages,' I said.

'Sure fing, Ed,' he said. 'Knew yah wouldn't let an old pal dahn an' if yah nab the brains be'ind the outfit bang to rights there'll be a nice bundle of lolly in it for yah.'

'How about a few quid walking about money?' I followed up fast.

CHAPTER FOUR

The old liver wasn't in very good nick the next morning, nor were the kidneys and brain cells. But I hadn't felt all that marvellous for some years and morning sickness had long been par for the course. I pulled on my trousers and crawled across the room to the corner wash-basin. I washed and shaved then rummaged about in the bottom drawer of the filing cabinet for a clean shirt. I couldn't find one and resolved there and then that this was going to be the day that I paid a visit to Wai Lim Fucs Chinese laundry in Brewer Street to get my shirts back. They had been there for something like two months and I had had to survive as best I could on a couple of polyester drip-drys. I put on the one I'd already worn for two days on the trot and filled the electric kettle with cold water.

As I settled down in the swivel chair behind my desk with a mug of Maxwell House instant coffee and my first smoke of the day the phone rang. It was Bert Fagley, the small claims manager at Acme Alliance.

'How's things going with Lady Leach's emerald neck-lace?' he asked in that squeaky voice of his.

'Fine,' I lied. 'I'm seeing a grass at lunch-time.'

'Splendid,' he shrilled. 'Then I can expect to have some good news from you this afternoon?'

'Maybe,' I said. 'Maybe not.'

His tone grew restive.

'Look, Ed, there's a board meeting tomorrow. Lady Leach is on the phone to me two or three times a day demanding a settlement of her claim and the chairman is going to want to know what progress you are making.'

I said: 'Tell him I'm working on it,' and took a deep drag on my cigarette. The smoke went down the wrong hole and I was seized by a nasty coughing spasm.

'Honestly, Ed,' cried Bert. 'If you don't stop chain-smoking you'll get cancer and die.'

'Thanks a lot, Bert,' I groaned. 'I'll be in touch.'

'Hold on, hold on,' he said. 'Look, I must have a written progress report from you before the board meeting in the morning.'

I said: 'I hope you get it,' and hung up.

Next on the line was Reg Mortimer. He sounded in less of a panic than he had the day before.

'How are you, Ed?' he started out. 'I hope you are well.'

'There's nothing wrong with me that a million quid and the love of a good woman wouldn't take care of,' I told him.

He ignored that and pressed on.

'I've explained the whole situation to Sir Henry and I'm happy to say that he feels just as I do. We owe it to his cousin's memory to try to clear the mystery up.'

'I was afraid he might,' I sighed.

'Really, Ed,' huffed Mortimer. 'I don't think that joke was in very good taste.'

'That was no joke, mate,' I came back at him. He chose to ignore me.

'Sir Henry feels that he should be the one to commission the investigation. I have to admit that I was hoping he would agree that your fees should be paid out of the estate, but he says that he would prefer to take the whole thing over himself.'

'Maybe he'd like to take the case to one of the big agencies up West,' I suggested hopefully.

'He is perfectly satisfied with my choice of investigator,' Reg assured me. 'I told him that you'd been highly recommended to me but of course he wants to meet you and discuss terms with you himself.'

'My charges are sky-high for out of London jobs,' I warned him quickly.

'I'll bring Sir Henry round to see you right away, if

that's convenient,' continued Reg, churlishly ignoring my warning.

'If you must, you must,' I sighed.

'We'll be with you in half an hour,' Reg clipped and hung up.

About thirty-five minutes later I heard the wheeze and clank of the old lift in the distance, trying to make up its mind whether it was working this morning. At the same moment my telephone jangled. I grabbed hold of the receiver and said: 'What's new?' into the mouthpiece.

It was Willy Paradis.

'They're on their way up nah,' he informed me.

'Who?' I asked.

'Reg Mortimer and the baronet geezer,' said Willy. 'An I wonna be sure as how yah goin' to treat 'im nice, Ed. No bunging 'im a load of old moody an' gettin' yahself aht of it, know what I mean?'

'I know what you mean,' I groaned.

'And don't overcharge 'im.'

'But I always charge fifty a day out of London,' I wailed.

'Firty-five top whack,' he informed me severely. 'And anuvva fing. My boys bin on his tail since 'e arrived at 'Eathrow and 'e's being followed. Know anything abaht that, do yer?'

'If he's got your boys on his tail, it stands to reason he's being followed,' I pointed out.

'Some uvva geezer's followin' 'im an' all,' Willy informed me. 'Geezer in a white Mercedes. I'd pop dahn and take a butchers at 'im when Sir 'Enry leaves, if I was you. 'E's parked across the street nah, outside the 'Amburger 'Aven.'

'I'll take a look,' I agreed. 'Better hang up now. I think they're here.' Two sets of purposeful footsteps were approaching down the passage.

'Keep in touch,' said Willy and rang off.

There was a rap at the door and I stood up to open it – just in case Willy had one of his boys watching through the window with a telescope to make sure I treated my guests respectfully, Reg Mortimer made the formal introductions.

'Sir Henry Baskerville,' he said. 'Ed Nelson.'

We shook hands, smiled unctuously and sized each other up like prize fighters at the weigh in.

'So pleased to meet you, Mr Nelson,' said the young baronet. 'Mortimer has told me so much about you and I am delighted that you have agreed to look into the suspicious circumstances surrounding my poor cousin's death.'

Members of the British aristocracy, as everyone knows, are always immaculately dressed, incredibly tall and handsome, devastatingly charming and debonair. They stand out in a crowd; girls swoon at the sight of them; policemen salute them and bank managers lend them money without the slightest hesitation. But the little rat-faced, wiry-haired bloke that had just walked in looked more like a door to door salesman than he did a peer of the realm.

Glancing at his watch, he marched across to the clients' leather chair and plonked himself down. Reg looked around for somewhere to settle and I waved to the sofa.

'I haven't very much time,' Sir Henry informed me in clipped tones. 'Got to get down the the F.O. and fill a few people in.'

I smiled secretly at what Willy might have made of that one had he heard it, and nodded Sir Henry my encouragement.

'As far as I can see, the best thing will be if you come down and stay at Baskerville Hall with me,' he informed me in a friendly but bossy tone. 'I gather that the couple called Barrymore that my cousin employed to look after the place have stayed on, so an extra guest should be no problem. How long do you expect the investigation to take you and what are your charges?'

'Thirty-five a day and expenses,' I said, taking the most important question first. 'I would certainly hope that it could be cleared up within a week.'

Reg Mortimer snorted: 'Most unlikely! If it was as easy as that, we local people would have got to the bottom of it already. I should reckon a month, Sir Henry, if I was you.'

I glared at Reg resentfully. Who'd asked him to interfere? All I was short of was a month in the sodding country.

'Well, if it turns out to be a week, fine,' said the rat-faced baronet. 'But if you find it takes longer, Mr Nelson, so be it. All the same, I don't want to have this hanging over my head for more than a month.'

'Me neither,' I agreed heartily.

He leaned back and put his stubby, well-manicured fingertips together. He gazed at me over them with pursed lips.

'That's fixed then,' he said. 'When do you want to start? I shan't be going down to Devon for a day or two as I have business to clear up in London, but you're welcome to go on ahead.'

'Not likely, guv,' I quickly assured him.

'Shall we say Thursday?' he asked, taking out his diary.

'I'm not sure that I'll be able to make it that soon,' I temporized. 'I'll let you know.'

He tucked his diary away again and I had a brain-wave.

'How about a glass of whisky to set the seal on our bargain?' I gave my new client a winning smile and bent down to yank open the Hankey Bannister drawer.

'Good God! Not at this hour!' exploded Reg Mortimer.

I gave him a reproachful look and said: 'I never expected to hear such sentiments from a Hankey Bannister drinker.'

To my surprise and relief, the brisk Sir Henry melted suddenly, and gave me a broad smile.

'It's quite wrong to think that there's a right time or a wrong time for a drink,' he informed us sagaciously. 'Look what opening hours have done to Britain. Lost us the Empire.'

I'd never heard that theory before but it seemed sensible enough to me. I warmed to this little wire-haired terrier of a multi-millionaire and grinned at Reg.

He put his hooter in the air and said: 'Well, I would have thought that we should discuss the new developments before a party spirit begins to prevail.'

'Quite right,' said Sir Henry, and glanced at his watch again. 'What's more I must be at the F.O. in fifteen minutes. I'm afraid I shall have to turn down the drink on this occasion, Mr Nelson – with many thanks, of course.' He gave me a companionable smile as I plonked the bottle on the desk. I poured a slug into the mug I'd been drinking coffee out of and lifted it to my lips.

'Only sorry you won't join me,' I told them both. 'What's this about new developments?'

'Mr Mortimer is referring, I take it, to the curious note that was delivered to me at the Savoy this morning,' said Sir Henry. He plunged a hand into an inside pocket, produced an envelope and took out a sheet of white quarto that had been folded into four.

Sir Henry handed me the note without a word and, with Reg craning his neck over my shoulder, I took a gander at it. Across the middle of the page a single sentence had been formed from words scissored from a newspaper and pasted to the paper. It read: 'As you value your life or your reason keep away from the moor.'

'What in thunder do you make of that, Ed?' Sir Henry demanded.

'Dunno,' I replied, thoughtfully. 'But it definitely looks like someone is trying to stick the frighteners on you.'

'That is quite obvious, I'd have thought,' Reg snapped impatiently.

'D'you mind if I hang on to it?' I asked, ignoring him. 'I'd like to make a few inquiries.'

Sir Henry bowed his agreement. 'The case is now in your hands,' he said.

I folded the note up again and slipped it into my pocket.

'That is certainly a very interesting and sinister development,' I told them, hoping that I was sounding impressive. 'Could be that the bloke who bumped off your cousin is now after you. We mustn't rule it out.'

The baronet took a hissing intake of breath and said: 'I certainly hope you're wrong.'

'Anything else dodgy happened?' I asked, wondering whether he'd noticed the white Mercedes that Willy said was following him around – or Willy's own boys for that matter.

Sir Henry stroked his chin thoughtfully. He hesitated a moment and then began to speak.

'Something slightly odd happened just as we were leaving the hotel, but it's such a minor matter I hardly think it's worth mentioning.'

'Better get it off your chest,' I encouraged him. 'You can never tell what's going to turn into a clue these days.'

'I should explain,' he began, 'that I came back from Kuwait with only the thinnest of tropical suits. Although it's only October, it's already quite chilly, so I popped out first thing this morning to the Savoy Taylors' Guild on the corner of the Strand and bought a couple of tweed jackets. I told them to send the jackets over to me at the hotel and walked across to the Grill to get some breakfast. When I went up to my room afterwards, the maid was just hanging up one of the jackets in my cupboard. The other hadn't arrived. The shop swore they'd sent it, but somehow it went missing between them and my room.'

'Have you mentioned it to your floor valet?' asked Reg.

'What would my floor valet want with a brand new jacket?' he inquired sensibly. 'But I'll ring for him after lunch, for what good it'll do.'

Reg said: 'I'm sure there is some perfectly innocent explanation.'

Sir Henry turned his attention to me.

'What do you think, Mr Nelson?' he asked. 'Quite a mystery wouldn't you say?'

'Not really,' I replied. 'People are lifting jackets that don't belong to them in hotels all over London.'

'Good heavens,' cried Sir Henry. 'Are they really? One gets so out of touch overseas.'

'It's the wallets and credit cards in the pockets, they're really after,' I explained.

'But surely any sneak thief would realize that he would be unlikely to find a wallet or credit cards in the pockets of a new jacket that was still in the wrapping paper from the shop at which it was purchased.'

I didn't have a quick answer to that. I shtoomed up and pondered the mystery. The thing that bugged me was that Sir Henry had said there were two of them. If the tea-leaf had half-inched the jacket, not for the contents of its pockets, but because it was brand new and maybe his size, why hadn't he swiped both of them?

I wasn't left much time for pondering, however. Having got the affair of the jacket off his chest Sir Henry jumped up and made for the door, braying at Reg to follow him at the double or he'd be late for his appointment at the F.O.

'Sorry to dash,' he said, giving my hand a brief muscular clasp. 'How about lunching with me at the Savoy tomorrow to talk things over?'

'I never turn down a good nosh,' I smiled.

'See you in the American bar at quarter to one,' he said and marched out of the office.

I gave them time to shut themselves in the lift and crank down a floor. Then I raced down the stairs.

I peeked out of my front door at the hurrying hurly-burly of Haymarket crowds and traffic. Reg and Sir Henry were waiting to cross the road at the lights. A white Mercedes was edging out into the traffic on the far side of the road. It was driven by a man with a bushy black beard and the licence plates read PHY 64 Q.

CHAPTER FIVE

I went and collected my clean shirts from the Chinese laundry as I had promised myself I would, and when I got back a little geezer from the Soho underworld called Second Thoughts Steegmuller was hanging about on the landing waiting for me.

'Wotcha, Second Thoughts,' I greeted him brightly. 'What's buzzing?'

'I wonna little rabbit wiv yer, Ed,' he said, out of the corner of his mouth.

'What about?'

'In the orffice,' he whispered. 'It'll be more private.'

'Okay,' I said and unlocked the door.

He followed me inside, glancing furtively about as though he expected the room to be full of CID.

'Take a seat, Second Thoughts,' I pointed at the clients' leather-upholstered chair. 'Fancy a slug of whisky?'

'On the wagon,' he muttered. 'Doctor's orders.'

'Best thing you can do,' I advised him, 'is change your doctor.'

I poured three fingers of Hankey Bannister's into my tooth-glass.

'I might be able ter do yah a bit a good,' said Second Thoughts. 'On the uvva 'and I might not.'

'Such as?' I grinned.

'Depends.'

'What on?'

'Wevva I get me whack of the reward money and yah don't grass me to the filth,' he replied sensibly. 'Or wevva I get nuffink and wind up gettin' me collar felt.'

'Ever known me to grass anyone?' I demanded.

'Wot abaht Meataxe 'Iggins?'

43

'I didn't grass Meataxe Higgins,' I snapped. 'I persuaded him to give himself up, over a police loudhailer,
when his gaff was staked out with armed marksmen after
he'd gone berserk down Wozzo Newman's spieler and
carved up most of French Henry's tearaways. He thanked
me for it afterwards and we still exchange Christmas
cards – he ought to get parole in four or five years if he
keeps his nose clean.'

'Maybe that's awright then,' said Second Thoughts.
'And maybe it ain't.'

I gulped some whisky and glanced impatiently at my
watch.

'Come on, son, cough it up,' I said. 'You going to do me
a bit of good, or aren't you?'

'Maybe I am,' he replied. 'And maybe . . .'

'Listen,' I interrupted him sharply. 'If you're thinking
of putting the bite on me for a few quid, you can forget it.
I'm skint as a church mouse and I owe a sackful of money
to loan sharks who are going to work me over good and
proper if I don't make a reduction on the interest by the
end of the week.'

'Yah don't 'ave to plead poverty to me, Ed,' said Second
Thoughts. 'I ain't on the ear'ole.'

'What is it then?'

'I 'eard a whisper around the manor that you're on the
look aht for Lady Leach's sparklers?'

If I hadn't been leaning back in the chair I'd have
kicked myself. I'd reckoned Second Thoughts was behind
it when Bert Fagley first told me the story of the emeralds.

'You saying you know where they are?' I asked. 'And
don't give me any of that old moody about maybe you do
and maybe you don't.'

A pained expression passed over Second Thoughts'
face. He didn't like being deprived of his performance, but
knew that if he messed me about beyond endurance I'd
boot him out on his ear. Very slowly he reached into his
raincoat pocket and pulled out a piece of cloth tied into a
small bundle with a length of blue ribbon.

My eyes widened with excitement as he dangled it enticingly in the air, between a forefinger and thumb, like the pendulum of a grandfather clock.

'Don't tell me,' I grinned. 'Let me guess. It was you who swiped Lady Leach's gems and they turn out to be too hot to handle so you want to give 'em back for a half share in the insurance reward lolly, right?'

He dumped the bundle on my ink blotter and sank back into the armchair.

'I ain't sayin' yah right,' he mumbled. 'And I ain't sayin' yah wrong – butcha right about the insurance money.'

I untied the ribbon and peeked inside. The glitter made my eyes bulge and took my breath away. I quickly shoved the gems out of sight in my desk drawer and gave Second Thoughts a penetrating stare.

'The Acme Alliance are bastards to deal with,' I told him straight. 'They won't pay out the ten per cent reward money unless all their conditions are met.' I paused for a slug of whisky. 'And that means the arrest and conviction of the guilty party as well as the return of the jewels.'

''Ow much they worf?' Second Thoughts inquired politely.

'They're insured for seventy-five grand,' I told him. 'But Acme will say they're not worth that much once they get 'em back.'

Second Thoughts did a sum in his head.

'Ten per cent of seventy-five grand is seven and a arf grand,' he said. 'That's three-seven-fifty apiece, Ed.'

'Listen, Second Thoughts,' I said in an unsteady voice. 'You ain't been taking any notice of a word I've said. Just because I hand 'em the tomfoolery back don't mean they'll hand over the reward lolly, just like that, but I do know the claims manager and I'll see what I can do.'

'Fair enough, Ed,' he said and stood up. 'I'll be in touch, then,' he added as he went out of the door.

'I'm not promising anything!' I shouted after him.

I opened the bottom drawer of the desk, took out the

Hankey Bannister's and gave myself a corpse reviver straight from the neck of the bottle. Then snatched the receiver off the hook and dialled the Yard.

'Inspector Lestrade,' I said to the switchboard operator.

'Who is that speaking?' she wanted to know.

'Philip Marlowe.'

'Hold the line please, Mr Marlowe.'

A moment or two later Lestrade's grammar school cadences came on the line saying:

'Listen, Ed, stop mucking my telephone girl about.'

'How did you know it was me?' I asked.

'Because you used the same gag last week,' he snapped. 'And the week before it was Philo Vance.'

'That's what I've always liked about you, Bill,' I replied. 'You're a man who can really take a joke.'

'What do you want?' he growled.

I kept it nice and casual.

'A run down on a licence plate.'

'What licence plate?'

'PHY 64 Q?'

'That's a west country lettering, registered in 1976,' he said. 'What else do you want to know about it?'

'Who owns the car?' I said. 'It's a white Mercedes.'

'What do you want to know for?' he inquired suspiciously.

'I'm thinking of buying it.'

The inspector shouted with laughter.

'Do me a favour, Ed! You couldn't even scrape together enough lolly for the hubcaps of a three year old Merc, let alone buy the whole motor.'

'You gonna find out who it belongs to for me or not?' I asked him flatly.

'Oh, sure,' sneered Lestrade. 'I'll get the whole flipping department on to it.'

I said: 'You're a toff, Bill,' and hung up.

I poured myself another slug of whisky, put my feet on the desk and scratched my head. Scratching your head is supposed to encourage the thought processes. It made me decide to give Willy a bell and report progress. I dialled the number of the Hide Away club.

''Ide Away,' said a kerb-stone voice at the other end of the line. 'Wotcha want?'

'Willy Paradis,' I said.

''Ang on a mo.'

'Yeah?' said Willy after a mo. 'Ooo is it?'

'Ed Nelson,' I said. 'Who do we know that goes in for laying threatening letters on people with words cut from newspapers and pasted to a sheet of paper?'

Willy laughed delightedly.

'Plenty of geezers arahnd up to that kinda stroke,' he said. 'Wot's the strengf?'

'My new client has just got one.'

'Wot, that bent antique dealer?'

'No, Sir Henry Baskerville.'

'Better fetch it dahn the club so's I can 'ave a butchers at it,' chortled Willy.

'Can't today,' I lied. 'Why don't you come round the office tomorrow?'

'I've got better fings to do that run arahnd after you, Ed,' he growled. 'But I might drop in.'

CHAPTER SIX

The Savoy doorman palmed my 10p tip for opening the cab door, looked me up and down and decided not to salute. I twirled through the revolving door and was about to take a left for the American Bar when I caught sight of Sir Henry at the reception desk.

As I ambled up behind him the wiry-haired baronet brought his fist down on the desk and began to shout. The line of reception clerks in braided uniforms huddled together to withstand the attack, looking slightly flustered but uncooperative.

'It's a disgrace that such things should be allowed to happen in a top class hotel,' yelled Sir Henry. 'I intend to warn all the foreign VIPs of my acquaintance against giving their custom to a pretentious dump that overcharges and is liable to lose them ever stick of clothing they've got on them.'

Fascinated, I watched the double-breasted manager hurry across the marble hall to the assistance of the clerks. He began by asking Sir Henry to lower his voice. The result was a deafening explosion.

'What the hell is it to do with you whether I choose to raise my voice – you pudding-faced menial!' Sir Henry swung round to glare at him.

Before I got spotted and dragged in on the act, I turned round, tiptoed speedily behind a pillar and out of the hall in the direction of the bar.

I settled myself at a comfortable window table, hoping that Sir Henry would sort out whatever it was that was eating him and turn up in time to pay for my drink.

I grabbed the opportunity of ordering my favourite cocktail and told the waiter to bring me a large whisky sour. They cost about three quid in the Savoy, but only a mug punter fails to take advantage if there's a good chance he's not in the chair.

The baronet tripped down the stairs into the bar about ten minutes later. He stood for a moment at the bottom looking around for me with his chin stuck out aggressively. Then he swanned over and dumped himself in the chair beside me. A spot of angry colour glowed on each of his cheeks.

'It's an absolute scandal, Ed,' he complained. 'I honestly wouldn't have believed that such things could take place at the Savoy hotel.'

'What's happened?' I inquired innocently. 'Room service forget to put the marmalade on your breakfast tray, did they?'

'No, no,' he bleated. 'You remember that I mentioned a new tweed sports jacket had disappeared on its way to my room?'

'Vaguely.'

'Well,' he went on, 'when I got back from the theatre last night I discovered that the new jacket had been returned to my room and an old Harris tweed jacket, that I have had for years, had been taken in its place. It was very worn and had leather patches on the elbows – but it was an old friend and I was attached to it.' He paused for a moment and then added. 'What is worse is that there was a solid gold cigarette case in an inside pocket.'

'You'll have to get on to Fernley Westall, the house dick,' I told him. 'It's an internal matter and the Savoy wouldn't thank me for meddling in it. Fern used to be in the West End Central shoplifting squad, so he's a dab hand at recovering gold cigarette cases and old tweed jackets – I know him from around so you can mention my name if you like.'

'Thanks, but I've just seen him,' snapped Sir Henry.

'Then the matter's in capable hands,' I assured him.

'He didn't impress me much, but if you say he's competent . . .' Sir Henry broke off, sighting a waiter

49

hurrying by a couple of tables away.

'You there,' he brayed, frightening the living daylights out of the poor man. The waiter stopped in his tracks and came to hover at Sir Henry's elbow.

'A double whisky and soda,' snapped the baronet. 'And . . . what are you drinking, Ed? Want another?'

'Large whisky sour,' I told him, quick as a flash.

Some time later Reg Mortimer joined us and we made our way to the dining-room. I scanned the menu for a decent fry-up, but the whole thing was written in French and being a bloke who doesn't know the difference between *Tête de Veau à la Crème* and *Caneton aux Cerises Noires* I settled, not very confidently, on *Boeuf Stroganoff*. What the other two ordered I'd have been hard put to pronounce, let alone eat.

After Sir Henry had put himself back in a good temper by pouring a blow by blow account of the missing jacket sensation horror into Reg's sympathetic ear, I felt it might be diplomatic to introduce a business note.

'Either of you got a black-bearded friend who drives a white Mercedes?' I asked.

'Don't think so,' and 'Not that I recall,' they chorused simultaneously.

'What makes you ask?' inquired Sir Henry.

I stopped shovelling down the *Stroganoff*, so's to make the most of my announcement.

'A white Mercedes, licence number PHY 64 Q, driven by a man with a bushy black beard has been following you round London ever since you touched down at Heathrow.'

Sir Henry dropped his knife and fork with a clatter and his face turned mud grey. He gazed at me with a look of horrified amazement.

'How do you know?' he gasped.

'A private eye likes to keep tabs on his client,' I pointed out reasonably. 'That's what he's paid for.'

'I call it pretty sinister,' said Reg seriously.

'What's more I don't intend to stand for it,' rasped Sir

Henry, recovering his poise. 'From now on, I shall travel by tube.'

'What about a man with a bushy black beard and forget about the car?' I asked. 'Can either of you think of someone who might fit the description?'

Both of them munched thoughtfully for a while, mentally running through their acquaintances. Then Reg brought the palm of his hand down on the table excitedly.

'I've thought of a possible,' he said.

'Let's have it,' I told him encouragingly.

'Barrymore, the butler down at Baskerville Hall, has one of those really big theatrical black beards.'

'That sounds just like it,' I enthused. 'What's the dope on the Barrymores?'

'What do you want to know about them?'

'How long they've been working at Baskerville Hall, what they did before that. You know, that kind of thing.'

He paused for thought then chose his words carefully.

'Well his name is John, as you know, and her name is Eliza. I understand that they are a theatrical couple who have fallen on hard times. John Barrymore once told me that he and his wife had run their own touring company at one time – they used to mount productions of the seldom seen plays of Sir John Irving and Oliver Goldsmith. But with the advent of colour television and so many beautiful old theatres being turned into bingo halls, their engagements became few and far between and eventually they were compelled to disband the company.' He paused for thought again. 'I am not entirely sure how they came to be in Sir Charles' employ, but I think it would be safe to assume that he advertised for a butler and housekeeper in *The Times* and possibly *Country Life* when he took possession of Baskerville Hall a little over two years ago.'

'Out of work actors will do anything,' I nodded knowledgeably. 'There's one I get to clean my office out every year or so, when the dust gets so thick it gives me sneezing fits.'

'I really can't see Barrymore coming up from the

51

country just to follow me around,' objected Sir Henry.

'Curiouser things have happened,' I informed him. 'At least this geezer is following you around in a Mercedes, not a flying saucer.'

'Very true,' nodded Reg anxiously. 'You have to remember that some very extraordinary things have been happening down at Muddicoombe.'

The rat-faced baronet's nose began to twitch with worry, as if a cat-faced predator was after him and he was less than clear how to escape.

'I can't say I like the idea of going down to the Hall without knowing whether it really is Barrymore who's been following me around.'

'Uncomfortable, I can see that,' I mused.

Then I had a brain-wave. I smiled indulgently on Sir Henry.

'I tell you what we'll do after lunch,' I said. 'We'll ring Baskerville Hall from your room and see if Barrymore's there.'

'Capital idea,' cried Sir Henry, a look of relief flooding his face. 'He can't be in London and Muddicoombe at the same time, after all. How long would it take him down the motorway, Reg?'

'Oh, four and a bit hours, even in light traffic,' Mortimer assured him.

'Christ, is it really as far as that?' I groaned.

'You'll fall under the spell of the moor like the rest of us, once you get there,' Reg encouraged me in a friendly manner.

'I doubt it,' I replied. 'Especially if I have to get mixed up with deadly flying saucers out to murder Sir Henry.'

'I wish you wouldn't talk like that,' the baronet snapped. 'Who on earth would want to murder me, anyway?'

I wasn't going to let him get away with that one.

'Who inherits the Baskerville millions when you snuff it?' I asked, leaning back and raising an eyebrow. He went rather white as he met my eyes across the table.

'It's an old parson fellow, some kind of second cousin.

He's pushing eighty, has a parish just outside Manchester and is called James Desmond, if my memory serves me right.'

'Any likelihood that he has a homicidal maniac for a son, with a bushy black beard and a taste in fast cars?' I inquired.

'None whatever,' snapped Sir Henry. 'He has one daughter who's a social worker.'

'That makes you look pretty safe,' I acknowledged. 'Have you made a will?'

'I haven't had time yet, but I intend to discuss it with my solicitor this week.'

'Money's always been my favourite murder motive. It seems a pity to rule it out,' I told them, as I toyed reflectively with another lump of *Stroganoff*. Then a thought struck me. 'What about Sir Charles' will?' I asked excitedly. 'Surely there must have been some other bequests as well as Sir Henry's windfall?'

Reg blushed to his eyebrows and gave a sickly smile.

'I was left a thousand, as a matter of fact,' he said. 'And the Barrymores got five hundred each.'

I shook my head.

'Doesn't sound like enough to me to push any of you into "murder one", as the Yanks call it.'

For the rest of the lunch Reg prattled on about the UFO sightings on Dartmoor, the wonderful collection of art treasures with which, under his guidance, Sir Charles had adorned Baskerville Hall and reiterated the suspicious circumstances that attended the sudden demise of his mentor. I was relieved when the meal was over and Sir Henry offered me a liqueur to go with my coffee.

'Large calvados,' I almost shouted.

'Splendid drink,' cried Sir Henry. 'I'll have the same.'

In fact, we had two each before leaving the restaurant.

Sir Henry had a lavish river suite, on the fifth floor, with enormous bay windows that gave a spectacular view of the

Thames, from St Paul's and Tower Bridge to the House of Commons. It was a breathtaking sight and probably cost him a hundred quid a day.

'Would you care for a drink, Ed?' Sir Henry asked hospitably, as we sank into the luxurious easy-chairs.

A man who has the taste knows no constraint.

'Don't mind if do,' I grinned.

'There are a few miniatures in my little refrigerator,' he said. 'But I doubt if there is any calvados. I'll ring room service. Better to stick to the same poison, eh?'

'Quite right,' I rejoined, enthusiastically, as Sir Henry ran his eye over the array of buttons, on the telephone table, which could bring any one of a variety of lackeys running to your door. He pressed 'room service' and I wondered idly if the 'chamber maid' would do a turn.

'Do you happen to know the telephone number of Baskerville Hall?' I asked no one in particular.

'Coombe Tracey 313,' said Reg.

Once Sir Henry had the important business of room service tied up I reached for the phone and gave Reg a sidelong glance.

'Any idea what the dialling code is?'

'029 6 double 8,' he said. 'Then the number.'

'You have to dial nine to get an outside line,' volunteered Sir Henry.

'Right,' I said. 'So that's 9029688313?'

The two men nodded their agreement. I lifted the receiver and got stuck in.

My first attempt was a dummy run – I dialled all the digits but wound up with a dead line in my ear. The second time a phone, a very long way off, began to ring, and a moment or two later a country woman's voice came on the line saying: 'Milton Damerel 323.'

'Sorry, luv,' I said, 'wrong number.'

I hung up the phone and lit a cigarette.

'Perhaps,' Sir Henry suggested good-naturedly, 'you had better go through the operator.'

'Okay,' I said. 'How do I get the operator?'

'Just dial 0.'

'Fine,' I said and did it.

The operator said: 'Number please?'

I said: '90296 double 8 313.'

'That's a ten number dialling code,' she scoffed. 'There are no ten number dialling codes in the STD system.'

'You don't need the nine if you're going through the operator,' whispered Sir Henry.

'Knock off the first nine,' I said into the phone.

'Could you repeat the number?' her voice had sharpened to a fine cutting edge.

'Err 029688313,' I said.

She said: 'That's 029688313?'

'Right,' I said.

'Hold the line, please.'

I waited and just as the floor waiter put in his welcome appearance, a voice from the other side of the world said, 'Sydney 88313.'

I slammed down the phone and buried my face in my hands.

'I can't take it,' I groaned. 'I'm chucking in the towel.'

'I quite take your point, Ed,' soothed Sir Henry. 'But I'm sure you'll feel better for a glass of calvados.'

'I think he's had enough,' whispered Reg.

'There's no such thing as enough calvados,' I shouted and waved my arms about in the air.

'Quite right,' Sir Henry agreed. 'A bottle of calvados and two glasses,' he told the waiter.

'Certainly, sir,' he said and departed with a superior smirk on his face.

Sir Henry ambled over to where I was sitting beside the telephone. 'While we're waiting for relief supplies to arrive, why don't I have a stab at Barrymore?' he grinned.

'On your own head be it,' I warned him.

He lifted the receiver confidently to his ear and dialled the operator.

'Ah, good afternoon, Sir Henry Baskerville here – suite

517.' He oozed more charm than a stock exchange con-man. 'Seem to be having a spot of bother getting through to the old ancestral seat in Devon – I say, that really is most fearfully kind of you. Yes, of course, Coombe Tracey 313. I'm sure you'll find it in the dialling code book. Good heavens, did you really? I say what a coincidence – Yes, yes I would be only too delighted to hold on.' He covered the receiver with the palm of his hand and gave me a wink. 'She says that she passed through Coombe Tracey on a caravan holiday with her parents last summer.'

'That doesn't surprise me,' I muttered and hoped that he wasn't going to keep on winking at me.

After a fairly lengthy pause Sir Henry handed me the phone.

'I'm putting you through now, Sir Henry,' purred the operator and in a jiffy a woman's voice of bell-like clarity came on the line saying: 'Baskerville Hall, Mrs Barrymore speaking.'

'GPO here,' I said. 'I have a telegram for Mr John Barrymore. Is he there?'

'He is up in the attic,' she said. 'But I am his wife, you can read it to me and I'll pass the message on to him.'

'It is the policy of the GPO to deliver telegrams only to those to whom they are addressed,' I said. 'Would you please call him to the phone.'

'I am his wife,' she came back at me testily. 'There's no law against telling me what's in the telegram, is there?'

'Not that I know of,' I said, sternly. 'But it's extremely irregular – do you have a pencil?'

'Yes.'

'Arrived from Kuwait last evening stop,' I adlibbed. 'Staying Savoy London for two days stop. Will advise train arrival time at Exeter stop. It is signed Sir Henry Baskerville.'

'Thank you,' she said. 'I'll tell him.'

'Would you like me to repeat it?' I asked.

'No,' she said and hung up.

Sir Henry grabbed the phone out of my hand and slammed it down.

'Why did you have to drag me into it?' he grated.

CHAPTER SEVEN

He sipped a half pint of lager and lime gloomily and said: 'It's not on, Ed, never in a month of Sundays.'

I knew, from personal experience, that *gloomily* is the only way you can sip a half pint of lager and lime. But what I couldn't make out was why he refused to rise to the bait.

'Do me a favour, Bert,' I said, persuasively. 'What the hell difference does it make to the Acme Alliance so long as Lady Leach gets her sparklers back?'

'It's company policy,' he replied stiffly. 'They will not pay out the ten per cent reward money unless all the conditions are met, and that includes the arrest and conviction of the criminal who stole them.'

'Suit yourself,' I shrugged. 'But, like I said, all I've had is a whisper from a nark who says that he might know a geezer, who knows a geezer who knows where the emeralds are. But the double-strong stipulation was – no law.'

Bert Fagley gave me a penetrating stare and the indisputable fact that he was the most boring dullard I'd ever met in my life did not prevent the uneasy feeling from creeping over me that he knew full well that Lady Leach's hot tomfoolery was burning a hole in my sky-rocket.

'Want another whisky, Ed,' he asked, with half smile.

I was trying to drink my way out of the awful calvados hangover that had hit me as I left the Savoy. I'd already polished off three or four large ones, but my head was still stuffed with cotton-wool and black dots danced before my eyes. Sir Henry had been very grumpy over my telegram stunt. I'd explained to him that it was the kind of subtlety that only top grade private eyes indulged in, but it had taken almost a whole bottle of the Savoy's finest calvados to convince him.

'Yes please, Bert,' I replied, gratefully. 'Make it a large one.'

He glanced at me reprovingly.

'You want to get your drinking under control, Ed,' he warned. 'Or you're going to end up with pickled kidneys and an enlarged liver.'

'Jesus Christ, Bert,' I wailed. 'Are we going to get down to cases about the old bird's emeralds or aren't we? – because if you think I'm going to stand here and take a bollocking from you about my state of health, you can bugger off and play hopscotch on the bleeding motorway.'

He'd got me rattled – I shouldn't have let that happen.

'All in good time, Ed,' he smirked. 'All in good time.'

He ordered me a large whisky and wisely forewent the mixed pleasures of another lager and lime for himself. Bert Fagley was not a drinking man.

'Cheers, Bert,' I said and swallowed half my drink. 'It's your move, sunshine.'

He watched me with shrewd, narrowed eyes for a while, then said: 'The real problem is the CID are involved and a blow up of the emeralds have been on Shaw Taylor's Police Five TV programme – perhaps you saw it?'

'Most TV goes on during opening hours,' I said. 'So I hardly ever see it – except maybe a bit of racing in afternoon drinking clubs.'

'If the company pay out reward money for the return of items that are subject to police investigation,' he prattled on doggedly. 'It would be tantamount to condoning the crime.'

'That's a load of old cobblers, Bert,' I sighed. 'And you know it – the Acme Alliance is as bent as any other insurance company. If they get the goods back they'll pay the lolly. As little or as much of it as they have to. Lady Leach's tomfoolery has got seventy-five grand cover, so the reward money at ten per cent comes to seven and a half. Taking into account the unusual circumstances I might be able to get my nark to pass it along that the Acme will cough up five grand.'

'Not on your life, Ed.' Bert Fagley was now in his element and enjoying the game. 'I might be able to wangle a grand out of the petty cash on the QT but that's tops.'

I said: 'Three.'

He said: 'Two.'

I said: 'Done – but I'll have to talk my party into it and I'll want it in readies and no questions asked.'

'Very well,' he said. 'But if you keep me waiting the price'll go down.'

'Have you got the lolly on you?' I asked.

'An experienced insurance agent is always prepared for any eventuality,' he said.

I looked him in the eyes measuringly and said: 'I'll have to make a phone call.'

He looked at his watch and said: 'All right, but be quick about it – the wife gets rather peevish when I get home late.'

I went into the telephone booth at the back of the saloon bar and dialled the number of the Hide Away club.

At the other end of the line the bell rang once only then a voice grated, 'Yeah,' in my ear. Bell ringing of any kind sticks the frighteners on gangsters. Shrinks would say it had to do with some deep rooted aversion they have to burglar alarms going off, and they may well be right for all I know. I don't recall the phone ringing down the Hide Away more than once before someone answered it, twice at most.

'Hello, Willy,' I drawled, 'it's me, Ed.'

'Yah don't say,' he came back at me menacingly. 'Where the bloody 'ell yah bin?'

'Lunching at the Savoy with the loaded hoi polloi,' I told him. 'Now I'm down the Half Moon in Duke Street, St James's.'

'Write it up in yah diary,' he replied tartly. 'I fort we 'ad a meet laid on so's I could 'ave a butchers at that freatenin' letter?'

'Sorry, mate,' I said. 'A bottle got in the light and I clean forgot. Let's make it tomorrow morning, okay?'

I glanced out of the window of the telephone booth. Bert Fagley was eyeing me suspiciously. I gave him a friendly wave. He nodded and put his back to me.

'Okay,' said Willy. 'Till termorrer then. And mind yah show up this time. I get the dead needle to the 'ired 'elp if they muck me abaht, see?'

'Don't hang up!' I shouted. 'Is Second Thoughts Steegmuller down there?'

'Yeah,' said Willy, ''e's losin' lolly 'e ain't got on the roulette wheel.

'Fetch him to the blower,' I said.

'Second Foughts!' bellowed Willy. 'There's a friend of yours wants to 'ave a little rabbit wiv yer.'

'Listen,' I said when he came on the line. 'I'm with the finger from Acme Alliance and two grand is top whack he'll go to – I'm gonna take it, okay?'

'Maybe it is,' said Second Thoughts. 'And maybe it ain't.'

The time up signal began to bleep and I shoved another coin into the box.

'Don't ponce me about, son,' I told him straight. 'It's the best deal I can make, so you'd better take it.'

'It's a long way orf seven and a arf grand,' he pointed out.

'How much are you down on the roulette?' I asked.

'A monkey.'

'Well that's five hundred you haven't got,' I snapped. 'And two grand is better than a poke in the eye with a sharp stick, isn't it?'

'Maybe it is,' he said. 'Maybe it isn't. Evva way it's a diabolical liberty when a geezer goes our riskin' 'is liberty and gets robbed.'

'We're wasting time,' I said. 'I'm going to take the two grand. Come round the office at noon tomorrow and I'll lay your whack on you.'

I hung up the phone and joined Bert Fagley at the bar.

'Let's go to the gents,' I said. 'My party reckons we can do business.'

'What a crafty chap you are, Ed,' said Bert as we stood shoulder to shoulder in the urinal with our cocks in our hands. 'I wondered if you had the emeralds in your pocket – but somehow I didn't really think you had the front.'

'Just hand over the two grand,' I smiled. 'And we'll call it quits.'

He zipped up his fly, crept off into a corner and examined the sparklers minutely through the jeweller's magnifying glass screwed into his eye. I kept watch on the door.

'They're Lady Leach's emeralds, all right,' he said. 'I don't suppose you'd tell me how you came by them?'

'You can read about it in my memoirs,' I replied impatiently. 'Now cough up the two grand and we can get out of here.'

He reached into the inside breast pocket of his charcoal-grey business suit and yanked out two sealed transparent packets with Barclays Bank printed on them. I snatched them out of his hand and looked them over. Both were £20 notes.

'They're brand spanking new,' I complained. 'Just come off the bleeding presses at the Royal sodding Mint. The bank is gonna have the serial numbers of them.'

'Sorry, Ed,' he smirked. 'You took me unawares and they were all I could lay my hands on at short notice.'

'You're a right bastard, Bert,' I told him hotly. 'This is the last time we're gonna do business together, I can tell you that for nothing.'

'Don't be like that, Ed,' he said, as he brushed by me. 'You know you don't mean it.'

I made an early night of it that night and pushed off home when the landlord of the Half Moon slung me out twenty minutes after closing time. That meant I woke early the next morning. It was only 9.15 when I started the working day by giving Bill Lestrade a bell at the Yard.

'Hello, Ed,' he said cheerily when the switchboard put me through to his extension. 'What can I do you for?'

'Nothing much,' I replied. 'I just wondered if you'd come up with anything on that motor?'

'Which motor's that, Ed?'

'PHY 64 Q?'

'Oh, yes,' Lestrade muttered absently. 'A white Mercedes, wasn't it?'

'You know very well it was, Bill,' I replied testily. 'Come on, what's the story on it?'

I could hear him shuffling papers around on his desk. I was fairly sure that he was jerking me about. Inspector Lestrade was a policeman who delighted in jerking people about.

'Ah, yes,' he said at last. 'Here it is – White 1976 Mercedes registered at Plymouth, Devon, to a man called Fletcher Robinson. That mean anything to you?'

Fletcher Robinson was the name of the *Western Morning News* hack who'd been writing up the UFO stories. But I decided, for the moment, not to share this titbit of information with Lestrade.

'Not a thing, Inspector,' I replied airily. 'Not a thing – just wondered why it was bird-dogging a friend of mine around town, that's all.'

'Robinson reported it nicked from a car park in Exeter two weeks ago,' he came back at me sharply. 'If you see it again get on to the stolen vehicle squad, all right?'

'Sure thing, Bill,' I said. 'One good turn deserves another.'

'You said it, chum,' he laughed. 'You owe me.'

'An arm or a leg?' I asked.

'We'll think of something, Ed.'

I said: 'Sure we will,' and hung up.

Willy came barging into the office at ten o'clock sharp snarling: 'Awright, loser, let's 'ave a butchers at the poison pen letter.'

'Yeah,' glowered Drummer Bill, standing sentinel at the door. 'The guv'nor's got a meet wiv the VAT geezer down the club at twelve so we ain't got much time left to cook the soddin' books.'

I took the envelope out of my inside pocket and passed it to Willy across the desk.

'Ta,' he said and looked the envelope over before he took the sheet of paper out. He studied it in silence with pursed lips for a minute or so, then made his pronouncement.

'Looks like the kind of type they print Sportin' Life wiv. 'Ere Drummer, yah still got yesterday's copy on yah?'

'Might 'ave, guv,' he said and dug into the capacious inside pocket of his overcoat. He produced four dog-eared editions·of the rag and threw them down on my desk.

'I mostly 'ang on to it,' he explained, 'so's I can check the winners in terdays agin the runners in yesterdays, see? I write me bets in the margin like.'

'Awright,' said Willy. 'Don't go on abaht it. Which day was it Value Life was in the two-firty at Kempton Park?'

Drummer scratched his head at the unaccustomed intellectual exercise.

'It weren't Fursday,' he opined. ''Cos I cleaned up on Bittersweet Fursday. And it weren't yesterday, cos that was 'Ungry 'Arry.' He stood thinking deeply. 'Tell you wot I fink it were,' he said at last. 'Day before yesterday.'

Willy grabbed Monday's paper out of the pile and turned to the list of runners and riders at Kempton Park.

'There yah are,' he cried, jabbing a forefinger at the 2.30. 'Value Life ridden by Lester Piggott and Asmoor ridden by Joe Mercer.'

I gazed at him with puzzled eyes and said: 'What's that got to do with anything?'

'They both lost, that's wot,' Drummer put in, ruefully.

'Stone me,' sighed Willy. 'Wot a right pair of bird-brained berks yah are.' He came around the desk and laid the open paper and the note in front of me, side by side. 'Nar do yer see wot I'm on abaht. The capital "V" in value and the capital "L" in life is the same in the bleedin' linen as it is in the note, right?'

'Right,' I agreed in amazement.

'And the first word in the note is "As" and the last is "moor", geddit?'

'Err, yes,' I replied a little more dubiously, glancing from the note to the racing column and back again. 'But I don't reckon that "As" was divided from "moor" with a pair of scissors, there isn't enough room.'

'Don't matter if there ain't,' snapped Willy. 'All yah gotta do is make sure yah don't cut frough the "m" in "moor" and getcha self a "As" from somewhere else in the linen. Same goes for the rest of the words.'

He cast his eye over an article about the chances of a nag called Persistence winning the 4 o'clock at Newbury.

'There yah are,' he shouted, then read aloud from the paper, putting emphasis on the words that also appeared on the sheet of paper. '"Persistence is a good sort and there is every *reason* to believe that she has a good chance of winning. But on past form wise investors may be tempted to *keep away from* her and back the favourite". The words "your", "you", "the", and "or" are all 'ere, look, there, there and there, right?'

'Well, I'm blowed, Willy,' I gasped. 'Buggered if I know how you do it.'

'Got an analytical brain, ain't I?' he said, casting his eyes modestly to the ground. 'The shrink in the slammer reckoned I got an IQ of a 'undred and firty.'

Drummer tapped his slanting, ape-like forehead.

'Well, yah wouldn't wind up guv'nor of the smoke if yah was a right berk, would yah?' he said.

I read the note aloud just to make sure Willy hadn't missed any important words out.

'"As you value your life or your reason keep away from the moor".'

'Sounds like a stiff from some old lag doin' chokey in Dartmoor nick,' said Drummer.

Since the Princetown prison is better known to the denizens of the underworld as 'the moor' is wasn't a bad assumption.

At 12 o'clock Second Thoughts Steegmuller came dashing into the office as though he was being chased by someone.

'Got my whack or ani'tcha?' he demanded to know.

I reached into the top drawer of the desk and tossed him one of the thousand pound packets that Bert Fagley had palmed off on me. Second Thoughts caught it in mid air and stuffed it into his trouser pocket.

'A word of warning, son,' I said as he headed for the door. 'The Acme Alliance shyster small claims manager worked a flanker on us.'

Second Thoughts stopped dead in his tracks and rounded on me with wide frightened eyes.

'It ain't fake is it?' he inquired querulously.

'Might as well be.' There was no way of breaking it to him gently. 'They're brand new notes, never been in circulation before. The bank'll have the serial numbers, so you'll have to do a spot of laundering. Moisher Katz, the fence, might give you seven fifty in used notes for a grand of new ones, if he's feeling big hearted, or five hundred the worst way. I'm not saying for definite that Acme have told Barclays Bank to send a list of the serial numbers to the Yard – but I wouldn't risk it if I was you, sunshine.'

'You know wot this kinda fing does to a 'onest tea-leaf, don'tcha, Ed?' he snarled.

'Makes him go straight?' I asked mildly.

'No it bloody don't,' Second Thoughts retorted savagely. 'It makes him turn mean – shall I tell yer wot I'm gonna do?'

'If you must.'

'I'm gonna go out and stick up a bank,' said Second Thoughts. 'I'm gonna go out and stick up two banks.'

CHAPTER EIGHT

I took the Bakerloo line to Paddington with a song in my heart and a spring in my step. Once I'd seen Reg and Sir Henry off to Devon, I intended to invest my retainer in the type of spectacular bender that brings a private eye to the peak of his form. If my new client and Willy Paradis both insisted that I pay a visit to the west country, I was going to make sure that I had alcoholic amnesia to help me through the rigours of country life.

I'd fixed to meet Sir Henry in the 'Travellers'' bar to have a farewell drink and receive my final instructions. He and Reg were crouched over their glasses at a corner table when I breezed in, with a welter of expensive luggage banked round them.

Having greeted them gaily, I bought a round and plonked myself down between a calf-skin hold-all and a trunk-sized blue leather suitcase.

'Travelling light, I see,' I quipped.

Sir Henry frowned thunderously and had a shot at grating his teeth. 'We give these bloody railmen rise after rise,' he said, 'but there isn't a porter to be found in the whole station.'

After a little humorous give and take about the nation's labour problems, Sir Henry got down to business.

'You'll be joining me at Baskerville Hall in two days' time. That's right isn't it, Ed?'

'Right,' I nodded, my spirits temporarily dampened by the prospect.

'Have you managed to get hold of that book on UFOs by Lord What's-his-name?'

'Damn,' I said, striking my thigh with my hand. 'I knew there was something I meant to do this morning – drop into Hatchards and see if I could get it for you. But I clean forgot.'

'Well, try to bring it down with you when you come,' Sir Henry admonished me.

So's to improve my image, I told them about the anonymous note being scissored from *Sporting Life* and who owned the white Mercedes.

'Jolly good work, Ed,' Reg enthused, but his surprised tone took the edge off the compliment.

'Now you come to mention it, I think I remember that journalist pottering around Muddicoombe in a rather flashy white car when he was interviewing people about the UFOs.'

'Have a bushy black beard, did he?' I asked.

'If the car's been stolen, it can't have been him driving it,' Sir Henry pointed out.

'And why would a car thief be so interested in you, Sir Henry? Why should he dog your footsteps day and night?' I leant across the table in order to sock it to him and watch his reaction closely.

But trained diplomats have poker faces. He lifted his sandy eyebrows and shrugged his shoulders.

'It's a mystery, isn't it?' he said imperturbably. 'But I haven't seen the car for the last couple of days. I think he must have given up.'

'So no one seems to have been following you lately?' I asked in an off-hand manner, raising my glass to my lips. I was interested to know whether he'd spotted Willy's tearaways.

Apparently he hadn't as he returned to the bearded berk in the Mercedes. 'Having discovered what a boring life I lead,' he said, 'your bearded friend seems to have given me up as a bad job.'

'He may have found out what he wanted and gone back to the west country,' suggested Reg. 'There must be some Devon connection if the car was pinched in Exeter.'

'Maybe it's some crazed tea-leaf from Muddicoombe who had a desperate yen to get his mitts on one of Sir

68

Henry's tweed jackets,' I put in.

Neither of them seemed to like my suggestion.

'Don't be an ass,' Reg frowned at me.

'Did Fernley Westall manage to get your jacket back yet?' I asked, not to be put down.

'No. I'm afraid it's gone for good,' sighed Sir Henry. 'And the gold cigarette case, more's the pity.'

A large group of spades who'd been sitting at the next-door table discussing their university entrance papers suddenly got up in a hurry and made for the door. Reg glanced at his watch.

'Better get going or we'll miss the train,' he said.

As I struggled past the ticket barrier, weighed down with Sir Henry's luggage, a murderous young skinhead from Willy's mob gave me a broad wink. I was tempted to suggest he lent me a hand, but when I looked up again he'd disappeared into the crowd.

Having piled the two of them bag and baggage into a first class compartment, I kept an eye on them from a safe distance until the massive pullman diesel slid smoothly out of the station. I turned to find the skinhead at my elbow.

'The guv'nor wants a rabbit wiv yah dahn the club,' he told me, then blew a nasty pink balloon of bubble gum and burst it with his tongue. ''E's doin' 'is nut sumink rotten, Ed. I wouldn't keep 'im 'angin' abaht if I wus yah.'

'Well, I ain't you, kid,' I said and walked away from him.

Underworld standards were certainly taking a nose dive if bubble gum-chewing skinheads were the only contenders to take advantage of Willy Paradis's latest recruiting drive. But then standards are declining all around I'm told.

What had got on Willy's wick was the fact that I hadn't climbed aboard the 1.45 express for Exeter along with the young baronet and the bent antique dealer. He was unimpressed by my need of a couple of days of heavy laying about on licenced premises, now that I'd got myself back on a steady salary. He seemed to think that Reg might be planning the biggest bulk movement of hot merchandise in the history of crime during the two days I intended to spend on the booze. Tearaways get like that when they've laid a few quid on you to do a job – they think they own you body and soul. So, come to think about it, do clients from all walks of life. When I win the football pools I'm going to give up being a private eye.

It took quite a while to calm him down and make sure that Drummer Bill wasn't going to give me an ears job. Then I asked Willy something that had been giving my addled brain a bit of stick.

'Do you think there's any connection between the little green goblins from outer space and the country house burglaries?'

''Course there bloody well is, yah cunt,' said Willy.

'I see,' I said, staring into my whisky glass and trying to figure it out. 'What is it?'

'Nah, yah askin' me!' he exploded. 'That's wot I bunged yah to find aht.'

'And the other geezer's bunging me to find out if his cousin was murdered by a flying saucer. It's going to be bloody difficult following up both angles at the same time.'

'No it ain't,' scoffed Willy.

'Was he murdered, d'you think?' I asked, pursuing the matter doggedly.

'Don't matter really,' the guv'nor assured me. 'Some geezer's fixed up this flyin' saucer bollocks as a cuvva for 'is receivin' business. Stands ter reason. What we want to know is 'oo's doin' it. That's wot yer've gotta suss out.'

'How?' I asked.

Willy gave a long-suffering shrug. 'Putcha self abaht rahnd the neighbour'ood. See'oo's there and get ter know 'em, like. Then tell me all abaht it and I'll suss aht 'oo it is, right?'

'Right,' I agreed.

Two unforgettable days later I popped upstairs and tapped lightly on the door of Black Satin Hotpants, the sizzling little hooker who did a roaring trade in the room directly above my office.

'Go away,' she trilled, sleepily. 'Come back at two o'clock.'

I glanced at my watch, it was a quarter to one. Black Satin Hotpants did not open for business until the early afternoon and she shut up shop at seven. She fixed up all her business on the phone nowadays and most of her clients were regulars – rich bankers from the city and government bureaucrats from Whitehall were the kind of blokes who beat a path to her door. She had a cushy life and it was a bit of a mystery to me why she was always so clapped out that she had to stay in bed half the day.

'It's Ed,' I yelled through the keyhole. 'Open up, I want to ask you something.'

There was the rustle of bed clothes and the patter of tiny feet, then the key turned in the lock and her sleepy eyes peered out at me around the half open door. She had on a pink satin shorty nighty that barely came down to her stock in trade and her tousled black curls hung limply around her disarmingly innocent little face. She was an eminently bedworthy dish and no man, except maybe a homosexual C of E bishop, would have denied that she'd chosen her profession wisely.

'Listen, Ed,' she pouted prettily. 'I know I said you could come up and have a short time on the house, any time you felt randy. But can't you come back later? It's too fucking early.'

I stepped over the threshold into her heavily scented, Fortnum & Mason's chocolate box of a bedroom. There was a slight crackle of electricity as she slid back between the pink nylon sheets.

I stuck a cigarette in the corner of my mouth and said: 'Look, the thing is I'm going away for a few days. I'll leave a note for the milkman, but would you be an angel and take my post in and generally keep an eye on the place –I'll leave my spare set of keys, okay?'

She peeped over the sheet and said: 'You on a case, lover?'

'Yeah,' I drawled and set light to the fag with a safety match.

She sat up in bed and clapped her hands together gleefully.

'How thrilling,' she trilled. 'What kind of case is it?'

'Murder.'

Her eyes widened and her forehead wrinkled into a serious little frown.

'I thought you never took on *murder* cases, Ed?'

I dropped my spare set of keys on her dressing table, said: 'I don't,' and went out.

My rusty, fourteen year-old Morris 1100 had landed up in dock again. There were nine hundred and ninety-nine thousand six hundred and thirty-four miles on her clock and I'd promised her a trip to Brighton for a breath of sea air if she made it to a hundred thousand. But she hadn't been at all well of late and tended to cough a lot and boil like a coffee pot even on short journeys. Greasy Gordon Lewis, the hot car licence-plate wringer, had been on at me for months to flog the old girl for scrap and buy a three-year-old Ford Cortina off him. He had resprayed the nasty little upstart shocking pink, and filed the engine numbers off it. His theory was that the filth would never tumble it, because only a complete nutcase would drive around town in a bent motor that colour. He was right about that – I told him to get stuffed.

It took a fair amount of cajoling and even a few threats before he agreed to look the 1100 over. But he still went right on complaining that it was beneath his dignity, as a craftsman, to have anything to do with such a disreputable old wreck and he refused to hold out even a glimmer of hope for her complete recovery.

Gordon had had the car in his tiny mews garage at Mornington Crescent for four or five days so I got him on the blower for a progress report.

'The old banger has blown a bleeding cylinder gasket,' he told me straight. 'I've put a new one in, but it won't get you very far, mate. Your piston rings are clapped out, your battery is on the blink, the brakes are knackered and your two front tyres are as bald as a baby's bum – sure you won't change your mind about the Cortina? She's a right little goer.'

'No thanks, Gordon,' I said. 'I'll be up to collect the 1100 in the morning – have it ready.'

'Sure you won't change your mind, Ed?' he persisted. 'I'll even take the old banger off your hands in part exchange, not that it's worth a light – can't say fairer than that, can I?'

'Leave off, son,' I snapped. 'I already told you enough times – can't you take *no* for an answer?'

'Don't be daft, Ed,' he sneered. 'When was the last time you met a car dealer who could take *no* for an answer?'

'Never have,' I conceded. 'See you tomorrow.'

Although it was a relief to have got shot of Lady Leach's emeralds, the vexing problem of what to do before I started west with my share of the pristine reward money still remained. I didn't fancy making a swap with Moisher Katz for seven fifty or five hundred in used notes for a grand in new ones. On the other hand I'd soon end up in the slammer if I started littering the pubs of Devon with hot lolly.

I decided to put off the irksome decision until I got back – if I ever did. By which time Second Thoughts would either have had his collar felt, made a swap with Moisher or blown the new £20s and got away with it. I hid the bundle under a loose floor board by the window and muttered: 'Please God, no burglars.'

CHAPTER NINE

The olive green 1100 beatled along the M4, gobbling up a mile a minute. Now and then, to overtake a slow coach, the needle of her speedometer crawled up to seventy, but she couldn't keep up that kind of speed for long and soon got winded, especially on hills. The heater had given up the ghost some time ago and I was grateful, on that chilly October morning, for the boiling engine heat that belched into the car through a filigree of rust in the metal floor. The accelerator and clutch pedals had become almost hot enough to blister the skin, but through the leather soles of my shoes they made ideal foot warmers.

I had covered just 60 miles of the 200 mile journey that lay before me when it happened. A jet of grey steam and rust-brown boiling water forced its way through a hole, that had once contained a wireless aerial, and shot several feet into the air – the rusty water splattered the windscreen and completely obliterated my view ahead. I quickly switched on the wipers and swerved limply on to the safety of the hard shoulder.

I had no idea where the hell I was or what the hell to do. I was stranded and, like most over emotional blokes are prone to do when they find themselves in a hopeless situation, I did my nut.

'Long Vehicles' loaded with tons of goods covered with flapping tarpaulin, spritely little sports cars, petrol tankers, charabancs crammed with old age pensioners on an outing and over-polished saloon cars towing caravans, belted past me in both directions at breakneck speed as I clambered out of the driver's seat. I slammed the door angrily, stormed around to the front of the car, glared at its steaming bonnet and screamed blue murder. Unable to

74

control myself, I fetched it off a mighty kick in the fender that almost broke my toe.

The motorway was flanked on either side by rough open country on which piebald cattle were dotted like currants in a cake. Close to tears I cast my panic-stricken eyes first to the right and then to the left. Several hundred yards away, in the opposite direction to that in which I had been travelling, I spotted what looked like a telephone box. I set off towards it with blasts of air, in the wake of heavy goods lorries, almost buffeting me off my feet.

There was no dial, just a notice in red capitals that said: LIFT RECEIVER AND WAIT. I did as I was told and a moment or two later there was a man's voice in my ear saying: 'Swindon police switching centre – where are you speaking from?'

'How the hell should I know?' I groaned. 'My motor has died on me on the sodding motorway.'

'What's the number of the box you're speaking from?' he clipped.

I glanced, hopelessly, around the inside and outside of the box and eventually spotted a number under the red notice.

'237,' I gasped.

A bloody great lorry roared by towing three massive trailers. The noise was so deafening that I didn't hear what he asked me next.

I stuck a finger in my other ear and yelled: 'What's that?'

'What's the licence number of your car?' he yelled.

'RUN 101 G,' I told him.

'What make of car is it?'

'Morris 1100.'

An oil tanker went by and I missed the next question, even with my finger in my ear.

'What?'

'Are you a member of the AA or the RAC?'

'Neither.'

'What, so far as you can tell, has caused you to break down?'

That was another of those questions to which there were a variety of possible answers. But I decided not to push my luck and said: 'I dunno – it's steaming like a turkish bath and the engine's packed up.'

'If you're lucky your thermostat's clogged,' he said. 'Otherwise you've probably blown your cylinder gasket.'

'Can't be that,' I replied, confidently. 'I've only just had a new one put in.'

'If you're not a member of the AA or the RAC, the only thing I can do is get on to a local garage in Swindon and ask them to come out and tow you off the motorway.'

Breaking down on the motorway, as I was rapidly finding out, was no joke. But the game had only just begun – there was a lot worse to come.

The filth called me back in about ten minutes and said that the tow truck would be out to fetch me in about half an hour and it was going to cost me fourteen quid.

'Thanks a lot, officer,' I crawled.

The 1100 had cooled off by the time I got back, and I decided to sneak a peek under the bonnet. There was a lot of rusty water and some oil splattered over the engine but apart from that I couldn't see anything wrong.

I closed the bonnet, got into the car, chain-smoked three cigarettes, then suddenly remembered the six bottles of Hankey Bannister's I'd had the foresight to pack in my case with my shirts, clean Y-fronts and my other suit. I had heeded Reg's warning that my favourite tipple was virtually impossible to come by in the west country.

The tow truck did not turn up in half an hour, nor even in an hour. By the time it eventually put in an appearance, two and a quarter hours after I had made the phone call, I had already seen off a good two thirds of a bottle and was not particularly surprised to find myself on cracking form.

'Where the bleeding hell have you been?' I asked the boiler-suited garage bloke when he tapped on the window.

'Been rushed off me feet all day, mate,' he said. 'Got held-up – what's up with your motor?'

'The carburetter splinge flange has overheated and

cocked up the valve rocker clearance,' I told him, straight-faced.

'You what?' he blinked.

'Well, if it ain't that,' I grinned. 'The cockle sprocket on the stroboscopic compression ratio analyser has buggered up the synchromesh transmission contact breaker gap.'

'Get away,' he said. 'You can't even do that on an old banger like this.'

I slugged a little more whisky, leered at him drunkenly and said: 'I'll have you know, my man, that this stately barouche is a dowager of the Queen's highway and there's nothing she won't stoop to or rise above.'

'Better take a look,' he said, went around to the front of the car and lifted the bonnet. His head disappeared from sight for not more than ten seconds, but when it came up again he had already diagnosed the trouble.

'Overheating, mate,' he shrugged. 'You boiled your oil as well as your water, blew a gasket and it's my guess we'll find you've buggered up the cylinder head once we take it to pieces and see.'

His voice became almost apologetic. 'Expensive job, mate, cost you two hundred, plus VAT, maybe more. A motor of this age is only worth two fifty, top whack, if it was in good condition – which this one isn't, with that rust all over the body work . . .'

'But I only had a new gasket put in yesterday,' I interrupted him, as though that ought to make the world of difference.

'Ah,' he sighed, 'that probably means your radiator is all rusted up – a gasket don't blow for no reason, mate. The mechanic who put in the new gasket ought to have cleaned the rust out of the radiator as well.'

'Thanks for telling me, son,' I said. 'A certain party is gonna hear from me about this when I get back to London – Okay, it's no good us standing around here talking about it – what are we going to do?'

The garage mechanic made an oblique reference, for the

first time, to the whisky fumes I had been breathing over him.

'Don't reckon you're in a fit state to steer the car if I give you a tow,' he said. 'I'll crank her front wheels off the deck on the winch and we'll tow her into Swindon like that –you can come up in the cab alongside me.'

As we pulled off the M4 at the Swindon junction I glanced out of the rear window. The sad old 1100, dangling from the hook at the end of the heavy chain from the winch, looked more like a beached whale that we were dragging along behind us than it did a car. I sucked on the bottle I had clasped to my chest and kidded myself that no more bad things could happen to me that day.

The vast, fenced-in compound we eventually fetched up at was piled high on every side with mountains of dead and gutted cars – it was a graveyard for cars that had died on the motorway. Some were the victims of multiple pile-ups but most, like my trusty old 1100, had given up the ghost from acute old age.

'You'll have to have a word with the boss,' said the mechanic, as he lurched to a halt. 'You'll find him over there in the office.'

The car undertaker's office was a makeshift shed, with a corrugated iron roof, tucked away in a corner of the compound and almost hidden from sight by the mountains of cars.

I tapped timidly on the door and a voice from within boomed: 'Come in.'

I grasped the door handle and pulled, but it wouldn't open.

'Push!' bellowed the voice from within.

I pushed and the door opened inwards taking me with it.

The tub of lard stuffed into the garish window-pane check-suit, seated at the broken-down roll-top desk against the wall, was a man I had never before clapped eyes on, but had known all my life.

He glanced at a slip of paper on his desk then turned his

revolting, side-of-beef face in my direction and said: 'Unless I'm very much mistaken you'll be RUN 101 G?'

'What kind of crack's that?' I slurred.

He cast the beady eye of the experienced scrap metal dealer over me and sighed with the mighty sigh of a man who knew the calamity of a motorway breakdown in all its horrifying guises.

The boiler-suited mechanic who had towed me in stuck his head around the door without warning and uttered a single sentence.

'Cracked cylinder head, boss, four months to go on the road tax disc.'

I whirled around, but he was gone before I could even catch a glimpse of him. When I turned back the fat man was wreathed in smiles but there was a cold appraising look in his china-blue eyes that told me that I was about to get screwed.

'Not worth getting it repaired,' he said, jovially. 'Cost more than it's worth.'

'Your man already told me that,' I came back at him. 'Make me an offer?'

He said: 'I'll give you ten quid for it.'

I said: 'Come off it.'

He said: 'Got the MOT?'

I searched in my pocket for my Ministry of Transport road worthiness certificate, knowing full well I didn't have it on me, and said: 'It's in my desk in London.'

He said: 'What about the log book, got that on you?'

'No.'

'Doesn't matter,' he grinned. 'Tell you what I'll do with you.'

'What?'

'I'll chuck in twelve 'n' half quid for the four months road tax. That'll make it twenty-two 'n' half quid. Got any tools in the boot?'

'I dunno.'

'I expect you've got a jack and a few odds and ends like that,' he said, jotting figures down on his note-pad.

'Why don't we say twenty-five quid all in?'

The whole thing had taken up so much time and given me so much aggravation I was almost ready to throw in the towel and let him have the clapped out old wreck for nothing.

'It's a deal,' I snapped. 'But Christ only knows what I'm going to do in the west country without any wheels.'

I shouldn't have said that. The fat man's face lit up like a Christmas tree.

'I can sell you a car *cheap*,' he replied, quick as a flash.

'Just hand over the twenty-five quid,' I retorted. 'I'll take the train and I'll send you the papers for the car when I get back to London.'

'Just as you like, Mr err?' he shrugged, pencil poised over his note-pad.

'Nelson,' I told him. 'Ed Nelson.'

'Address?'

'Three Regent Chambers, London, West one.'

'And what line of business are you in, Mr Nelson?'

'I'm a private detective,' I drawled. 'And I'm supposed to be investigating a *murder* case down in Devon, not breaking down on the bloody motorway or sodding about haggling with you, guv.'

He yanked a massive wad of grubby notes out of his hip pocket and leafed five fivers off it with a fleshy clubbed thumb.

'We get all kinds come in here,' he said, handing me the money. 'Doctors, actors, farmers, you name it – we've had 'em.' He scratched his thinning scalp with the end of his biro. 'But I've got to admit you're our first private detective.'

I trousered the £25 and said: 'Who were the actors?'

'What actors?'

'The actors you said you'd had in here.'

He smiled broadly and puffed out his chest with pride.

''Ad Penelope Keith in last week,' he said, and added, 'back axle.'

'Who's she?' I hiccuped, trying to get one cigarette out

of the two packets of Rothmans that had mysteriously appeared in my two left hands.

'Wot?' he almost shouted. 'You never 'eard of Penelope Keith?'

I looked up apologetically. 'Name rings a bell somehow,' I said. 'But I can't put a face to it. Who is she?'

'Only the biggest TV actress wot's going,' he sneered.

'Ah! That explains it,' I smirked. 'Don't watch TV myself. Had any stage actors, have you?'

'Well, now, let me see.' He stroked his chin reflectively. 'We had a couple in with their pantechnicon quite a while back. Couple wot put shows on, like. That's wot they were. I remember because my Jenny went to see their "Aladdin" with 'er school friends – must 'ave bin five or six years back, and the name stuck in me mind, Barrymore it was.'

I froze with the fag I'd finally shaken from a pack halfway to my lips. 'What did you say their name was?' I shrieked.

The fat man seemed taken aback by my excitement.

'What's it to you?' he asked suspiciously.

'It matters to me, mate,' I assured him. 'Remember I said I was a private detective? Well, it might tie up with a case I'm working on.'

A crafty light entered his eye. 'Now ain't that a coincidence?' he said. 'I had it just now – but it's gone again. What a memory I got!'

'Okay,' I said. 'How about if I give you the twenty-five quid back – any chance that might jog your memory?'

He held out his meaty paw and nodded his massive head.

I returned the money to him and said: 'Let's have it?'

'Barrymore was their name – it was written on the side of their removal van in big black letters.' He made a half moon in the air with a forefinger and thumb. ' "The Barrymore Travelling Theatre Company" – I never forget anything that goes on in my yard. Seeing someone break down on the M4 is like getting a look at their soul – they nearly

81

all do their nuts and everything about them is right there on the surface, if you get my meaning, Mr Nelson.'

'Yes, yes,' I said. 'But is there anything else you remember about the Barrymores?'

'They was a man and a woman, sort of middle-aged, I'd say. They were travelling west down the M4 in a big pantechnicon. I think they had a busted half shaft, or maybe a big end went. Anyway, we had a spare of whatever it was so we fixed them up without too much trouble.'

'What was in the pantechnicon?' I asked excitedly.

'Can't tell you that,' he said. 'Now you come to mention it I did think it was a bit fishy at the time – they wouldn't let my mechanic open up the back to get any tools out or anything. Said there was a load of valuable antiques in the back and they wouldn't let no one near them.'

'Now then,' I said. 'How long ago was it?'

'Well over a year ago, must've been at least that long ago.'

'Sounds as if it must be them,' I said. 'Can you remember what either of them looked like at all?'

'You mean the bushy black beard he had – just like a sea captain?' the fat man asked.

'That clinches it.' I pointed at the phone on the edge of his desk. 'Mind if I use your blower?'

He sank back in his chair and made an expansive gesture with his banana hands.

'Help yourself, Mr Nelson.'

I snatched up the receiver, dialled 100, asked the operator to get me Coombe Tracey 313 and in less than a minute Sir Henry Baskerville was on the line saying: 'Hallo, old man, how very nice to hear from you – when are you coming down?'

'Never mind about that,' I said excitedly. 'Just tell me this. Do the Barrymores have a large pantechnicon with them at the Hall with "The Barrymore Travelling Theatre Company" written on the side in big black letters?'

'Not to my knowledge,' replied the baronet in a mystified tone.

'Then watch your step,' I told him. 'They're the number one suspects.'

'Good God,' he gasped with horror. 'What on earth have you discovered, Ed?'

'I'll tell you when I get there,' I told him. 'I've broken down on the motorway and I'll have to come on by train.'

'Would you like Barrymore to meet you at Exeter in the Rolls?' he asked.

'Not bloody likely,' I growled. 'I'll rent a car and be with you late tonight.'

'Just as you like, Ed,' he replied in a slightly amused voice. 'There'll be a hot meal and a warm bed waiting for you.'

I replaced the receiver and looked at the fat man.

'How much do I owe you for the phone call and where's the railway station?'

'The phone call is on the house, Mr Nelson.' He plucked a half hunter out of his waistcoat pocket and lamped the dial. 'The station is just up the road and the next fast train from London to Exeter arrives at Swindon Junction in twenty minutes – if you look lively you'll catch it easily.'

'Thanks, guv,' I said. 'That bit of info you gave me has made the case I'm investigating as clear as mud.'

'Don't mention it.' His many chins trembled in a merry chuckle. 'The wife won't believe me when I tell her about all the excitement that's been going on here this afternoon.'

'So long,' I said, and made for the door.

'Have a nice day, safe journey, take care, adios,' the fat man called after me.

CHAPTER TEN

I dumped my suitcase, containing the five remaining bottles of Hankey Bannister's, in the overhead luggage rack and slumped into a corner seat in a second class compartment. There was only one other passenger in it, a wizened old man with gnarled fingers, an aquiline nose and skin like parchment. He was wearing a tweed deer-stalker hat, flecked with brown, and an ankle-length cloak with a cape attached to the shoulder. The cloak matched the deerstalker and beneath it he had on plus-four trousers in a lighter coloured tweed, long green woollen socks and stout brown brogues. He was puffing on an outsized hooked meerschaum pipe with a black stem and the compartment was filled with a dense fog of evil smelling tobacco smoke.

He gave me a one-toothed smile as I sat down. I gave him a nod but said nothing. I was a bit cheesed off at having left the remains of the bottle of Hankey Bannister's in the cab of the breakdown truck. The overpowering desire to escape from the car graveyard had outweighed all other considerations. I turned up the collar of my invincible trench-coat and settled down for a nice long kip.

'I differentiate between people by the bone structure of their faces,' croaked the old man.

'What's that?' I grunted, half opening one eye.

'It's the difference between one person's face and another's that makes them easily identifiable,' he explained.

I opened the other eye and squinted at him through the clouds of smoke.

'Yeah,' I faltered. 'It's the same thing with me.'

'Well, I never,' he exclaimed eagerly. 'What a small world it is. Of course, I have made a life-long study of people's faces and I have discovered that each differs quite considerably from any other.'

I wrote him off as an old loony and closed my eyes again.

'It's a little more difficult with identical twins,' he persisted. 'But even with twins there is very often a marked difference between one and another if you take the trouble to observe them closely.'

He was obviously not going to let me get any shut eye, so I lit a cigarette and added my own contribution to the pollution of the compartment.

'What about the Chinese?' I asked.

He gave me his one-toothed smile again.

'Now with ethnic groups there are very great differences between one face and another which may not at first be discernible to the Western eye,' he told me. 'But to a Chinaman another Chinaman is easily recognizable by his facial characteristics – particularly if they happen to be related by blood or marriage or, indeed, if they are acquainted with each other socially. I happen to have had the good fortune to travel widely in the Orient, as a young man, and astonishing as it may seem I have always found this to be the case.'

I threw both hands in the air deprecatingly.

'I never argue with an expert,' I said.

He changed the subject abruptly. 'How old do you think I am, young man?'

I took a stab in the dark. 'A hundred and ten?'

'Good grief,' he stammered. 'That is my exact age – how on earth did you know?'

'Just a lucky guess,' I smirked. 'You must be the oldest man in England?'

'I am,' he chuckled. 'Holmes is my name – Dr Barnardo Holmes. Perhaps you've heard of me? I was quite well known as a private investigator during the reign of Queen Victoria. But at the turn of the century I turned my back on such frivolities and devoted the remainder of my active life to giving shelter to orphaned and destitute children.'

I reached across the gangway and shook his scaly paw.

'Ed Nelson's the name,' I said. 'No, I don't think I have ever heard of you, Dr Holmes. But that's not all that surprising on account of I expect you had retired from public life before I was even born.'

'Quite so,' he sighed and puffed savagely on his pipe. 'There is no one alive now who was around in my young days.'

'Thing is, Dr Holmes,' I ventured hesitantly. 'It so happens that I am also a private detective and I am on my way to Devon to investigate a case right now.'

A gleam of interest lit up the old man's feeble eyes.

'You don't say?' he croaked delightedly. 'Is it a nice juicy murder case?'

'As it happens, I rather think it is,' I replied. 'But I don't usually take on murder investigations. I got lumbered with this one more or less by accident. A titled bloke called Baskerville snuffed it in the grounds of his stately home and . . .'

The old man leaned forward, his eyes bright with interest.

'Baskerville,' he interrupted me. 'Did you say Baskerville?'

'That's right,' I said. 'Does the name mean anything to you, Dr Holmes?'

'Does it mean anything to me?' he cackled. 'I should say it does! The hound of the Baskervilles was one of my most celebrated cases.' A mist of sadness clouded his eyes for a moment, then he smiled secretly to himself as though recalling some distant but pleasurable memory. 'My dear friend Dr Watson, now long deceased alas, wrote the whole thing up for *The Strand* magazine – in 1901 if my memory serves me correctly.'

'Stone me, Dr Holmes,' I gulped. 'The bloke who asked me to investigate the death of his friend Sir Charles Baskerville mentioned something about the footprints of a gigantic hound – but I don't reckon it could be the same one. I've never heard of a dog living for seventy-nine years.'

'No, no it couldn't be,' said Dr Holmes. 'I emptied five barrels of my revolver into its flank and shot it dead.'

'Quite a coincidence your having worked for a Baskerville, all the same,' I said. 'D'you think it's the same family?'

'Does your one live at Baskerville Hall, on the edge of the moor, not far from Coombe Tracey?' he inquired.

'It's a Coombe Tracey phone number,' I enthused. 'Must be the same lot. What was the full strength of your hound caper?'

'My memory is not what it was,' Dr Barnardo Holmes confessed. 'But there is a curse on the house of Baskerville, that I do remember. The legend of the spectral hound, when I looked into the matter almost eighty years ago, proved to be entirely false. It was a long and somewhat complicated investigation, as I recall, but the upshot of the matter was that a man with a sinister reputation, named Vandeleurs, had been plotting to lay his hands on the Baskerville estate and fortune. He was distantly related to the baronet through a younger son. Eventually, in the hope of achieving his evil aims, he acquired an enormous dog which was said to be a cross between a bloodhound and a bullmastiff. Vandeleurs was well aware that the Baskervilles of the male line had, for several generations, suffered from a serious heart condition and it was from this knowledge that this desperate man hatched his foul plot to do away with Sir Charles, the then incumbent of Baskerville Hall.'

'What did he do?' I asked excitedly. 'What did he do?'

'He half starved the poor hound in a derelict tin mine in a remote, and seldom visited, part of Dartmoor,' said Holmes. 'Then one night, at a time when he knew that Sir Charles would be taking his evening constitutional, Vandeleurs covered the wretched beast with a preparation of phosphorus and let it loose in the grounds of Baskerville Hall, in the hope that it would frighten old Sir Charles to death. And that, Mr Nelson, is exactly what happened.

The poor man's heart stopped beating as soon as the ravenous hell hound reared up before him.'

Two burly men in tight-fitting raincoats, with copper written all over them, suddenly appeared at the compartment door and leered at us through the window.

'Did Vandeleurs get captured, Dr Holmes?' I inquired urgently, in the hope of hearing the end of the story before the intruders invaded our compartment.

Holmes eyed the two men suspiciously and whispered.

'He perished upon the moor – sucked under in Grimpen Mire.'

The more bulky of the two men slid open the compartment door and entered, still smiling.

''Allo, Arthur,' he said to the old man. There was a touch of menace in his voice. 'Where the 'ell you bin? Me an' Tom 'ave bin searchin' all over the train for you.'

Guilt and fear came into the old gent's eyes, but he said nothing.

The big bloke turned his attention to me and said: 'I 'ope Arthur 'asn't bin a bovva to you, sir?'

I said: 'What do you mean *Arthur*? His name is Dr Barnardo Holmes and who are you, anyway?'

The man at the door exploded with laughter and bellowed: 'He's been pulling your leg, sir – old Arthur can come out with a pretty convincing line of chat when he's on form.' He eyed the old man reproachfully and a note of sarcasm crept into his voice. 'He's as harmless as a fly, sir, but he has got this thing about thinking he's a cross between Sherlock Holmes and Dr Barnardo, the founder of the famous orphanage chain. That's why we let 'im dress up in them funny clothes, see?'

'Yeah,' the one who was towering over me put in. ''E also gets people to guess 'is age and 'e'll agree to anyfing over ninety – wot figure did you come up wiv, sir?'

'A hundred and ten.'

'Cor,' he chuckled. 'That's the top whack yet – 'e's an oldster, awright, but seventy-eight is 'is proper age.'

I glanced across at the poor old fellow. His face was a

picture of utter desolation. Two thin rivulets of tears dribbled down his cheeks.

I glowered first at one man and then the other.

'What a pair of right bastards you are,' I snapped. 'You couldn't've smashed an inoffensive old chap's dream world more completely if you'd taken a bloody great sledge-hammer to his skull – who the sodding hell are you anyway?'

The big man drew himself up to his full height and adopted the tone of voice that officious twits like the filth, prison screws, income tax inspectors, jumped-up politicians, lunatic high court judges and other government servants, who are doled a little power to abuse, all go in for.

'We are male nurses from Black Tamerton mental institution,' he said. 'Arthur 'as bin looked after there for fifty years on account of 'e can't maintain 'imself in any uvva environment. We 'ave just escorted 'im up to London to see a 'Arley Street specialist about 'is ticker, wot's bin playin' 'im up lately. You may fink we don't give a monkeys about the patients in our care, sir – but you'd be wrong.'

'Well don't take the piss out of him, then,' I said.

'Arthur enjoys a joke with the best of them,' retorted the bloke at the door. 'Isn't that right, Arthur?'

Arthur blew his nose into a big red polka dot hankerchief and gave us his one-tooth smile.

'Any chance of a cup of tea and a bun, Mr Jenkins?' he asked the big man.

''Course there is,' he replied. 'Come along now, Arthur, we'll be at Exeter soon and the van will be waitin'.'

The crafty old codger got himself to his feet with the aid of a stout walking stick and he shuffled slowly towards the door, with the heavy either supporting or restraining him by the arm – I couldn't tell which. He paused at the door and gave me a sidelong glance.

'Don't forget what I told you about the Baskervilles, young fella,' he croaked. 'There's a curse on that family, take my word for it – and be careful upon the moor. The mire has claimed many a good man as well as desperate villains.'

Then he disappeared from sight along the corridor sandwiched between the two male nurses. I thought about getting a second bottle of Hankey Bannister's out of my suitcase, but changed my mind. Reg Mortimer had warned me that Muddicoombe-in-the-Moor was well over an hour's drive from Exeter and I didn't fancy getting off on the wrong foot by finding myself being asked to blow into a Devonshire Constabulary breathalyser.

CHAPTER ELEVEN

The gaunt granite turrets of Baskerville Hall loomed out of the swirling Dartmoor mist like a bad movie set for Dracula's castle. As the wheels of my hired Hillman crunched up the gravel drive it crossed my mind that you would have been hard put to it to conjure up a more fitting venue for murder.

Electric light filtered through the curtains in the downstairs windows of the house and I sent up a silent prayer that if a remote pile like this had managed to get itself plugged into the telephone and electricity grid, it had also succeeded in getting itself connected to the mains water supply and a septic tank.

The huge iron-studded door swung open, as I got out of the car, and an unmistakable squat silhouette was etched against the warm yellow light from within.

'Hello there,' he called. 'Is that you, Ed?'

'No,' I called back. 'It's Bela Lugosi. Is this the residence of the Baron Frankenstein?'

'You bloody fool!' he laughed. 'Do come in out of this filthy weather.'

I climbed the short flight of stone steps that went up to the front door and shook his extended hand. A large drop of freezing water escaped from a leaky gutter above and landed on the nape of my neck.

'Welcome to Baskerville Hall, Ed,' smiled Sir Henry.

'Yeah,' I said and followed him inside.

'Dump your suitcases anywhere,' he told me, 'and don't make a racket. I want to have a word about this Barrymore business before they know you're here.'

I glanced around the hallway nervously expecting to see a crouched bearded figure lurking in the shadows.

'In here,' hissed the baronet.

On iron dogs, in a fire-grate that took up a third of the drawingroom wall, enough wood to build a staircase was blazing.

My host had the good sense and common decency to make for the silver-gilt drinks tray on the sideboard.

'Whisky?' he inquired.

'About a pint,' I nodded, 'with a splash of soda and a cube of ice in it.'

He brought it across to me, the flickering firelight painting his rat-face rosy as he observed me suspiciously under frowning brows. His bonhomie seemed to have disappeared now he'd got me in his den.

'Where did you phone from?' he snapped.

'Swindon,' I said.

'Then what was all this nonsense about a pantechnicon?' The tone was not friendly.

'It was the most fantastic coincidence,' I enthused. I took a deep draught from my whisky tumbler and sighed with pleasure. 'Mind if I sit down?' I asked.

'Go ahead,' he agreed without cracking a smile. 'But I want an explanation of your wild accusations about my butler and housekeeper – and I want it now.'

'Okay, okay,' I soothed and let myself down into the luxurious depths of a big leather library chair. Sir Henry stood tensely with his back to the fire, his feet slightly apart, his hands in his bulging pockets and the firelight flickering on his neat little corduroy backside. I wondered for a moment whether the bulge in his right hand pocket could have been a fire-arm. Then I remembered that I was in Devon, not Soho. More likely a pair of secateurs, I told myself, and relaxed. Sir Henry's beady little eyes were fixed on me measuringly.

'Shoot,' he ordered, in unbecoming slang.

I told him about my breakdown and what the garage man had said about the Barrymore pantechnicon. He cross-questioned me about it closely, but finally his brow lightened and he let out a bark of laughter.

'So your reason for suspecting the Barrymores is that they once owned a pantechnicon which they've now got rid of?' He made it sound as silly as he could possibly manage. Grinning broadly he wandered over towards the drinks tray and took the stopper out of a decanter of port.

'There are plenty of reasons for suspecting the Barrymores,' I came back at him. 'He's got a bushy black beard for a start – or has he shaved it off?'

'The fungus is still in evidence,' Sir Henry assured me as he tipped the decanter over a small glass.

'Then there's the mystery of the disappearing pantechnicon which they wouldn't let the garage man look inside.'

I was about to carry on and point out that they were presumably using it to run container loads of hot antiques to Plymouth, when I was seized by unaccustomed caution. It was Willy's business anyway. He might be the biggest mobster since Reggie Kray, but as long as he was a client of mine he deserved the same guarantee of confidentiality as anyone else I worked for.

'And they were working here at the time Sir Charles died,' I finished lamely.

Sir Henry picked up his glass of ruby liquid and held it up to the light. 'Clear as a bell,' he murmured with satisfaction. 'Horribly cloudy last time. I had to show Barrymore how to filter it myself.' Then he turned to me and gave me a crooked smirk.

'I don't see that you've anything on the Barrymores, Ed,' he said. 'And I certainly wouldn't want you to have. They turn out to be the best thing my cousin's left me. She's a really inspired cook and he floats around playing the butler out of some play Oscar Wilde would have written if he'd thought of it. I was really horrified when I got your phone call. I can't see how I could live in this draughty old pile without them.'

I took another deep and satisfying belt of whisky and wagged my finger at him. 'Take care,' I warned. 'Don't let the Barrymores off the hook too lightly.'

'Tell you what we'll do,' he said. 'We'll have Barrymore in and you can ask him about the pantechnicon yourself.' He went over to the fireplace and pulled a white porcelain nob out of the wall and shoved it back again. A moment or two later an elegant looking bloke in soup and fish, sporting a black, shaggy beard, came silently into the room. It wasn't the geezer who had been bird-dogging Sir Henry all over the place in the white Mercedes.

'May I be of service to you, sir?' he inquired politely, in a rich baritone voice.

It struck me that he was hamming it up a bit, but what else can you expect from an actor, on stage or off?

'This is my friend Mr Nelson, Barrymore,' Sir Henry explained. 'He wants to put one or two questions to you.'

Barrymore turned towards me and bowed with just the right degree of servility for an 1890s melodrama.

'If I can be of any assistance, sir?' He managed to turn the phrase into an interrogative.

'Yeah,' I said, as I rolled myself over to face him in Sir Henry's deep leather chair. 'Where have you and the missus stashed that pantechnicon of yours?' I was gambling on shock tactics, but the servile gaze he had directed at me didn't even flicker.

'I beg your pardon, sir?' he came back at me as if he hadn't followed my drift.

'Are you denying that you and your wife used to run the Barrymore Travelling Theatre Company and drove a large pantechnicon with its name painted all over the sides?'

The so distinguished butler struck a martyred pose – it looked like St Sebastian without the arrows.

'Unfortunately, sir,' the martyr informed me, 'the taxation authorities saw fit to take possession of the company's wheels as part payment of some outstanding liabilities.' He sighed deeply. 'That proved the death blow to our thespian ambitions.'

'But you were driving through Swindon in it less than two years ago,' I objected. 'Surely by that time you'd packed up the company and come to work for Sir Charles?'

Barrymore cast me the kind of despising glance that a maths master might cast a sticky-fingered schoolboy who'd failed to master vulgar fractions.

'When we first came to Baskerville Hall,' he explained, 'we had not discharged the whole of our previous liabilities.'

'In other words,' Sir Henry translated for my benefit, 'they didn't wind up the theatre company and settle with the Inland Revenue until after they started work here. Surely you can follow that, Ed?'

'Okay, okay,' I said. 'It's as clear as mud and I suppose it lets you and your wife off the hook as far as doing in Sir Charles is concerned.'

'You can serve Mr Nelson's dinner now, Barrymore,' rapped Sir Henry, to cover up my *faux pas*.

Most domestic staff nowadays would get the dead needle, pack their bags and leave if their employer spoke to them like that. But not Barrymore, he simply bowed slightly, said: 'Certainly, sir,' and made a discreet exit, down stage left.

The pheasant was the best thing I'd tasted since a client took me to Wheeler's fish restaurant in Old Compton Street, Soho, a year or two ago and introduced me to the oyster. It was too good to throw up in the dead of night so I flatly refused Sir Henry's insistence that I pour a bottle of *Chateau Lynch Bages* 1967 on top of the whisky.

I took a shufty round the dining-room in which Sir Charles had installed low sexy lighting, just like a London restaurant. The walls were hung with sinister portraits of old geezers in kit dating back to a time in English history when you could get a gallon and a half of whisky for a groat, and tearaways, like my friend Willy Paradis, were hanged in chains at Tyburn. Most of the furniture, though old in design, didn't look distressed enough to be genuine antique. The same had been true in the drawingroom and I reckoned they were all reproductions supplied by Reg Mortimer.

The young baronet sat beside me at the snooker-sized dining-table while I ate, chatting aimlessly about this and that. His exciting plans for the home farm, restocking the dairy herd and reclaiming the marshland that was beginning to encroach on the Baskerville estate. Then suddenly, as I mashed the last crispy golden brown roast potato into the remaining dregs of delicious gravy, he looked me straight in the eye and said:

'How and when will you begin your investigation into the circumstances surrounding the mysterious death of my cousin?'

'Dunno,' I shrugged. 'Probably play it by ear, the same as always – that's the advantage that a private eye has over the CID. They have strict procedures they have to stick to. Taking down statements, threatening the guilty and innocent alike – you know, that kind of stuff. But a private eye who knows his business stays loose – just nosing around here and there until he comes up with something.'

'Well, I hope to God it isn't going to take too long, Ed.'

I held my hands palms inwards about six inches apart.

'It might take as long as that, Sir Henry.' I threw my arms open to their fullest extent. 'Or it might take that long.'

Barrymore swanned in to clear the table.

'My compliments to the chef,' I told him contentedly.

'Thank you, sir,' he replied. 'My wife will be pleased.'

'Coffee, Ed?' asked Sir Henry.

'No thanks.' I gave my gut a resounding slap. 'I'm knackered. Today has been one of the worst I have ever lived through. What I need is a good long kip.'

'Good idea,' he said. 'I'm sure we could all do with a good night's sleep.'

The airy bedroom that my host showed me into was as cold as a witch's tit and not quite as big as the Lyceum ballroom. It was dominated by a vast catafalque of a four-poster bed with tapestry hangings and a brightly coloured patchwork quilt.

'What do you want me to do?' I asked. 'Sleep in here or invite three or four dozen of my most entertaining friends down from London and throw a party?'

'Barrymore has put a hot water bottle in the bed,' he smiled. 'I'm sure you'll be quite comfortable.'

'Thanks a lot,' I said. 'Good-night.'

'Good-night, old boy,' he said and went out.

It was some time later when I was suddenly aroused from my drunken torpor by the sound of a woman sobbing outside my door.

'Stone the crows,' I groaned and buried my head under the bed covers. 'The bloody house is haunted.'

CHAPTER TWELVE

I woke up with a jolt next morning a little after eight, sat bolt upright and grabbed my head. I never find waking up in the morning easy, even when I'm kipping on the sofa in the familiar surroundings of my office. But I get the horrors when I wake up in a strange bed; most often it means I'm in some scrubber's bedsit who I picked up pissed in a boozer the night before and occasionally it means a police station cell.

I glanced wildly about and it was a full three minutes before the circumstances that had brought me to this place came flooding back. I threw back the covers and swung my legs over the side of the dirty great bed; it was so high off the deck my feet did not touch the floor. I jumped the remaining couple of inches, slightly twisted my ankle, limped over to the window and drew the curtains.

The fog had cleared and I was now able to see the surroundings. There were a lot of fat grey clouds in the sky, but enough blue here and there to make a pair of sailor's trousers. The rough bracken-covered landscape of Dartmoor rolled away to the horizon beyond the garden. There were a few stunted, wind-bent trees dotted about with all of their branches pointing to the west. It was almost as though the branches had been pruned into that strange shape with a buzz-saw. In the distance mysterious rocky tors climbed out of the ground, like neolithic giants. There was also an occasional patch of green on which diminutive Dartmoor ponies and cattle grazed.

I got my trench-coat off a hook on the back of the door, slipped it on over my pyjamas and sat down in a chair. I lit a cigarette and got my morning smokers' hack over with. There was a door ajar, half a mile away, on the far side of the room and when I trecked over there barefoot and pushed it open with the palm of my hand a well equipped modern bathroom came into view.

A scalding hot bath, close shave, clean Y-fronts and a crisply laundered shirt made a new man of me. I trotted down the great carved staircase with a spring in my step, struck a red topped match on a suit of armour in the hall, lit the second fag of the day and pranced into the drawing-room.

Sir Henry was seated in an armchair next to the crackling log fire, reading the *Financial Times*. He looked up as I came in and gave a friendly nod.

'Morning,' he said. 'I expect you'll be wanting some breakfast. Did you sleep all right?'

'Like a top,' I replied, cheerily. 'Only got woken up once – by a woman blubbing outside my door.'

'Surely not,' he said. 'You must have dreamt it.'

'I dream about women from time to time,' I conceded. 'They are usually naked and doing naughty things to me, but so far none of them have ever cried about it.'

He shrugged. 'There's only one woman living in the house,' he said, 'and that's Mrs Barrymore. She doesn't strike me as the type to wander round the house crying in the middle of the night, though I've only known her for a couple of days, of course.'

'Unless your house is haunted,' I told him, 'it's got to be her. What's she like?'

'You can see for yourself,' he replied, 'and order some breakfast at the same time.'

He reached over and pulled the bell. In next to no time the other half of the Barrymore double-act put in an appearance. She was a woman of Wagnerian proportions in a forget-me-not patterned pinafore. She had a mountain of auburn hair piled on her head and loosely secured by tortoise-shell combs; to judge by the scarlet highlights, its colouring was artificial. Her face itself was plastered with make-up as if she was about to take the boards as Desdemona or Hedda Gabler.

She had given her eyes bright purple shadows, while her lashes were blackened and curled upwards. The eye itself was outlined in black pencil, but I thought I could detect red inflammation under the lining – as if the make-up was designed to cover tell-tale traces of her tears.

'Mrs Barrymore?' I said.

'Yes, sir,' she said.

I mustered a warm friendly smile, the one I use to get women grovelling at my feet.

'I must thank you for the wonderful pheasant you served up for my dinner last night, Mrs Barrymore.'

'How kind of you to mention it,' she gushed and turned a glinting smile on her employer. 'I was *Cordon Bleu* trained before going into the theatre, you know, Sir Henry. I'm frightfully rusty, of course, but it's such blissful fun having a go at the old *haute cuisine* again after all these years.'

'Really? I hadn't realized that,' muttered Sir Henry, momentarily thrown off balance by her intimate revelations.

Mrs Barrymore rounded on me. 'I suppose you'll be wanting the works,' she giggled winsomely. 'Orange juice, museli, bacon, egg and sausage. What about muffins? It's no trouble to fix them.'

Her menu had a horrid effect on my stomach muscles. Even the idea of it brought me close to throwing up. I hoped she didn't notice I'd turned an interesting shade of green.

'Just toast and coffee,' I told her quickly.

'Ah, a continental breakfast,' she nodded crestfallen. But she braved up to the disappointment and gave me a toothy leer. 'I'll pop my head round the door and shout cooee when it's ready,' she informed me.

Sir Henry buried his head in the *Financial Times* hoping, I presumed, to discourage further conversation. I gave Mrs Barrymore a flashing smile and said: 'Strong black coffee with plenty of sugar.'

Over breakfast we discussed a number of vital issues.

'Eyes red-rimmed and bloodshot under the war-paint,' I maintained vehemently.

'If you smother your face in as much gunge as that, it's certain to make your eyes water,' Sir Henry objected.

'Want a bet?' I asked, jamming a golden corner of toast into my mouth liberally smeared with dairy butter and home-made marmalade.

'Fifty pee,' the millionaire agreed crisply.

Then I told him about the old boy I'd met in the train the night before who'd said his name was Dr Barnardo Holmes, but turned out to be a loony called Arthur.

'Any truth in his theory that there's a curse on the house of Baskerville?' I inquired.

'The legend of the hound is common knowledge,' Sir Henry scoffed. 'We certainly had a very badly behaved ancestor, around the time of the Cavaliers and Round-heads, I think, who hunted down an innocent village girl with his pack of hounds and is supposed to have brought a curse on the family. It's a load of moonshine, if you ask me.'

'So my batty old friend knew what he was talking about,' I exclaimed with surprise. I carried a brimming cup of black coffee, heavily laced with sugar, to my lips; it was a lot stronger than I'd bargained for and I fell about coughing my guts out for a minute or two. Sir Henry slugged me on the back in the hope of speeding my recovery and the paroxysm passed.

'What about one of your ancestors being frightened to death by a faked up hound? I asked.

Sir Henry groaned and leant back in his chair.

'It's one of those tiresome things one never hears the end of,' he explained, 'if one happens to have the surname Baskerville.'

'Oh, yes?' I murmured, wondering whether to risk some more coffee.

'Have you ever heard of a writer called Conan Doyle?'

'It rings a bell somehow,' I frowned, trying to remember why.

'Well, somewhere around 1900 he wrote this story called *The Hound of the Baskervilles*. He was quite a friend of the family at the time, I believe, and he'd heard the legend of Sir Hugo and the hell hound. He made up this silly murder story around the legend and had his fictional detective Sherlock Holmes investigate it. He didn't even have the decency to change our name to something else. I mean, if he'd called it *The Hound of the Barrington-Smythes* or something, no one would have minded.'

'Sounds a bit of a bounder to me,' I grinned encouragingly.

'The family were frightfully upset, of course. And Conan Doyle was never invited down here again – even after he was knighted, I believe.'

'Quite right,' I said, allowing my knife to squeak on the plate as I scraped the last bit of delicious marmalade on to my toast.

'The book was a big success,' Sir Henry continued plaintively. 'And the upshot is that whenever one says one's name is Baskerville, people ask if one's related to the hound. I must have explained the whole thing to hundreds of people by now.'

'So what about my friend on the train?' I asked.

'I imagine he'd read the book too, and being a loony, decided he was Sherlock Holmes himself. It's quite common. Masses of people think they're Napoleon and Hitler and things.'

CHAPTER THIRTEEN

At ten o'clock Reg Mortimer came striding up the drive
with a funny looking creature trotting along at his heels
that looked like a furry tea-cosy. I saw him approaching
through the drawingroom window and went out to meet
him.

'Ah, there you are, Ed,' he cried, as I came abreast of
him. 'I hope you didn't have too much trouble finding the
old place. Most people do. It's a bit off the beaten track.'

The furry tea-cosy yapped, jumped up at me and left
muddy paw marks on the trousers of my best blue suit.

'Down, Scruffy,' shouted Reg. 'Down!'

I eyed the little mutt closely but couldn't make head nor
tail of it except that one end wagged and the other had a
long pink tongue hanging out of it. I made a half-hearted
attempt to brush the mud off my trousers and the furry
tea-cosy, thinking I wanted to play, wagged its rear end
furiously, yap yap yapped and jumped up at me several
more times.

'Down Scruffy, down Scruffy, down!' Reg shouted again
and again.

But the little bugger kept right on jumping up at me
until my jacket and trousers were stamped with his muddy
paw prints, like arrows on a Victorian convict's prison
uniform.

'You're a very disobedient little dog,' Reg scolded him,
good-naturedly. 'You must excuse him, Ed. He's only
trying to be friendly – I'm sure the mud will brush off
without too much difficulty once it's dry.'

'It's my best suit,' I grated, eyeing the tea-cosy savagely
and wondering whether Reg would ever speak to me again
if I gave it the kick it deserved.

'I thought you might like a guided tour of Coombe Tracey,' Reg explained, folding his arms and kicking the gravel while he spoke. 'It might be a useful start to your investigations if I introduce you to one or two people.'

He was obviously hoping to horn in on my operation and keep tabs on what I was doing. He should have been busy in his antique shop after spending a week away from it in London. But that was no skin off my nose.

'Right,' I said. 'What time do the pubs open round here?'

'I think the Devil's Stone Inn opens at ten-thirty,' said Reg, a disapproving frown appearing on his brow. 'But it's a good three-quarters of an hour walk, so we won't be there before eleven.'

'Walk, did you say?' I stammered in amazement. 'You can walk if you like but I'm taking the car.'

'It's such a fine morning – just the weather for walking,' Reg argued.

'Even better for driving,' I told him adamantly.

I popped back into the house to tell Sir Henry what I was doing and pick up my trench-coat.

'What time can I expect you back?' he asked.

'When you see me,' I informed him.

Scruffy was sitting panting beside my hired car with his tongue hanging out when I came out of the house. He looked as if he had just rolled in a cow pat. I backed off as he scampered towards me and hid behind Reg.

'My trench-coat is not going to get the same treatment as my suit,' I remarked, sharply. 'If that little bugger is coming with us, he can ride in the boot.'

'He'll behave himself,' Reg assured me. 'He can curl up on my lap.'

'Errk,' I sniffed, disdainfully. 'Rather you than me.'

As we started down the drive I asked Reg to give me a run down on the locals I needed to treat as possible suspects.

'This is a very sparsely populated corner of the country,' he pointed out. 'You can count almost all the locals on the fingers of one hand.'

'Go ahead,' I invited him.

'Well, to begin with there's Giles Stapleton and his sister Margaret who live in Merripit House. Giles runs a tomato and long-stem roses nursery on the few acres that belong to the house and Margaret has recently opened a sort of whole food restaurant.'

'What's a sort of whole food restaurant?' I asked.

Reg explained: 'She only serves meat and vegetables that have not been contaminated by chemical additives or insecticides.'

I said: 'I think I know what you mean – it's what they call "ethnic", isn't it?'

'I believe you're right,' agreed Reg. 'I haven't had a meal there myself yet, but it's said to be very good for you.'

'Anything sus about them?' I asked.

'Sus?'

'Suspicious, mate?'

'Not that I know of.' He went on hurriedly. 'Giles is about forty, but his sister is considerably younger and a very attractive girl. They have lived at Merripit House for about four years, but I'm afraid I can't tell you where they came from before that.'

'So much for the Stapletons,' I said. 'Who's next?'

'Well, there's old Ivor Frankland at Lafter Hall. He writes for the *Spectator*.'

'He the nut who keeps spotting UFOs through his telescope?' I asked.

'That's right,' Reg replied.

'What else can you tell me about him?'

'Oh, lots,' he cried. 'Mr Frankland is a very well known character in these parts. He's a great chum of Jeremy Thorpe, the former liberal party leader, who you will remember was acquitted at the Old Bailey last year of plotting to murder his what was said to be one-time boy-friend. Thorpe has a cottage in Devon, you know.'

'You don't say! Tell me more.'

'Ivor is the son of the famous novelist and wit, Evelyn Frankland – perhaps you have read his books?'

'Never read a book in my life' I grunted. 'And I'm not starting now.'

'His most famous work was *The Decline and Fall of Rupert Goldsmith*. I'm sure you've heard of that, Ed?'

'Saw the movie of it with Laurence Olivier and Joan Collins,' I admitted crustily. 'Anything else?'

'I have, on several occasions, read reports in the press about libel actions brought against him by people he has written awful things about in the *Spectator*. And I once read that the editor had almost been persuaded by his lawyers to discontinue Frankland's column altogether because the out of court settlements had grown so large.'

'Did he have a go at Sir Charles Baskerville in his column?' I asked.

'No, but they hated the sight of each other,' Reg replied. 'Frankland couldn't stand the idea that Sir Charles, a self-made man, had enough money to reclaim Baskerville Hall and set himself up as a country squire. They had several heated arguments in the early days, but in more recent times Frankland simply cut him.'

'That makes Frankland my number one suspect,' I said. 'Unless you can come up with a more likely candidate.'

'Surely you don't mean it, Ed,' Reg spluttered. 'Frankland may be a bit dotty, but he certainly isn't capable of murdering anyone.'

'Anyone can commit murder if they set their mind to it,' I told him. 'That's why most murderers are first offenders – they lose control just once in their lives and that's it.'

I cast a glance at Reg and said: 'Any more?'

'Well, there's old Lavender, the vicar. There are a few hill farmers scattered about the moor and the local trades people in the village. Besides that, there's only the residents of the ghastly caravan park at Great Sourton. Some of them seem to live there all year round. I've no idea what they do for a living; perhaps they commute into Exeter. They all seem to have large cars.'

We crunched into the old world gravel car park of the Devil's Stone Inn at exactly 10.35. It was one of those picturesque, rose-covered dumps on the outside but the interior had been invaded by Axminster and horse-brasses. It was littered with fruit machines and complicated electrical TV games that made uncanny, supernatural pinging noises.

A buxom country wench with a frizzy hair-do, defying the chilly weather in an off-the-shoulder cotton blouse, came over and gave me the prettiest smile I'd seen since I arrived in these parts.

'What be you 'avin, zur?' she asked in a lilting Devonshire accent.

'Large whisky.' I glanced at Reg. 'What's yours?'

'I'll just have half of lager, if I may, Molly,' he said to the girl.

There was one very old geezer with a muddy jacket and gumboots leaning over the fire with a pint pot of bitter at his side, but otherwise we had the place to ourselves.

Scruffy made the most of it, dashing up and down and in and out of the chairs yapping. After shouting at him ineffectually a few times, Reg produced a lead and tied him securely to the leg of the table to which we'd carried our drinks.

The pretty girl busied herself unpacking a cardboard box of potato crisps.

After he'd downed his glass of lager, Reg suggested we push off and make a tour of the village.

'Quite unnecessary,' I assured him. 'If we stay here the suspects will come to us without our having to shlap around and look for them.'

'But some of them don't use the pub,' Reg objected. 'Especially not on a weekday morning.'

'Those are not the kind of people I wish to meet,' I told him severely.

After a while he turned huffy and, having made some snide allusions to my proclivity for drink, he told me he had far too much to do to waste the morning in a pub.

'See you around, then,' I told him kindly.

He still hovered as if in two minds as to whether he should leave me.

'I tell you what,' he suggested. 'Why don't you come up to the shop and have a bit of lunch later on?'

'I wouldn't like to promise,' I told him cautiously. 'I might get tied up here.'

'The pub closes at two,' he pointed out.

'Does it really?' I gasped. 'As early as that? In that case I'll drop into your shop around 2.15.'

'I'll see if we can knock up a bit of salad,' he said, turning to leave with a cheery smile and calling his unruly mutt to heel.

'What do you take me for,' I said under my breath, 'a rabbit?'

'What's that?' he asked.

'Nothing.'

I spent the next hour or so very pleasantly chatting up the comely barmaid. Crumpet can be very thin on the ground in the country, but what little there is can often get bowled over by the glib patter of a travelling salesman from the Smoke, or even a down-at-heel private eye, come to that. I showered her with compliments about her peaches and cream complexion and a load of old moody about what a big wheel I was in the 'import and export business'. She seemed impressed and I hoped that it would pay dividends some lonely and chilly night.

Around 12.30 the pub gradually began to fill up. Apple-cheeked plough boys, with long hair and blue jeans, lumbered in and ordered pints of bitter and packets of cheese and onion crisps. They crowded the bar swapping rowdy stories about tractors and the chances of the local team thrashing the team from the neighbouring village in the darts tournament that night.

Molly got rushed off her feet pulling pints of ale and didn't have any more time for me. So I slid off my bar stool and wandered over to the fire, a glass of whisky clutched tightly in my fist. A man in brown corduroys, checked shirt and open-weave sweater smiled at me and said:

'You're Ed Nelson, aren't you?'

I stared at him in amazement. 'How did you know?' I asked.

'No mystery about it really,' he laughed. 'Reg Mortimer told me you were coming down and we don't get many new faces round here. In fact, you and Sir Henry in one week is pretty much a record.'

'So you just guessed who I was?' I inquired, still suspicious.

'That's right,' he said, smiling. 'For all I knew you could have been Sir Henry. But for my money you looked more like a private eye than a diplomat.'

He held out his hand to me. 'Stapleton's the name,' he said. 'But everyone round here calls me Giles.'

I transferred the whisky glass to my left hand and shook his horny toiler's fist. Its surface was scratchy and there was mud ingrained in the pores.

We settled at a corner table and started to rabbit.

'You've come down to look into the UFO business, haven't you?' he asked, 'and whether it had any connection with Sir Charles' death?'

'You seem to be pretty well informed,' I told him.

'Reg Mortimer's an old mate of mine,' he explained. 'Have you formed any views yet?'

'I've only just arrived,' I said, then lowered my voice to a mysterious note: 'But I've got one or two ideas which I can't really talk about.'

I was rather pleased with the effect.

'Quite right to be discreet, I'm sure,' Giles commended me. 'It's a very strange business and quite frightening. It was brave of Sir Henry to decide to settle here.'

'But surely this UFO business is a load of cobblers?' I remonstrated.

'More like moonshine,' he told me with a long face. 'It glows, this thing people keep seeing. Some say it's cigar-shaped and some say it's saucer-shaped but they all agree it hovers and glows.'

'Have you seen it yourself?' I asked incredulously.

'Only once,' he replied with a nod. 'I'd been over to Coombe Tracey and walked back across the moor. It was dusk and I was on the cart track that skirts the famous Grimpen Mire – and suddenly there it was in the distance. A large glowing object hovering over the mire.'

'Do people always see it in the same place?' I queried.

'It's over Grimpen Mire that most people have sighted it,' he agreed. 'But poor Sir Charles kept seeing it around Baskerville Hall. It was certainly sending him off his rocker, if you ask me.'

'Do you think it could be some optical illusion to do with marsh gas?' I suggested.

'Hardly,' he replied. 'Did you read about it chasing a light aircraft yesterday near Plymouth?'

'Blimey, no,' I gasped.

He stood up.

'Hang on,' he said 'and I'll see if Molly can dig up the paper.'

He came back five minutes later with another round of drinks and a copy of the *Western Morning News*.

'There you are,' he said. 'Front page story.'

I grabbed the paper and read avidly.

The piece was by Fletcher Robinson again, clearly a hard-working hack. What he said had happened was this. A small business-man's plane had taken off at Plymouth intending to fly up to Manchester at around five in the evening. Shortly after take-off the pilot noticed a glowing object in his rear view mirror. The glowing object followed him for about five minutes and then seemed to accelerate and come after him. He tried changing course and altitude but the mysterious 'thing' followed him, getting closer all the time. Finally he panicked and turned back into Plymouth. It was only as he was dropping down into the airport that the 'thing' sheered away and disappeared into the night.

'What an extraordinary story,' I said, putting the paper down.

'It does seem to confirm that there's some kind of

"Unidentified" object around, doesn't it?'

'I suppose it does look that way,' I agreed hesitantly.

Although he was a long way behind me, Stapleton had had a drink or two by now.

'I must have a slash,' he confided. 'Don't let anyone bag my seat.'

'Okay,' I agreed.

As he disappeared I noticed that a girl in a voluminous ankle-length dress was pushing her way towards me through the revellers. She was staring at me intently and a tight little frown creased her brow. She plonked herself uninvited in Giles Stapleton's chair, and grabbed my arm.

'Don't stay here,' she breathed in a low vibrant voice. 'For God's sake go back to London. It's not safe for you here.' Her breath was heavy with garlic.

I leant as far away from her as I could.

'What do you mean?' I asked, 'and who are you?'

'That doesn't matter,' she told me urgently. 'Don't you understand a warning? You're not safe here. Your life is in danger.'

Before I had time to inquire any further as to what she was on about, Giles returned.

Oh, hi there, Margaret,' he said with a grin. 'I see you've introduced yourself to Ed. What are you drinking?'

Her eyes flickered at me as if she'd prefer it if I stayed shtoom. Then she smiled prettily at Giles and said: 'Half a shandy, please, love.'

He pushed his way over to the bar, turning his back to us. And she grabbed me again.

'Please, please forget what I said,' she implored me. 'I didn't realize who you were. I thought you were Sir Henry.'

CHAPTER FOURTEEN

Coombe Tracey had a smaller population than Regent Chambers, the old building in the Smoke where I have my office. The Devil's Stone Inn was the only pub. There were half a dozen or so houses dotted around the village green, a Post Office-cum-grocery-provisions-shop and that, apart from the church with its steeple-clock stuck at a quarter to six, was more or less it. It was the kind of place where people spread malicious gossip about you if they see your bedroom light on after ten o'clock at night.

Reg's junk shop was two hundred yards or so down the road from the pub and I lurched in through the door at about a quarter past two.

'Where'sh my lunch?' I shouted.

'Coming up right away,' cooed a wispy-haired lady who was lurking behind the till.

'So glad you've made it,' said Reg heartily, coming forward. 'You haven't met my wife.'

'Wife?' I slurred in amazement. 'You never told me you had one of them.'

'He keeps it quiet,' giggled the wispy-haired lady.

'Margery, this is Ed,' Reg introduced us.

'Hello, Margery,' I said. 'Let's have the grub.'

'I'll just warm up the soup,' she said, breaking away from me and making for the door. 'I'll give a shout when it's ready.'

In the meantime Reg insisted on showing me round the shop.

Most of the rubbish on display looked as though it had fallen off the back of the rural district garbage truck. There were dozens of dirty old sauce, coffee and medicine bottles. Rusty biscuit tins, with chipped and faded pictures of horses, dogs, cats and royalty printed on the lids. Mounds of old brass door knobs, fire tongs and antiquated carpentry tools. He waved a hand expansively over his treasures and said: 'There's a fortune to be made out of old Victorian rubbish tips.'

'You don't say?' I shrugged.

'Yes, yes,' he insisted. 'Those bottles over there are worth three or four pounds each, depending on their condition. A Victorian chamber pot uncracked or chipped will fetch as much as ten pounds, even more if you export it to America. I have platoons of school-children digging up old rubbish tips for me at weekends and in the summer holidays. They turn up some marvellous things. Last year two little boys dug up a wonderful marble bust of Prince Albert – it had lain in the ground for almost a century but it was in beautiful condition. It fetched three hundred pounds at auction. I keep most of my better quality merchandise in a warehouse in Plymouth – you don't get any call for the really good stuff in a small village like this.'

'Did you say you'd got a warehouse in Plymouth?' I almost shouted.

'Yes, why?' Reg looked at me, surprised.

'Bears out everything Willy was saying,' I enthused, leaning over the back of a bust kitchen chair.

'Do be careful of that Windsor,' admonished Reg. 'It's quite a good one.' Then ignoring my drunken interjection he went on with his lecture.

'Take that Welsh dresser over there.' He pointed towards the back of the shop. 'I bought it for five pounds from an old lady over near West Trentworthy. She was having a modern kitchen unit installed in her cottage so she had no further use for it. It may not look like much now with all those layers of paint on it, but once I've soaked it in an acid bath and stripped it down to the beautiful grained pine that it was originally built from, a century ago, you wouldn't recognize it. You can't find wonderful, straightforward, artisan craftsmanship like that anywhere in the world today. By the time I've finished with it a New

York dealer will be able to hang a price tag on it for fifteen hundred dollars.'

A musical call of 'Cooee' from the upper regions was a welcome rescue. It was accompanied by a good deal of yap-yapping which seemed to indicate that Scruffy was also waiting for us above.

'I can't think what you see in that frightful little dog,' I groaned.

The hot, thick vegetable soup had the effect of sobering me down. I turned down the salad course but got stuck into some bread and cheese for afters.

To keep the conversation going I gave the Mortimers a pepped-up version of my Dr Barnardo Holmes anecdote. 'And Sir Henry told me over breakfast that the curse and the hound legend are quite true,' I finished with a flourish. 'I wouldn't want to hang around a spooky old pile like Baskerville Hall with a curse on my head, I can tell you.'

'Interesting you should have bumped into the Baskerville legend like that,' said Reg. 'The person who knows all about it is old Lavender, the vicar, of course. I'm not sure that he hasn't even got a copy of the original document.'

'I'll go up there after lunch,' I said. 'The Rev ought to be checked out anyway. And, for all we know, this UFO business may be the latest manifestation of the ancient curse.'

'Have you seen today's *Western Morning News*?' said Margery, trying to keep her end up.

'Yes,' I told her shortly.

The Rev Lavender was the kind of old style country parson you used to see in English wartime movies like *Mrs Miniver*. He was not too tall, fairly old and had unruly wisps of snow-white hair poking out from under his floppy brimmed felt hat. I found him in the garden of his rectory armed with a giant butterfly net.

'Mr Lavender?' I called out to him. 'Mr Lavender?'

He glanced about in every direction except mine, then looked up at the sky in case the voice he had heard belonged to his governor.

I cupped my hands around my mouth and called to him again.

'Good heavens,' he cried in a trembling voice. 'Where on earth did you spring from?'

'Name's Ed Nelson,' I shouted. 'I want a word with you.'

The old boy picked up his hat and hurried towards me smiling. The dog-collar was several sizes too large for him and hung loosely around his scrawny neck, like a hoop-la ring. His two-piece suit was pretty tatty and frayed at the cuffs. But there was a merry twinkle in his watery grey eyes and he spoke in a kind of sing-song voice as though chanting a psalm.

'Extraordinary, extraordinary,' he gasped as he came up to me. 'I do believe I saw a small tortoise-shell butterfly on the buddleia. I certainly wouldn't have expected to see one as late in October as this. It is one of the most familiar butterflies to be found in this part of the world. Actually it is very common everywhere, but it does illustrate a number of fascinating aspects of butterfly lore.'

'You don't say?'

'But I do, Mr Nelson,' he replied happily. 'I most certainly do. Did you know, for example, that the mother tortoise-shell has the ability to distinguish one species of plant from all the others that grow upon the moor? Unerringly she lays her eggs on the stinging nettle.'

'No,' I told him. 'I didn't know that.'

'This is not her own food plant, of course, but some strange instinct tells her that the nettle leaves are the favourite food of small tortoise-shell caterpillars.'

His enthusiasm was infectious and I found myself joining in the spirit of the thing.

'Now I call that flipping amazing,' I exclaimed. 'If you'll excuse my French, vicar.'

'Quite so,' he chuckled. 'The small tortoise-shell is undoubtedly a little miracle of Our Lord's creations. It actually passes through two generations in a single year and it is one of the few British butterflies that hibernates as a perfect insect. Most of our other butterflies perish before winter sets in, but the small tortoise-shell goes to sleep instead, sometimes spending six months, or even longer, in a torpid condition.'

'Lucky little chap,' I said. 'It's the kind of thing I often feel like doing myself.'

'One final point.' The Rev Lavender waggled a finger in my face. 'The plucky little tortoise-shell is a migrant. Vast numbers of them may have come, like the cuckoos and swallows, from lands that lie further south.'

'Blow me,' I came back at him excitedly. 'Just goes to show you, doesn't it? Thing is, parson, I wanted to have a little chat with you about the Baskervilles.'

He glanced up at the steeple-clock of his church. It was still stuck at a quarter to six.

'Perhaps you would care for a cup of tea?' he said. 'I usually have tea at this hour.'

Over a cup of strong Indian tea provided by his ancient housekeeper I explained my interest in the Baskerville legend.

Rev Lavender stood up abruptly and marched over to a heavy oak bookcase.

'Let me show you, Mr Nelson,' he said and reached down a weighty old tome bound in faded red leather. 'Come over here, will you?'

Embossed on the cover in gold leaf was a large cross, some kind of latin text and, *'Ye Coombe Tracey Parish'*, in ancient type.

He opened it at a yellowing, paper bookmark and jabbed a bony forefinger at the top of the page.

'There you are,' he said, standing aside. 'You may read it for yourself.'

I set light to a cig and leaned forward. The heading, in curly old-world lettering said: *'Ye Curfe of ye Baſkervilles'* and under it, *'Anno Dom 1742'*. I puffed a cloud of smoke into the air and had a bash at the dodgy looking lingo.

'Juſtice which puniſhes sin may alſo moſt graciouſly forgive it.' I glanced down the page in search of a juicy bit. *'It came to*

116

pafs that Hugo Bafkerville, of this parifh, in his evil paffion for the daughter of a yeoman who held lands next to the Bafkerville eftate did, one Chriftmas eve, carry off the maiden intent upon a long caroufe as was his nightly cuftom.'

I scratched my head and gave the old devil dodger a sidelong glance.

'Can't make head or tail or it, vicar,' I said. 'Looks like it was written by a bloke with false teeth.'

'Ah, yes,' he smiled, 'the written English of the eighteenth century can be very baffling if you are not accustomed to it. Spelling had not yet been formalized and the use of an "f" instead of an "s" was common practice, though never at the end of a word.'

'You live and learn,' I said.

'Perhaps you might find it a little easier to follow if I read it aloud to you?' he suggested.

'I doubt it,' I replied. 'Why don't you just give me the gist of it?'

What he came up with was this. The bad baronet Sir Hugo Baskerville, circa 1650, and some of his companions had carried off the innocent daughter of a local farmer. They locked her in an upstairs room at Baskerville Hall while they had a booze-up. When Hugo went up to have it off with her, she'd climbed out of the window and had it away down the ivy.

So Hugo got out his hounds and hunted her down across the moor. But this ungentlemanly behaviour was not approved of by the Almighty. He dispatched a hell hound to look after Sir Hugo in his turn. When his friends caught up with him on the moor, there was the village maiden stretched out cold. Beside her were Sir Hugo's hounds, huddled together and whimpering, while Sir Hugo himself was stretched on the ground with a vast hell hound, breathing fire, in the act of biting out his neck.

'And ever since a terrible curse has hung over the Baskerville family,' finished the vicar, shaking his head sadly.

I thanked him profusely for all his help and he pointed

me in the direction of the Devil's Stone Inn where I'd left the car.

It was half trying to rain, with a lowering grey sky and low flying clouds scudding by, that looked as though they'd knock over the steeple. The weather and puffs of wet wind that tried to knock me over, made the church-yard a sinister and threatening place. I glanced here and there at the inscriptions on the grave stones that crowded together on every side, like commuters in the London rush hour.

One to a kid of nine went:

> *Ah lovely flower! Soon snatch'd away*
> *To bloom in realms divine.*
> *Thousands will wish at judgment day*
> *Their lives were as short as thine.*

It made me wonder how my own epitaph would turn out. I let myself out of the thatched lychgate into the road, muttering to myself:

> *Here lies Ed Nelson private eye*
> *Gone to the great pub in the sky.*
> *In life he was a berk and a loser.*
> *You'll find him in the Heavenly boozer.*

When I got back to my car, parked outside the Devil's Stone Inn, a dog the size of a house came bounding towards me up the street wagging its bull-whip of a tail. It looked like a cross between a bloodhound and a Great Dane. I wrenched the car door open and leapt behind the wheel. But I'd left the window wound down and as I fumbled frantically in my trench-coat pocket for the keys the bloody thing stuck its massive head in through the window and licked me on the face with a vast expanse of pink tongue.

'Bugger off you bloody great softy,' I shrilled. 'Go and pick on someone your own size.'

A girl's voice, some way off, trilled: 'Heel, Tiny, heel.' The dog lost interest in me long enough to wind the window up.

A pretty young lass came hurrying towards me, scolding the dog. 'Bad boy, Tiny, bad boy. You mustn't go around licking strangers – if I've told you once I've told you a hundred times!'

The big dog cowered away from her with its head hanging in shame and its tail between its legs.

I wound down the window and shouted: 'Yeah, Tiny, you never know where strangers have been.'

'Sorry about that,' said the girl. 'He only wants to be friendly, that's all.'

'It's okay,' I said and drove off hell-for-leather up the street.

CHAPTER FIFTEEN

The day was dying in long hard shadows across the moor as I nosed the Hillman along the narrow country lanes, watching out for signposts for Muddicoombe. Setting out for Coombe Tracey, after breakfast, with Reg Mortimer in the passenger seat to direct me, had been a piece of cake. But I had paid no attention to the left and right turns he'd told me to make, and the return journey was proving a little more testing.

Getting to Coombe Tracey had taken ten minutes but now, flanked by steep banks of rustic hedges, the lanes with their hairpin bends seemed to go on forever. After half an hour I had to reluctantly admit to myself that I was well and truly lost. And a panicky little thought flitted across my mind that if I didn't get back to Baskerville Hall before night fell out of the sky I'd eventually run out of juice and get lost on the wild and desolate moor.

The thought popped out of my mind as quickly as it had popped in. A bloody great milk tanker came batting around a blind S-bend and threatened to take care of me right there and then. I instinctively swung the car away from the oncoming tanker, but there wasn't really anywhere to go. The Hillman, somehow, climbed a bracken-covered bank and clung there like a fly on a wall long enough for the tanker to shave by.

The sodding thing missed me by only a whisker and belted off down the lane and out of sight, sounding its klaxon triumphantly, but not noticeably slackening its speed. I should have been dead – the rest of my life has been borrowed time.

That was my first shattering experience but if the Baskerville caper was to teach me anything it was to keep off Devon roads.

Tanker drivers in the west country are under orders from the Milk Marketing Board in Whitehall to kill any motorist they meet on sight. An unsuspecting towny or even a local, for that matter, is taking his life in his hands every time he sets out in his car to travel from A to B. It's safer to drive paralytic drunk round Hyde Park Corner in rush hour traffic than it is to venture forth on to the Devonshire lanes in the daytime. At night it's a little less risky – at least you can see the glowing headlights of what's coming at you from some way off.

A couple of miles further on I came to a crossroads infested with white police cars with blue lights whirling and a large sign in red lettering on a white background that said: 'HALT POLICE'. I thought for a moment that the milk tanker had claimed another victim. But as I pulled up and yanked on the handbrake I could see no dead bodies in the road, no wrecked family saloons nor even an ambulance. I reckoned they must be doing spot checks with their breath test equipment. I hadn't had a drink since I got turfed out of the Devil's Stone Inn at 2 o'clock and it was now close to six. Whisky travels through my system at a rate of knots so there was a better than even chance that I'd show up negative.

A florid-faced country sergeant, with a violent orange, sleeveless wind-cheater over his blue tunic, ambled over and leaned on the roof of the car to get a better look at me through the window. Several feet away more filth congregated. They too were wearing orange wind-cheaters and one of them cradled a shotgun in the crook of his arm.

'What's up, officer?' I asked the florid-faced sergeant.

'Where be you goin', zur?'

'Baskerville Hall,' I smiled. 'I'm a guest of Sir Henry.' He didn't return my smile.

'Youm bain't on the right road, zur.' He eyed me suspiciously. 'Us'll 'ave to ask youm to get out of the car.'

'What for?'

'Just do what I tells you, zur.' His voice was hard at the edges and his mate with the shotgun had moved a little closer. 'This be a road block, zur.'

I made no reply and got out of the car. A uniformed inspector with pips on his epaulettes and silver scrambled egg on the peak of his cap ambled over and said: 'What have we here, Sergeant?' He didn't have a Devon accent.

'Dunno yet, zur,' he said and then to me. 'What be the licence number of this car, zur?'

'I don't know,' I shrugged. 'It's on the front and the rear licence plate – look for yourself.'

The inspector got stroppy.

'So you don't know the number of your own car?'

'It's not my car,' I told him. 'I hired it in Exeter yesterday.'

'Name?'

'Hertz Car Rental.'

'Your name, sir?' snapped the inspector.

'What the hell's all this about?'

The bogey with the shotgun moved even closer.

'I want your name,' the inspector demanded. 'And some means of identification.'

'Ed Nelson.' I looked at the shotgun. 'All right if I get my driving licence out of my inside pocket?'

The inspector said: 'Yes, but no monkey business.'

I slipped my hand under my trench into the inside pocket of my jacket and produced the document. The inspector snatched it out of my hand and lamped it with an eagle eye.

It was one of those flimsy green slips from Swansea that expire in the year 2000 with endorsements in coded letters, decipherable only to the expert eye.

'I see you got a DR30 five years ago, Mr Nelson,' the inspector said.

'A what?'

'A DR30,' he repeated. 'Driving whilst unfit through drink.'

'Oh, that,' I replied sheepishly. 'I was young and stupid

in those days. Now I'm older and still stupid – but a reformed character.'

He glanced at the sergeant and said: 'Search the car.'

'Yes, zur,' the sergeant said. He sloped off to the rear of the car and opened the boot.

I put on the kind of cringingly deferential voice that I know, from long experience, never fails to win the filth over and said: 'Can you, please, tell me what's going on, Inspector?'

'Decided to cooperate, have you, sir?' he clipped.

'Yes, of course,' I simpered. 'Please tell me how I can be of help?'

'Axeman Selden, the famous bank robber has escaped from Princetown prison,' he told me. 'Have you seen a desperate looking man on the road?'

'Yeah,' I said. 'A madman tried to mow me down in a milk tanker a mile or two back – licence number TGS 79 S. Do you think the escaped convict pinched it to make his get-away in?'

'I doubt it,' he replied sternly. 'The prison alarm bell only rang half an hour ago – he wouldn't't've had time to steal a milk tanker.'

'I guess not,' I agreed.

The sergeant came around from the back of the car and glanced into the passenger seats.

'There bain't nothin' 'ere, zur,' he told his superior.

The inspector returned my driving licence.

'All right, Mr Nelson, you can go.'

'Thanks a lot,' I said. 'Can you put me on the right road to Baskerville Hall?'

'It be back the way you came, zur,' the sergeant volunteered. 'Left at Pixton Cross and right at Crow Tor letterbox.'

'Thanks,' I said, got behind the wheel and nearly ran over the toe of the bloke with the shotgun as I made a U-turn.

Axeman Selden, like Willy Paradis, was an old style post-war tearaway who had climbed to the top of his profession the hard way. He was a crack peterman and I can well remember being lost in admiration of his talented history when I met him one night down the Hide Away club. He'd busted into his mother's gas meter when he was only five years old and blown his first peter in a sub-post office when he was just thirteen. After that, between lengthy lay-offs in the slammer, he went from strength to strength – blowing bank vaults all over the country, picking locks on diamond merchants' strong-rooms with little more than a hair pin and hi-jacking armour-plated security trucks stuffed with used ten pound notes. He wound up in the dock at the Old Bailey again about three years ago for blowing four bank vaults in a week. His total haul was not known for sure, but was estimated to be around half a million in readies and negotiable bonds, most of which had not been recovered. The judge had got a bit peeved and told him he was, 'A menace to society'. He was sentenced to thirty years. With all that money stashed away, there wasn't a high security nick in the country he couldn't buy his way out of. It was also pretty much on the cards that Willy Paradis had lent a hand in getting him sprung.

The sergeant's directions worked out more or less okay, not that naming the turnings did me much good. But I took a left at the first crossroads I came to and a right a mile or two further on at a corner, where I spotted a small red letterbox buried in the hedge. A few miles after that I thought I recognized a gnarled old oak tree that I'd driven past on my way into Coombe Tracey and ten minutes later I fetched up at Baskerville Hall.

Sir Henry listened, without comment, to my riveting report of the day's activities. I had a sneaking sus that he had other things on his mind, but he didn't say what they were and I didn't ask him.

Being in the cheerless, under-populated west country for a whole day and a night was something else, and it was beginning to get to me. I was already homesick for the lively pubs, sleazy gambling dens and tart-infested streets of Soho. My host's heavy after dinner port cast me down and I cleared off to my room at 11 o'clock, got into my pyjamas and knocked myself out with four or six hefty slugs of Hankey Bannister's.

In the dead of night the woman went blubbing past my bed chamber again. I slipped out of bed, tiptoed across the room and barricaded the door with a big carved chair, tilted backwards and jammed under the handle.

CHAPTER SIXTEEN

I woke up next morning with my usual start. And my spirits plummeted when it came back to me which neck of the woods I'd fetched up in. A swift butchers out of the window revealed great gusts of torrential rain falling out of a leaden sky.

'I'm jacking this caper in today and going back to London,' I muttered, as I set off on the mile long trek to my private bathroom.

Country capers were definitely not up my street. I didn't really give a monkeys whether Sir Charles kicked the bucket from heart failure or got the life frightened out of him by a flying saucer or a gigantic hound. It was not as though he had been one of our own or I owed him any favours. And to top things off there was the added certainty that if I set foot outside the house I would catch pneumonia and die. Even my invincible trench-coat would be no match for the monsoon that thrashed against the granite walls of Baskerville Hall with the fury of an avenging angel.

'Rather inclement weather, sir,' Barrymore, the old ham, commented as he poured my black coffee.

'Yeah,' I drawled, and then added sharply, in the hope of taking him off his guard: 'Who's the bird who wanders around the house in the middle of the night making with the water works?'

'I beg your pardon, sir?'

'Don't give me all that, Barrymore,' I sneered. 'There's a woman roaming around this gaff after lights out bawling her head off – she's done it two nights on the trot and I want to know who it is.'

'Unless you and Sir Henry have been having a bit on the

side, under cover of darkness,' snapped Barrymore dangerously, his servile mask slipping, 'there's only one woman in the house – and that's my wife.'

I pounced. 'How do you account for the red rings around your wife's eyes?'

Sir Henry strolled into the dining-room and sat down at the end of the table. Barrymore snapped to attention and replaced the servile simper on his face.

'Your wife is the only woman in the household, Barrymore,' Sir Henry observed mildly. 'It stands to reason that it must be she who is doing the crying – I certainly would not want to pry into any personal problems you and your wife may have, but in the circumstances I think it might be wise if you made a clean breast of it.'

The butler glanced wildly from me to his master and then back again. Then he gave a big draughty sigh.

'I'm afraid your ears have mistaken you a little,' he said, 'though I must apologize for your being disturbed.'

'Thought you'd know all about it,' I smirked with satisfaction and gave Sir Henry a knowing wink. 'You'll have to pay up, you know,' I reminded him.

'Come on, let's have it, Barrymore,' said the baronet.

'Well, it's like this, sir,' Barrymore began, bending a little at the waist and rearranging the table napkin on his arm. 'My wife has this little dog, a fox terrier, which we keep in the kitchen quarters. He's not as young as he was – we've had him for fifteen years now. And he's developed this nasty abcess on one of his upper teeth. When he's in pain he snuffles and sobs just like a human being. You must have heard him as the wife went past carrying him up to bed with her.'

Sir Henry struck the table with his hand and gave a bark of laughter. 'There you are, Ed,' he snorted. 'There's your sobbing woman for you. You owe me fifty pee.'

I put my hand in my pocket and came up with a fistful of change. I didn't believe a word of the old moody that the thespian had bunged us about his smelly little dog. But he probably had some dark reason for inventing the yarn, and I'd be more likely to tumble what his game was if I kept shtoom.

I came face to face with Mrs Barrymore half an hour later under the powerful electric light in the hall. There were red rings round her eyes okay.

The jangle of chimes Sir Charles had installed in the hall had summoned both of us to the front door. I wouldn't have gone if I hadn't seen it was Giles Stapleton, my boozing partner of the day before. I'd watched him through the drawingroom window jump out of a van and scamper for the door with a newspaper over his head. I couldn't leave the poor sod out in the pissing rain.

In the event Mrs Barrymore opened the front door and I sauntered up behind her.

'Hi, Liz,' Giles greeted her. 'I've brought the tomatoes. If it's convenient I'll fetch them in.'

'Super of you,' breathed Eliza. 'But you shouldn't have bothered in this frightful weather.'

'Can't let a spot of rain bother you if you want to make a living,' Giles assured her with a soppy grin.

'Depends how you earn your living,' I told him, joining them at the door.

'Morning, Ed,' said Giles.

'Private eyes never go out in the rain,' I told him.

'In that case, I suppose you're not going to give me a hand with the tomatoes,' he returned cheekily.

'You must be a mind reader, son.'

Mrs Barrymore gave me a disparaging look out of her great red, black and blue eyes. Giles squelched out to his van and came staggering back loaded with twenty or so wooden trays of tomatoes. He dumped them inside the hall door with a 'Phew!' just as Sir Henry came down the stairs.

'Sir Henry,' I called. 'Here's your neighbour, Giles Stapleton. You wanted to meet him, didn't you?'

I'd told him about my meeting with the Stapletons down at the Devil's Stone Inn and Margaret's strange warning. He'd looked decidedly hipped at the bird wanting him to clear off before she'd even met him and expressed a strong desire to meet the brother and sister act at the earliest opportunity.

The little wiry-haired baronet trod purposefully across the hall and observed Giles through narrowed eyes as they shook hands.

'Your Mrs B is helping out with my tomato glut,' grinned Giles winningly. 'Frightful this time of year. Everyone's tomatoes come on together and it's hard to get rid of them even at rock bottom prices.'

'Won't you come in for a moment?' Sir Henry invited him. 'I'm sure Mrs Barrymore can rustle up some coffee.'

'Right away,' she chirped and the rest of us filed into the drawingroom.

What Sir Henry was really after, of course, was a chance of meeting Margaret and finding out in person what the warning was all about. After we'd sat around jawing for a while, he suggested we push off down to the pub.

'I'm afraid I'm practically out of booze here,' he lied diplomatically.

'I'm not going out in that,' I said, pointing out of the window.

'I'll get the Rolls out,' he smiled. 'You won't get wet.'

'How about the bit between your front door and the car?' I said. 'And the bit at the other end, between the car and the pub – I've already completely buggered up my suede shoes since I've been here.'

Sir Henry looked me over and a faintly amused grin spread over his boat.

'Yes, Ed,' he said. 'I have to admit that you are not exactly kitted out for the country.'

'Never had any use for plus-fours,' I told him. 'They chap my crotch – at least I'm sure they would if I ever tried them on.'

'I'm sure that Barrymore can provide you with galoshes and an umbrella,' he persisted.

'Oh, all right,' I groaned and followed him out into the hall.

Giles left his tomato truck in the drive and we all piled into Sir Henry's Rolls. It was really Sir Charles' Rolls, of course. The new baronet liked slopping around in muddy corduroys and an old tweed jacket. He looked a bit out of place in the dirty great property tycoon's car. And, being a little squirt, he could only just see over the steering-wheel.

We called in at Merripit House to pick up Margaret. This was my suggestion, subtly designed to please my employer. We found her surrounded by plastic demi-johns, decanting some elder-flower wine to serve in her health food dump. She didn't take any persuading to ditch this boring occupation in favour of a few drinks with a titled millionaire in a Rolls. She'd jumped into the passenger seat beside Sir Henry before you could say Fletcher Robinson, and was chatting away nineteen to the dozen.

She was wearing the same ethnic skirt as the day before and I noticed that the bare feet in sandals which peeped below its hem were decidedly on the grubby side. She had wavy auburn hair which hung in a long uncombed mat down to her waist. On the other hand, she had a very pretty country girl's face, untouched by the products of Revlon, Elizabeth Arden or Helena Rubinstein. And her line of chat was quite jolly and amusing.

I could tell that Sir Henry took a shine to her straight off. Once we got to the boozer I dragged Giles off to the bar and pestered him with intimate questions about tomatoes while we ordered the drinks. I added a few difficult extras to the orders so's to spin out Margaret and Sir Henry's *tête à tête* which was clearly going great guns over at a corner table. Giles kept fidgeting and glancing over at them suspiciously. But I took no notice and asked Molly for ten packets of Rothmans in one go, explaining to Giles the dangers of running out when you were marooned in a dump like Baskerville Hall and surrounded by non-smokers. Molly had to go out to the store-room and rummage around for a new carton to deal with my shipping order.

When she got back I fired a number of questions at her about the history of the pub.

'Carved over the door outside is the date 1784,' I said. 'Have they really been pulling pints of ale in here ever since?'

Country folk love to bend your ear about the romantic history of their hostelries. She went into a long rigmarole about how the Devil's Stone Inn was named after a dirty great lump of rock that had been lying about in the Coombe Tracey churchyard since the beginning of time. Museum experts and archaelogists who still came to have a butchers at it from time to time remained undecided about how it got there – but everyone reckoned it was definitely a force for evil and able to wreak mischief upon life and limb. One old yokel who gave it a hefty kick busted his ankle and was lame for the rest of his days, and a young damsel who got screwed behind it by a randy plough boy, one summer's night, gave birth to Siamese twins – joined together at the nose.

When she'd finished telling me all that, I asked for two packets of potato crips, specifying one smoky bacon and one salt 'n vinegar. That took quite a while to sort out as well.

I was repaid for hanging things out by a glowing look from the baronet when we finally tottered over with the drinks. Giles had definitely gone off me. He plonked himself down between Margaret and Sir Henry and did his best to ruin the budding romance. He hardly bothered to acknowledge my existence.

Sir Henry told me later what Margaret's warning had been about. Being a simple soul, she was wholly convinced that the UFOs were genuine. She also believed that they had some special connection with Baskerville Hall and whoever owned it.

'There are these fantastic vibrations round the Hall,' she'd told him. 'You can feel them if you're psychic and they're really terrible.'

According to her, Sir Charles' death demonstrated that the extra-terrestrial agency behind the vibrations was hostile to Baskervilles. And if Sir Henry didn't watch out they'd do him in too.

'Jolly sweet of her to care,' Sir Henry told me in a soppy kind of tone that implied softening of the brain. He seemed to have forgotten that the bird had given the same warning to me before she'd cottoned who I was. But I didn't point this out as he was obviously pretty pleased with the idea that buxom Margaret was out to protect him.

Sir Henry drove the whole party back to Baskerville Hall at closing time, since Giles had left his truck there and needed to pick it up. Margaret just came for the ride.

As we reached the crest of the steep hill out of Coombe Tracey, and the russet moorland stretched before us, Giles called to the baronet to draw into a lay-by for a moment.

'Call of nature, eh?' laughed Sir Henry as the Rolls purred to a standstill.

'No. It's not that,' snapped Giles. 'I wanted you to look over there.' He pointed to a stretch of bright luscious green pasture that edged a spiky rock-crowned tor.

'Looks an edible bit of grass,' I said. 'Funny none of the sheep are having a lunch-time nibble.'

'They are sometimes deceived like you,' Giles told me with blood-chilling severity. 'That is the Grimpen Mire. It has claimed too many lives to number, many of them beasts, more than a few humans.'

In the silence that followed his pronouncement, even our breathing could be heard in the car.

'That lush and tempting green spells certain death to those who trespass on its surface. The unfortunate man or beast is sucked under – slowly, with inevitable certainty and no recourse. It is there, hovering over the mire, that hikers and villagers have seen the mysterious glowing saucer-shape.'

CHAPTER SEVENTEEN

Lafter Hall was one of those dirty great white elephants that the nouveau-skint gentry hand over to the National Trust in lieu of death duties. Baskerville Hall, which was no slouch when it came to boasting about how many drafty corridors and icy bedrooms it had, looked like a cottage by comparison.

It was Margaret Stapleton who'd got Sir Henry all roared up about making Ivor Frankland's acquaintance.

'You get this wonderful feeling of empathy with him,' she'd told the baronet. 'He's the number one real original who lives round here and, of course, the house is cluttered with fantastic antiques.'

Sir Henry had passed this info on to me, adding that Frankland was something of a national as well as a local celebrity, since anyone who was anyone read his column in the *Spectator*.

'You can't impress me that easily,' I told him. 'Never read the drivel in my life.'

'That doesn't surprise me,' he came back at me unkindly. 'You've never read anything at all as far as I can see.'

The upshot was that he dragged me off to Lafter Hall in the pissing rain to make the acquaintance of the notorious quill-pusher.

I gaped up at the terrifying pile in open-mouthed astonishment and gasped: 'We're not actually going in there, are we?'

'Don't see why not, old boy,' Sir Henry replied. 'Got to break the ice with the neighbours sooner or later.'

'You go in,' I said. 'I'll wait in the car.'

He said: 'No, no that wouldn't do at all.'

I said: 'Why not? I couldn't care less about meeting Mr Frankland.'

He said: 'I've brought you along because I want you to meet him.'

I said: 'You're an upper-class nob and Frankland is an upper-class nob. I'm sure the pair of you will get along like peaches and cream, without me around droppin' me aitches and making dim-witted jokes about the oil paintings and second-hand furniture.'

He glanced at me with intense irritation and his lips began to twitch, characteristic early warning signals of a dissatisfied client about to blow his stack. I had seen them so often I could now recognize them a hundred yards off.

'Two days ago,' he snapped, 'you were telling me that Frankland was your number one suspect. And now you don't even want to meet him. I'm beginning to wonder what the hell I'm paying you for.'

'I've been meaning to have a word with you about that, Sir Henry,' I stuttered. 'Fact is, I don't really think that this is my kind of case – I get nervous if I see a blade of grass, let alone wander about the countryside exposed to the elements. On Dartmoor that goes double – nasty foggy place and so dark most of the time you never know what you're going to tread in next. Tell you what I'll do with you, Sir Henry. I'll just scoot off back to London and I won't even send you a bill, right?'

He gave me a speculative look and for a glorious moment I thought he was going to agree to my suggestion.

Then he said: 'I've taken you on to sort out whether my cousin could have been murdered. I shan't be satisfied until you've come to a definite conclusion. Otherwise there'll always be talk.'

He grasped the car door, threw it open and stepped out into the rain.

'Come on, you ass,' he called to me.

The old woman who opened the front door, in answer to Sir Henry's echoing crashes with the great iron knocker, was dressed in black from head to toe and was bent almost double from the grinding toil of a lifetime's floor scrubbing and furniture polishing.

'Good morning, my good woman,' Sir Henry twittered. 'Kindly inform Mr Frankland that Sir Henry Baskerville has called to see him.'

'Yez, zur,' she mumbled and showed her face for the first time.

Frankland would certainly have no need for a gigantic hound to chase off unwelcome visitors. She had the most hideous boatrace I'd ever laid eyes on. Her wart-infested, hooked nose met her bristled chin on its upward path and her sunken lips were barely visible until the corners of her mouth twitched into a gummy smile. She'd have made a fortune in horror movies.

I took a couple of paces backwards and would have taken to my heels if Sir Henry had not locked a vice-like grip about my wrist.

'Youm better come in, zurz,' the old hag cackled. 'Wait in the 'all while us be findin' Mr Frankland.'

She departed into the dark hall, in a flurry of skirts, like a big black bat.

'Let's go, Sir Henry,' I pleaded. 'We're never going to get out of this place alive.'

'Nonsense, Ed,' he snapped. 'We have called to see Mr Frankland, and I'm not leaving until I've met him.'

He was a lot younger than I thought he was going to be, about forty-five or so. His hair, what there was of it, was fair to ginger, longish at the nape of his neck but no sideburns. He had an intelligent-looking face and a forehead that glistened pink right the way back and out of sight over the horizon of a billiard ball head. Perched on his long thin nose was a pair of gold-wire framed specs with spherical lenses. He was togged up, rather surprisingly, in a battered old three-piece chalk-striped business suit. The waistcoat strained at the buttons over a gut that looked like it had been bloated at great expense on good vintage wine rather than cheap ale. He was about five feet eight, but looked shorter.

'Mrs Weynolds, my housekeeper, tells me that one of you is Baskerville,' he said as he came storming towards us across the tiled hall. 'Which one is it and who's the other one?'

Sir Henry stepped forward and declared: 'My name is Baskerville.' He glanced at me. 'And this is my friend, Mr Nelson.'

The little chap moved in on us with a nasty glint flashing a warning from behind his specs.

'Sir Henwy,' he snarled, savagely rolling his Rs into Ws. 'Kindly wemove yourself fwom my house and get that Wolls Woyce out of my dwive.'

The blood drained out of Sir Henry's cheeks and fury set light to his eyes.

'Good grief . . . I have never ever been spoken to like that in my entire life,' he babbled. 'I am Sir Henry Basker-ville – Do you realize, sir, to whom you are speaking?'

A wicked, almost impish, smile spread over Frankland's face.

'I will not tell you again, Sir Henwy,' he said. 'You are twespassing on my pwoperty and I will take measures to have you wemoved if you do not leave.'

'I have never been so insulted,' the baronet cried.

'Vewy well,' said Frankland. 'If you will not get out, you leave me no other alternative.' He turned away from us and shouted into the body of the vast house. 'Mrs Wey-nolds, Mrs Weynolds, put in your dentures and bite Sir Henwy Baskerville on the backside and keep on biting until you have seen him off the pwemises.'

I thought it was a joke, but the smile died on my lips when out of the darkness the crazed bat-like witch scuttled towards us gnashing the most ferocious set of National Health choppers I have ever seen.

Sir Henry, hardly able to believe his eyes, backed off a few paces and then made a bolt for the door. Laughing hysterically, I pounded across the hall hard on his heels.

'Mr Nelson,' Frankland called. 'You may stay. I wish to

speak to you – Mrs Weynolds, don't bite Mr Nelson – just that accursed Baskerville fellow.'

Sir Henry jerked the massive front door open and flew down the stone steps yelling: 'Get away from me, you loathsome woman, get away. . .'

I peeked out of my hiding place behind the door and watched the fun. Mrs Reynolds was gaining on her quarry, and was almost upon him as he reached the Rolls. He made it by a whisker and got the motor running while she snapped and snarled at him through the closed window. Then the car tore off down the drive, hell-for-leather, and disappeared from sight. Still foaming at the mouth, Mrs Reynolds gobbled like an enraged turkey and stood there in the teeming rain, gazing after the Rolls.

Mr Frankland came to the door and looked out at her.

'Thank you, Mrs Weynolds,' he shouted. 'We shall be two for lunch.'

'Blimey,' I gasped. 'You ought to put a sign up saying *Beware of the Housekeeper*, mate.'

'Wouldn't dweam of it, Mr Nelson,' he smiled sardonically. 'That would spoil half the fun. There is nothing that Mrs Weynolds enjoys more than sinking her dentures into a tender wump.'

I gave him a penetrating look and chuckled nervously.

'You're putting me on,' I said. 'She's not for real, is she?'

'Oh, yes,' he replied, offhandedly. 'Mrs Weynolds is vewy weal indeed, an absolute tweasure, Mr Nelson, an absolute tweasure. Come into the dwawingwoom – you'll stay to lunch, of course?'

'All right,' I said. 'But only on the understanding that I am not the main course.'

'Vewy weasonable condition.' His face was wreathed in smiles. 'Vewy weasonable indeed.'

I found myself liking him – how can you help liking a bloke who gets his housekeeper to bite unwelcome intruders?

Except for the vastness in size, the drawingroom differed little from the one at Baskerville Hall. There was the obligatory five and a half miles of dusty leather-bound books, a log fire blazing brightly in a grate the size of my London office and ancestral portraits littered the walls. They seemed to be of a better quality than Sir Henry's collection.

'I'm so pleased to meet you, Mr Nelson,' Frankland said and offered me his hand. 'I have seen you dwiving along the moorland road in that yellow Hillman of yours. I also saw you in St Luke's churchyard the day before yesterday.'

I shook his hand and said: 'You been spying on me?'

'I keep an eye on everwything that goes on in the distwict,' he told me. 'But I was particularly interwested in you. I've never watched a pwivate eye at work before.'

'How did you know I was a private detective?' I asked.

'It's all over the village,' he pointed out. 'No one fwom the outside world can visit these parts without the locals finding out exactly who they are within a few hours. It gets a little more difficult in the touwist season, but they manage it somehow.'

'Stone me,' I said. 'The sooner I get out of here the better.'

'No, no,' said Frankland. 'You mustn't cheat us of your company. I was hoping your investigations might make quite a hilawious column in the little magazine I wite for.'

I said: 'Leave my name out of it will you?'

Mrs Reynolds may have been a terrific watchdog but she was a bloody awful cook. You can't have everything, I suppose. She served up some revolting stew, fluffy grey-tinted boiled spuds and cabbage – the whole lot was cold. I sussed that this might be because the kitchen was a mile and a half away from the dining-room. I swallowed one mouthful of the sick-making mess and spent the rest of the time pushing the stuff around the plate with my fork.

Frankland, on the other hand, wolfed the muck down with relish, demanded seconds, then looked at my plate and said: 'Not hungwy, Mr Nelson?'

'Not particularly.'

'Perhaps you'd like some cheese?'

'Yes please.'

The bat-witch came billowing into the room in a flurry of black skirts in answer to his tinkle of a small silver handbell.

'Cheese, Mrs Weynolds,' he said, 'and cwackers.'

Back in the drawingroom, sipping tepid black coffee by the fire, I decided to test out his views on the Baskerville caper.

'Do you reckon there's anything in the rumour that's buzzing around that Sir Charles was murdered?' I asked.

'Vewy good idea,' he grinned. 'I wouldn't know if it was twue, but it would have been a vewy good idea to bump him off. I hope Sir Henwy's for it too. Dweadful bunch, the Baskervilles, except for young Pevewille who was killed in the war.'

'What's wrong with them?' I inquired.

'Wevolting family – I can scarcely bwing myself to speak their name. The best thing that ever happened in the county was when old Sir Hugo died in 1945 and the estate was sold up. Then two or thwee years ago that fwightful Sir Charles weturned to the Hall and wenovated the place with the help of that dweadful man Mortimer.'

'What about the curse?' I asked. 'Any truth in that, do you think?'

'The curse is that the Baskervilles ever weturned to this part of the countwy,' he replied flatly, and got to his feet. 'Would you like to come and see my observatorwy?' he asked.

'Observatory?'

'Someone must have told you about the powerful telescope I keep on the woof, surely?' He looked at me over the top of his specs in surprise. 'The life of a witer is so borwing, you know,' he explained. 'One has to have one or two little hobbies to keep one going. I've got my telescope and my libel actions – they're quite fun too, as a matter of fact.'

I stood up to follow him.

'Do you really believe that you've seen UFOs flitting around the moor?' I asked. 'Or are you just enjoying a leg pull?'

'Gwacious, no,' he said. 'I have observed the saucer many times. It is definitely a materwial object and it glows. I've weported many sightings to the Woyal Astwonomical Society in London. They merely think I am a twouble-making cwank and dismiss my sightings out of hand, but others have seen them too and one day my theowy will be pwoved that an invasion of Gweat Bwitain by the Martian hordes has been taking place on the moor since the time of neolithic man.'

I said: 'If they've been arriving for that long you'd think they'd all be here by now.'

'Many hundweds of thousands of them have,' he replied. 'They are all awound us if we could but see them.'

I glanced about nervously.

'Where are they?'

'In this vewy woom, Mr Nelson,' he said. 'But they are invisible.'

'Right,' I said and followed him out of the door and up the stairs to the very top of the house.

His powerful telescope stood on a tripod, near a small window, in an attic room. The window looked out over Coombe Tracey and the moor beyond to the horizon. Drawing-pinned to the walls were several complicated astronomical charts and a large ordnance survey map of, I guessed, the area that could be seen out of the window.

'So this is where you keep an eye on things?' I remarked cheerily.

'Quite wight, Mr Nelson,' he beamed, and stroked the telescope. 'I can see ten miles in any diwection with the aid of this instwument. Even further on a clear day – would you care to look?'

'Sure.'

'Just swivel it awound until the lens is pointing out of the window.' He pointed to a brass fitting on the side. 'Then twiddle that knob when you want to get anything into focus – you can enlarge a slate on the church woof until it seems as big as a house and you can almost wead the menu in dear Margwet Stapleton's little westauwant.'

I closed one eye and squinted down the telescope with the other. I jumped back immediately and gasped: 'There's a bloody spider in it.'

Frankland looked for himself.

'You're wight,' he exclaimed. 'It's spinning a web in the bwacken, two or thwee miles away on the moor.' He glanced at a distance gauge on the side of the telescope. 'Two miles, five hundwed yards to be exact – look again.'

I swivelled the thing around a bit and took another gander. This time the rooftops of Coombe Tracey came clearly into view.

'Terrific, Mr Frankland,' I said. 'I'm getting the hang of it now. It's the kind of aid to vision that no private eye should be without – it would come in double handy for divorce snooping jobs in Brighton hotel bedrooms. Blimey, I'd even be able to testify under oath to the exact colour of a platinum blonde's pubic hair.'

I zoomed it around a bit more and a white Mercedes towing a caravan sprang into view, travelling at speed along the moorland road. I tracked it with the lens like an assassin with the heart of his victim locked in his telescopic sights. I adjusted the focus a little and the licence plate on the back of the caravan jumped into my eye like a newspaper headline: PHY 64 Q!

CHAPTER EIGHTEEN

I flung out of the room and belted down the stairs two steps at a time, yelling over my shoulder at Frankland: 'How do you get to Great Sourton caravan park from here?'

I'd left him a long way behind, but his surprised tones echoed after me with bell-like clarity.

'It's wight and wight again, Mr Nelson. But why are you leaving in such a huwwy – is it something I said?'

I turned the last bend and accelerated for the hundred yard dash across the tiled hall.

'The game's afoot, there's not a moment to lose,' I yelled. 'Gotta capture a bloke with fungus on his chops, towing a flipping caravan!'

I yanked open the front door and started into the driveway. The rain had left off, but little rivulets were speeding their way down the drive while trees, rose-bushes and anything else in sight were heavy with water and dripping.

After the first, two squelchy steps, realization flooded over me. I hadn't got a jamjar. Sir Henry had brought me over in the Rolls and abandoned me.

I cursed Our Saviour, shook a fist at the heavens and turned slowly to retrace my steps.

Puffing slightly and pink with the unaccustomed exertion of running down the mile and a half of staircase, Frankland appeared in the open doorway.

'Whatever got into you, Mr Nelson?' he demanded to know. 'You're not going to wun all the way, are you? It's over two miles, you know.'

'Slipped my mind I hadn't got any wheels,' I told him laconically.

For a minute or two we stood there in silence while the

inclement weather did its thing around us, with Lafter Hall's blocked gutters cascading like a Niagara in the background. When Frankland had got his breath back, he turned to me and said: 'You want to interview a suspect in a cawavan?'

I nodded.

'Tell you what,' he suggested, taking a fat gold watch from his waistcoat pocket and glancing at its face. 'I'll wun you over there in the Mowwis.'

'Best offer I've had all day,' I enthused warmly.

'One doesn't get the opportunity to twavel wound with a pwivate eye evewy day.' He smiled at me broadly over his gold-rimmed specs. 'I should get a pawagwaph or two out of it.'

It was a clapped out old banger that Frankland fetched from the back of the house, rusting at the seams and coated from stem to stern with layer upon layer of rich Devonshire mud. He drove like a man possessed by demons, skidding around blind bramble thickets on two wheels and hurtling down one in four hills towards blind corners.

'I'm afwaid the bwakes aren't much good,' he confessed as the car became airborne over a humpback bridge.

The Kamikaze syndrome of belting around in junkyard motors was as familiar to me as the life-line on my right hand. But there's a world of difference between driving that kind of wreck yourself and sitting in the passenger seat with some bloody lunatic behind the wheel. I sat there ashen-faced and speechless from fear with my sphincter going two bob, half a crown, two bob, half a crown all the way. By the time we reached our destination I'd kept no less than six nervous breakdowns to myself.

The Great Sourton caravan park was stacked out with mobile homes, infested with snotty nosed kids and their middle-aged, middle class mothers with low slung behinds. But a thorough search of the place failed to come up with the Mercedes or the geezer with the beard.

I sorted out the superintendent in charge of the dump, a beefy strawberry-nosed local, and asked him if he'd seen a

Mercedes, licence number PHY 64 Q, in the last couple of hours.

He thought long and hard and scratched his arse.

'May 'ave, zur, may not 'ave,' he foxed.

'You wonna give me nine quid for a tenner?' I asked.

'That be very kind of you, zur.' He counted nine grubby ones off a plump wad. I exchanged my crisp tenner for them.

'Well?' I prompted him.

'Gen'leman in a Mercedes, he were round with 'is caravan not 'arf 'n 'our back, now us comes to think of it, zur,' said strawberry-nose. 'Dropped it off 'e did, so's 'e could use it weekends is what 'im said. Why, you'm only just missed 'un.'

'Thanks a lot,' I groaned. 'Where did he leave the caravan?'

'Bottom of the field, down yonder, zur.' He pointed off into the middle distance. 'Third from the right, you can't miss 'un.'

Frankland and I sloshed off down the muddy, caravan-lined avenue that the superintendent indicated.

'Smart work with the bwibe there,' Frankland congratulated me. 'I didn't understand for a moment what you were offerwing him.'

'Sort of stroke you always have to be ready to pull in my game,' I replied nonchalantly. 'Nothing is for nothing in this world, as the saying goes.'

We found it in the end, axle-deep in mud, parked in the most out of the way spot of the mucky and depressing caravan site. A plate with the licence number of the car was still attached to the rear end. 'PHY 64 Q' it announced as bold as brass. It had very bad taste plastic curtains pulled across its windows. I tried the door handle, but it was locked up tighter than a police cell. I tried to climb up and peek through a chink in one of the curtains. But all that did for me was bark my shin and splatter mud down the front of my trench. We plodded all the way back to the superintendent's office.

'You'm find 'un, okay?' he inquired politely.

'We found it,' I replied shortly. 'Do your clients have to fill in any kind of papers when they dump their nasty mobile homes here?'

'Zertainly they does. But that be confidential like, zur,' he said with a speculative glint in his eye.

I slipped him another quid and he rifled through the papers on his desk until he came up with a printed form hurriedly completed in a scrawling hand. I took it from him and scanned it to find the client's name, address and telephone number.

Then my eyes nearly jumped out of my head.

'Holy mackerel,' I exclaimed.

'What is it? What is it?' asked Frankland excitedly peering over my shoulder. 'Don't tell me there is a new twist to the investigation?'

'Dead right, there is, mate,' I said.

'What twemendous fun,' he gurgled. 'I can't see anything wemotely interwesting on that dweadful form. Do tell me what it is?'

I pointed to the third line down. 'Doesn't that name mean anything to you?' I asked.

'Fletcher Wobinson?' he said. 'I think it does wing some sort of bell.'

'The journalist geezer who's been writing all that stuff about the UFOs,' I reminded him. 'Didn't he come to see you?'

Frankland struck his head with his hand and laughed.

'The waving lunatic from the *Western Morning News*, of course. I wemember having quite a long chat with him but he hardly pwinted anything I told him.'

'Did he have a black beard?' I asked sharply.

'No. He was a young, clean shaven twit,' Frankland informed me. 'One of those gangling boys, twemendously keen but dim.'

I'd forgotten the strawberry-nosed superintendent while we had this discussion. But apparently he'd been plugged in and listening with interest.

'Gen'leman as left us 'is caravan 'ad a big black beard, zur,' he interposed at this point.

'Good gwacious!' exclaimed Frankland. 'And he signed his name Fletcher Wobinson. I think I smell a fwaud.'

'Not in front of the help,' I mouthed at him, jerking my head at strawberry-nose.

I scribbled down the address and phone number bearded had put on the form and we left.

Frankland said he'd drop me at the gates of Baskerville Hall and he drove along at his usual breakneck speed chattering nineteen to the dozen about the Fletcher Robinson mystery.

'Hold it,' I told him sharply, as we flashed past the hamlet of Muddicoombe. I'd spotted a red telephone box. 'Stop the car, will you. I need to make a phone call.'

We slithered to a halt through a series of richly piled cow pats.

I jumped out of the car and dialled the number I'd scribbled down at the caravan park.

After one ring a girl's voice came on the line.

'Western Morning News,' she said with a soft Devon lilt.

'Can I speak to Fletcher Robinson?' I asked her.

'No, zur,' she replied. 'Mr Robinson be away this week. Can anyone else help you?'

'Do you know him by sight?' I asked her.

'Oh, yes, zur,' she giggled. 'We all know Fletcher Robinson.'

'Has he grown a big black beard?'

'Heavens, no,' she squealed.

CHAPTER NINETEEN

I was sipping my black coffee moodily next morning, wondering what to do with the day, when Barrymore came in to tell me there was a gentleman on the phone for me from London. The sarcasm he threw into his pronunciation of the word 'gentleman' led me to believe there was something double dodgy about the call.

I put the receiver gingerly to my ear and said: 'Ed Nelson speaking.'

''Ow yah getting along then?' chortled Willy Paradis. 'Long time no 'ear.'

'Oh, hallo Willy,' I sighed. 'Any hope of persuading you I've been down here long enough and ought to come home?'

'Depends 'ow yah bin doin', son,' he told me. 'Tumbled anyfing yet, 'ave yah?'

'Plenty,' I assured him. 'I should think you'll get to the bottom of it, once I've told you all the stuff I've found out.'

'Let's 'ear some of it,' he snapped.

'Well,' I thought for a moment, then told him: 'Reg Mortimer has a warehouse in Plymouth where he keeps his posh junk.'

'Go on,' said Willy.

I told him about the Barrymores and their pantechnicon, and about Fletcher Robinson, and about Frankland.

'And Stapleton has a big van for delivering tomatoes,' I concluded. 'I expect you could pack the odd container of hot merchandise into it if you tried.'

'Yah not doin' too badly,' Willy conceded generously. 'Butcha better 'ang abaht and do a bit more ear'olin'. Sounds ter me as 'ow yah might wind up wiv some innerestin' developments.'

'Oh no,' I groaned.

'Buck up me 'ole mate,' Willy encouraged me. 'I'll see yah awright.'

When he'd rung off I mooched around for a while, then decided I'd take a spin over to Tavistock, more to get away from Sir Henry than anything else.

Like the rest of the market towns in Devonshire, it was as pretty as a picture postcard and as lively as a Church of England funeral.

When the landlord gave me the slingers out of my lunchtime pub at 2 o'clock, I pointed the nose of the Hillman listlessly towards home again. In Coombe Tracey I stopped off at the village shop and ambled in to buy some fags. Molly, the comely barmaid, was buying stamps at the tiny Post Office counter. She gave me a demure little smile and said: 'Arternoon, zur.'

The hollowness of depression that had been dashing my spirits all day suddenly ebbed away and I beamed at her like a searchlight.

'Hallo, Molly,' I replied. 'How's it all going on, then?'

She tucked her stamps into her purse and turned towards me.

'I be awright, zur,' she trilled and headed for the door.

'Hang on a mo,' I called after her. 'I want to talk to you.'

The old woman behind the counter gave me an inquiring glance.

'Forty Rothmans King Size,' I said and handed her a fiver.

She gave me the cigarettes and change without uttering a word. Molly was waiting for me on the pavement outside.

'I 'ave to be gettin' 'ome, zur,' she said. 'Mother be waitin' for I.'

'Get in the car,' I said. 'I'll give you a lift.'

'Don't live far, zur,' she smiled. 'Just over the other side of the village.'

I opened the car door and said: 'Get in – we'll be able to talk more privately.'

148

She glanced up and down the street, then did as I asked.

'What be you wanting to talk to me about, zur?' she asked as I started the engine.

'Nothing much,' I grinned. 'Call me Ed.'

'Be it somethin' to do with they Baskervilles?'

'That depends.'

She gave me a sidelong glance.

'On what, Ed?'

I flicked the indicator and pulled away from the kerb.

'On how much you know about them.'

Out of nowhere a white police car sirened through the village at breakneck speed. I pulled over to let it get by and almost ran over a cat.

'Wonder where they're off to in such a hurry?' I muttered.

Molly was far more concerned about the cat.

'Poor little pussy,' she cried. 'Us've frightened 'im out of six of 'is lives.'

I placed a comforting hand on the damsel's thigh.

'There, there,' I patted her gently. 'Don't upset yourself – the moggy got away all right.'

She looked at my hand and then into my eyes. The message she read there made her blush and look away.

'This be a bad time of the month, Ed,' she whispered. 'An' mother be worried if I bain't 'ome soon.'

I sighed heavily and drove her home.

As I reached the crest of the steep hill out of Coombe Tracey, a couple came in view walking down the road hand in hand ahead of me. They were quite a long way away and it took me a moment or two to recognize Sir Henry and Margaret Stapleton.

In order to avoid offering them a lift, I pulled into the handy lay-by where we'd stopped in Sir Henry's Rolls to take a gander at Grimpen Mire. I cut the engine and lit a fag, then sat back and glowered at the wild, uninhabited, bloody moorland that stretched all around me. As I was staring morosely at the bright green splash of Grimpen Mire glinting in the distance towards Baskerville Hall, a car came bumping along a rough cart track that seemed to run down the edge of the mire.

I followed it with my eyes as it rounded a bracken-clad hillock and turned into the main road about a mile away. It was pointed towards Coombe Tracey and I waited idly for it to pass the spot where I was parked to see if I knew the driver.

But it never reached me. Sir Henry and Margaret Stapleton broke apart guiltily as the car approached them. I watched it stop. Then the door flew open and Giles Stapleton leapt out waving his arms about angrily and shouting. Things seemed to be getting interesting and I'd got a seat in the front row of the stalls.

As Giles came abreast of the couple he was really doing his nut and it looked for a moment as though he and the baronet were going to have a punch-up right there and then. But Margaret talked to first one and then the other, and in a moment or two the whole thing dissolved into nothing worse than mouthed oaths and a certain amount of finger pointing. Giles then escorted his sister to his car with a hand encircling her wrist. He pushed her into the passenger seat, banged the door on her and got behind the wheel.

Sir Henry cringed into the hedge as the car accelerated past him down the road. By the time it reached me, Giles and Margaret seemed to be having a good old ding-dong.

I started the car engine and coasted the two hundred yards or so to where Sir Henry was standing. I pulled up beside him and wound down the window.

'Want a lift?' I asked.

He glared at me with smouldering eyes.

'What's that you say?'

'Would you like a lift up to the Hall, Sir Henry?' I asked him a second time.

He stalked around the front of the car and got into the passenger seat without another word.

'Having a spot of girl trouble?' I inquired lightly.

'My personal life is no concern of yours, damn it,' he

snapped. 'Kindly investigate what you've been paid to investigate and keep your nose out of my personal life.'

'Sometimes difficult to know where to draw the line,' I shrugged. 'One avenue of inquiry overlaps another – if you get my meaning.'

'No, I don't get your meaning,' he blazed. 'If you cannot stick to your brief I will dispense with your services forthwith – do you understand?'

'Oh, sure,' I grinned. 'I always understand that kind of talk. When do you want me to leave?'

'Look here, old chap,' he said, calming down a little. 'I didn't mean it. Sorry to snap at you like that.'

'Don't mention it,' I replied easily. 'People jump down my throat so often, I don't take any notice no more – occupational hazard of being a private eye.'

'Very good of you to take it like that,' he sighed. 'May I tell you something in confidence?'

'Fire away.'

'Well, you see, the thing is,' he began sheepishly. 'Margaret Stapleton and I have formed rather a strong attachment to each other.'

'That's nice,' I said. 'Love at first sight was it?'

'Good Lord, Ed,' he cried, blushing fiercely. 'You make me sound like a goofy schoolboy. I wouldn't go as far as to say "love at first sight", but we do find that we have various common interests and enjoy each other's company tremendously.'

I never did understand why the upper-crust bottled up their emotions so tightly. If he fancied the bird double strong why couldn't he come right out with it and say so? Not the done thing, I suppose.

'Sounds cosy,' I said.

'Trouble is,' Sir Henry went on, 'her brother Giles disapproves and he won't allow us to be alone together – it really is most distressing. He seems to follow her around everywhere she goes.'

I drew up outside Baskerville Hall, jerked on the handbrake and cut the engine.

'Margaret is a big girl,' I pointed out. 'And from what I've seen of her she seems to have a mind of her own.'

'I know, I know,' he bleated. 'But her brother seems to have some kind of hold over her.'

'Want me to find out what it is?' I asked.

'Only if you can do it discreetly.'

'No sweat, Sir Henry,' I said and got out of the car.

For a time we stood side by side looking out over the moor.

'Did you ever see such a spectacular view, Ed?' he asked.

'Prefer bricks and mortar and a few neon lights myself,' I admitted.

Suddenly from far out on the moor an unearthly scream rent the air.

'Blimey,' I gasped, 'what the hell was that?'

'One comes to expect rather unnerving cries to come from the moor,' he replied unperturbed. 'It could be almost anything – a pony who has stumbled into the mire, a screech owl, or even, of course, a human being.'

'Sounded like the baying of a hound to me,' I muttered. 'Could be that hell hound that's got it in for your family.'

'Keep a hold on your imagination, Ed,' Sir Henry advised me with a disparaging laugh as he turned into the house.

I gave some thought to methods for discreetly rumbling Giles Stapleton's maniacal possessiveness as I knocked back my bedtime Hankey Bannister's in the privacy of my room. One way was to ask Reg Mortimer. A second was to get Giles blind pissed and see if he confided in me. The second seemed more attractive and I decided to attend to it the very next day.

But in the event it proved unnecessary. We'd hardly finished breakfast next morning, Sir Henry was still barricaded behind his *Financial Times*, when Barrymore ushered Stapleton into the dining-room.

'I've come to apologize, Sir Henry,' said Giles, bouncing over to the baronet with a look of boyish appeal on his mug. 'It was simply frightful of me to behave like that yesterday. Could we have a quiet word and I'll explain.'

Both of them turned to look at me meaningfully. I scraped back my chair and stood up.

'Okay, okay,' I said, 'I'm off. You'll find me in the rose garden if either of you need any detection done for you.'

'But we haven't got a rose garden,' objected Sir Henry.

'Then try the Devil's Stone Inn at ten-thirty,' I advised him and shambled out of the room.

Sir Henry passed on the gist of Stapleton's yarn later. His sister had had a stormy affair with an international playboy two years before and ended up with a real corker of a nervous breakdown. After the loony bin had got nowhere with electric shocks and group therapy, Giles had stepped in and picked up the pieces. He'd brought Margaret down to Devon and installed her at Merripit House. Gradually, through love and affection he'd got her over it. Six months ago she'd started up her health food restaurant and the roaring trade she'd done with the summer tourists had bucked her right up.

But that was not to say, according to Giles, that things could not go wrong again. He was very worried, for instance, by how much hash Margaret was smoking. It meant she wasn't quite in touch with reality. And if she now got involved in another steaming affair with the bad baronet, the precarious balance of her reason might be expected to slip at any minute.

He begged Sir Henry to take things easy. If he must go on seeing Margaret, to try to behave like a friend rather than a lover. At least for a while till it became clear how Margaret was taking it.

The obliging baronet apparently agreed to hold his passion in check for a while. And that was that, I didn't believe a word of it.

CHAPTER TWENTY

'Gotcha!' I snarled and threw myself headlong into the darkened room, brandishing my gun. 'Who the hell have you been signalling to with that torch?'

The Barrymores whirled around as I snapped on the light and stared at me ashen-faced from their crouched position by the window. John had a powerful 'Ever Ready' headlamp gripped tightly in his fist and his wife was wringing her hanky.

'I seen you,' I told them bluntly, 'so there's no good in denying it. You were signalling to someone on the moor and someone signalled back. I seen 'em do it through the window in the passage. So you might as well come clean, right?'

'What the devil is going on here?' barked a voice behind me.

I whirled around, pointed the .38 pistol at Sir Henry's midriff and in the excitement of the moment almost pulled the sodding trigger.

'Never creep up on a bloke with a gun in his hand,' I shouted at him. 'You're liable to get a nasty little hole in your tummy.'

'For heaven's sake do put that silly thing away, Ed,' he commanded. 'Good gracious, where on earth do you think you are? This, in case you may have forgotten, is Baskerville Hall, not a barrelhouse in Chicago.'

I tucked the gun sheepishly into my belt and said: 'These two have been signalling to someone out on the moor. It seems double suspicious to me. I think you should ask them how they did in your cousin. And what they've got in store for you, for that matter.'

Sir Henry turned on the Barrymores with beatling brows.

'Is this true?' he asked. 'Who have you been signalling to?'

'How did that bleeder find us?' snapped Barrymore, playing the crook for a change. 'Your room's in the other bleeding wing.'

I cocked an eyebrow at him disapprovingly.

'When private eyes are woken up by footsteps clumping past their room at three o'clock in the morning,' I told him, 'they sometimes pop out to investigate. Not always, I'll admit. Sometimes they just stick their fingers in their ears.'

'You'd better keep a civil tongue in your head, Barrymore,' Sir Henry told him crisply. 'I'm going to get to the bottom of all this. Take your wife down to the drawing-room and we'll have it out there.'

John Barrymore got up off the floor, rose to his full height, pointed his nose arrogantly at the ceiling and headed for the door with the resolute bearing of an aristocrat going to the guillotine. Eliza followed him, with her head bowed, still weeping and I tagged on to the end of the little procession as it snailed its way along the landing to the head of the stairs.

'Half a mo,' I said. 'Be right with you – just got to get something.'

Sir Henry glanced around at me and nodded. I beatled back to my room and rummaged in my suitcase for a bottle of Hankey Bannister's. Stocks were getting low – there were only two full bottles left and the remains of the one that had deprived me of my senses the night before. I grabbed it by the neck and went downstairs muttering: 'This caper had better come up with its denouement before the whisky runs out or it's going to have to solve itself.'

Sir Henry appeared to be having a fierce argument with Barrymore when I strolled into the drawingroom. The baronet snapped his lips shut in a hard line at the sight of me and the flow of invective was stopped in mid-stream.

'Don't mind me,' I told them. 'Just carry on.'

But neither smiled or spoke.

The butler joined his wife on the sofa, Sir Henry heaved half an oak tree on to the dying embers of the fire and I went over to the sideboard and slopped some whisky into a tumbler. I didn't ask anyone to join me.

'I do hope that you are not going to get drunk, Ed,' the baronet chided me gently.

'If I didn't drink, then I'd have to take a handful of sleeping pills every night,' I told him straight. 'A private eye who is hooked on sleeping pills is about as much use to his clients as Rip Van Winkle.' I slugged some whisky, lit a cigarette, cast an eye over the assembled company, and added: 'Let's get on with it – we can have a long heart to heart about my drinking problem some other time.'

Sir Henry eyed his butler and said: 'Very well, Barrymore, out with it – who were you signalling to on the moor?'

I slumped back in my fireside chair and watched everyone closely with half-closed eyes.

'It's Peter,' boomed John, dramatically. 'Peter Selden, the convict who has escaped from Princetown prison.'

I suppose that Axeman Selden had been referred to by his Christian name in *The Times* and *Daily Telegraph* when his sensational Old Bailey trial hit the headlines. But they are not linens that I normally read and I'd never known him by any other name than Axeman.

He'd got the nickname when he was just a kid because of his neat ploy of chopping jangling burglar alarms off bank walls and other premises he had unlawfully entered, with a long-handled woodman's axe. But he was a gentle soul deep down and had never, to my knowledge, used violence in the furtherance of a crime. Peter seemed like a soft enough name for him – Flossy or Prendergast would've done equally well.

'The escaped convict,' Sir Henry echoed in astonishment. 'What possible reason could you have for signalling to him on the moor?'

Barrymore cast his eyes to the floor. 'He is my brother-in-law, sir.'

I tried to stifle a burst of laughter with a mouthful of whisky and almost choked to death.

'Pull the other one,' I coughed, 'it's got bells on.'

'It's true,' sobbed Eliza. 'Peter is my younger brother.'

'Well strike me pink,' I said. 'That's one up for the book, I must say. Don't tell me that you two sprung him from the slammer?'

'No, no,' the butler put in hurriedly. 'We knew that he was planning to escape if he ever got the chance. Both my wife and I did everything mortally possible to dissuade him – but a man facing a thirty year sentence can be driven to desperate things – by persecution or hopelessness.'

I had a thought.

'You applied for a position here, when Sir Charles advertised for staff, so that you could be close to the nick and be able to see Axeman on visiting days – right or wrong?'

'Don't even call him by that insulting name, Mr Nelson,' bleated Eliza through renewed tears. 'To me his name will always be Peter, whatever those frightful London underworld gangsters may have called him. He is my little brother Peter and always will be.'

'Sorry, Mrs Barrymore,' I said, 'just a slip of the tongue. He couldn't have had it away on his toes without outside help – the security in that joint nowadays is as tight as a bank manager's fist. They've got TV cameras on top of the walls, guard dog patrols night and day – the lot. If you didn't help him escape who did?'

'He hasn't told us because we haven't asked, right?' snapped John.

'Sounds possible,' I agreed.

'He told us that he'd got a break planned when we visited him a week ago,' Barrymore explained to his employer. 'That was the day you came down, Sir Henry, and that was why my wife was so upset.'

'And you tried to make me believe it was your little doggie that was crying,' I sneered.

'The last thing the wife could have handled was you sticking your nose into the affair,' he retorted.

'So how did Selden keep in touch?' I asked, ignoring his impertinence.

'We heard about the break on the six o'clock news down in the kitchen. He telephoned here a few hours later and we made the arrangement about signalling late at night when he was on the moor. He keeps the signal going so we can go out and find him and have a chat about how he's doing and what he needs.'

'So you've actually seen him?' I asked eagerly.

They exchanged some kind of glance.

'Only once,' said Eliza. 'And we did everything we could to persuade him to give himself up . . .'

'No go, eh?'

The pseudo-butler looked me straight in the eyes.

'Would you give yourself up if you were facing a thirty year prison sentence, mate?'

'Not bloody likely,' I said.

Sir Henry broke his silence and pointed towards the uncurtained window.

'Look, look,' he exclaimed, excitedly. 'There it is again! The light, the light, see it, see it? Quite close to Grimpen Mire, I'd say, judging by the direction.'

We all sprang to our feet and dashed over to the window. Sir Henry was right. Someone was out on the moor with a flashlight, waving it from side to side in the inky darkness.

'Come on, Ed,' the young baronet cried enthusiastically. 'Let's nab him!'

'Not me, guv'nor,' I replied emphatically. 'If it ever got out that I helped put the finger on Axeman Selden, I'd never be able to raise my head in respectable society again.'

'Very well,' he snapped. 'I'll go alone.'

'No, sir, no sir!' the Barrymores chorused. 'You can't!'

'I wouldn't advise it, Sir Henry,' I told him kindly. 'You would never catch him on a filthy night like this and you'd stand a good chance of stumbling into the mire.'

'Quite so, Mr Nelson,' John agreed. 'Grimpen Mire has sucked many men to a muddy grave.'

'Stand aside,' commanded Sir Henry and marched resolutely out of the room.

'The man's a flaming nut-case,' I groaned and dashed out after him.

Short of caving his bonce in with the iron-spiked club the suit of armour had clasped in its mailed fist, there was no way I could stop the stupid idiot from rampaging out on to the moor. He had already pulled on his wellington boots and was fighting his way into a heavy khaki waterproof.

'This is sheer madness, Sir Henry,' I pleaded with him. 'Call the filth if you must, but don't go out on the moor.'

'It is the duty of every law abiding man to make a citizen's arrest when the opportunity presents itself,' he replied.

Without another word he made his way to the front door, threw back the heavy bolts and disappeared into the night. I grabbed my trench off the hatstand and beatled after him.

'Mr Nelson,' Mrs Barrymore called after me from the drawingroom door. 'Please don't let him take my brother back to that awful prison!'

'Not if I can help it,' I called back and dived down the porch steps two at a time.

The torrential rain that had been falling out of the sky for the past eighteen hours had let up a bit and been replaced by a thin, freezing spray.

'Sir Henry!' I shouted. 'Where the hell are you?'

He beamed his flashlight on me along the full length of the yew alley and shouted back: 'I'm here – hurry if you want to be in at the kill.'

I raced to his side in my sodden Hush Puppies and out we went through the wicket gate on to the moor, very likely never to be seen alive again.

He flashed the torch along the never ending sea of

elephant grass and tangled bracken and said: 'I think the signalling came from over there to the south west.'

I said: 'Anything you say, Sir Henry,' and squelched along beside him in that direction.

It was heavy going and after about fifteen minutes we paused, blowing like cart-horses, to rest in the partial shelter of a big rock that reared up out of the ground like a ghostly giant.

'We're not going to find him,' I said. 'Let's turn back?'

'Oh, ye of little faith,' he chuckled. 'He's around here somewhere, I'm sure of it.'

The silly bugger was actually enjoying himself.

I sat down on a jagged boulder, lit a fag and wished to Christ that I'd remembered to bring the bottle with me. Then suddenly I pricked up my ears and grabbed Sir Henry's arm.

'What the hell's that noise?' I gasped.

'What noise?'

'Listen.'

A faint humming sound drifted across the moor.

I said: 'There it is again,' and strained my ears to try to discover what direction it was coming from.

'Christ, you're right, Ed,' Sir Henry whispered, as the noise grew louder. 'I wonder what it can be – maybe it's the wind humming through the electricity pylons?'

'Could be.' I jerked a thumb over my shoulder, 'It's coming from behind us.'

We crept stealthily around the tor and there hovering in the night sky about a quarter of a mile away, was a glowing saucer-like object about ten or twelve feet across and three feet thick, tapering at the top into what might have been a cockpit.

CHAPTER TWENTY ONE

I didn't bother to take a second look. I just bolted.

The heather and the bracken kept getting tangled up with my feet and every few yards I stumbled and fell over some sodding rock.

Sir Henry dashed past me, more or less at the off, shouting: 'Don't bother with Selden. Back to the Hall!'

Like most public school twits, he had obviously been a pretty good athlete in his day, and took off across the moor like a greyhound after the hare at White City Stadium. I pounded after him as fast as my legs would carry me, but twenty years of booze and chain-smoking is not exactly the ideal type of training for the hundred yard dash, and in no time at all he had disappeared into the night ahead of me.

For the first five minutes I was so crazed with blind terror that I didn't even wonder about where I was going. I just knew I had to escape.

Some time later, when it was out of sight, and I was out of breath, I paused and stood for a moment panting heavily. I didn't think I could hear the hum of its engine any longer, but I wasn't sure as the blood was making such a racket drumming in my ears.

It was then that I realized I hadn't an earthly where I was or how to get back to the Hall. I couldn't see because it was dark — completely dark — and Sir Henry had made off with the torch. There might be precipices, bogs, potholes, slithering snakes or ravening beasts in any or every direction. How could I tell? I couldn't see anything.

Panic began to clutch at my heart. I sat down to try and work out what do do. I didn't get any ideas for a while but then, over to the right, I heard the unmistakable sound of a car belting along a road. I peered through the darkness and saw the glimmer of its headlights in the distance.

A road meant civilization, so I stood up and began to stumble towards it. The car disappeared soon enough but I tried to keep a fix on where it had been and keep going in that direction.

After twenty minutes or so, I saw a distant twinkling and the lighted windows of Baskerville Hall loomed up on the horizon. With a whoop of relief I began to quicken my pace. The next thing I knew I was up to my ankles in the dreaded Grimpen Mire. In seconds its tenacious grip had sucked me down thigh deep, and it looked as though it was curtains.

I tried to shout: 'Help!' but I was so exhausted and short of breath that I could hardly even hear it myself. I felt myself being sucked, slowly inevitably deeper and deeper into the morass.

Then, maybe because I had never given a sucker an even break or even helped an old lady cross the road, my feet came into contact with something solid, a log perhaps or the skull of the last bloke to get sucked under or maybe even firmer ground at the bottom of this particular bit of the mire. My slow descent into an unmarked grave suddenly stopped, halfway up my chest. And with the aid of some tufts of firmly rooted elephant grass I somehow managed to ease my way out of the bubbling gunge. In my final lunge for safety, and all the years of penury that lay ahead, the slimy mire claimed forever my right suede shoe.

I slithered up the steps of Baskerville Hall and barged through the front door dripping fetid decomposing slime on to the marble tiles.

Sir Henry rushed out of the drawingroom to greet me, closely followed by Barrymore.

'We were just planning to put out a search party,' he exclaimed. 'Thank God, you're all right.'

'If you call being caked from head to foot in nauseous slime being all right,' I told him, 'you're a less fastidious bloke than I took you for.'

'But you're alive,' he cried and turned to Barrymore.

'Give the police station another buzz and tell them he's turned up after all, will you?'

And then they gave me a hero's welcome. Barrymore carried off my slimy clothes and wrapped me in a soft, clean towelling dressing-gown, the property of the late Sir Charles Baskerville. Sir Henry poured something approaching a full bottle of whisky down my parched throat while Mrs Barrymore knocked me up a midnight feast of devilled kidneys and peaches in brandy.

It was gone five when I finally reached my bedchamber but I was on top form. I poured myself a piping hot bath and rolled around in it, singing 'On Top of Old Smokey', using my fine baritone voice *fortissimo*. The acoustics of my private bathroom proved to be excellent.

After smoking one final gasper in front of the crackling fire in my bedroom, kindly lit by one or other of the Barrymores, I found my eyes beginning to close. I was starting to scale the heights of my mountain of a four-poster, when there came a very faint tap on the door.

The dip in Grimpen Mire had clogged up my shooter with green slime. I had planned to take it to bits and give it a clean as soon as I found the time but for the moment had left it soaking in the lavatory cistern. I nipped into the bathroom, fished it out, shook some of the water off it and crept towards the door. If forced to pull the trigger I'd probably squirt a jet of water into my intruder's eye. But wet or dry no one likes to have a gun pointed at them and you very seldom actually have to shoot anyone.

The light tap came again and I jerked the door open saying: 'One false move and you're a gonner!'

John Barrymore blinked down the barrel of the gun and said: 'Don't shoot, sir, it's only me.'

I lowered the gun and hid it behind my back like a guilty schoolboy caught with a catapult.

'Come in,' I faltered. 'What do you want?'

He glanced furtively up and down the passage, to make sure the coast was clear, then came into the room.

'You won't tell the police that you have seen my

brother-in-law signalling on the moor will you, sir?'

'Not me, mate,' I assured him. 'Axeman . . . er Peter Selden hasn't got anything to do with my end of this investigation as far as I know – in any case I never go around grassing on escaped cons unless they're right bastards and there's a reward.'

'Oh, thank you, sir,' sighed Barrymore. 'Thank you very much indeed. My wife is so desperately worried about him. I think we have persuaded Sir Henry against turning him in. And if it's all right by you too, then she'll be so relieved. Thank you so very much.'

Barrymore seemed to have packed in playing a crook and reverted to the familiar butler routine. I wondered if there was a real Barrymore somewhere lurking underneath it all.

'Don't mention it,' I grunted in reply to his effusive thanks. 'Look, I've had a tough day and I'd like to get to bed.'

'Yes, sir,' he said. 'I won't keep you a moment.

He reached into the inside pocket of his jacket, took out a plain white envelope and handed it to me.

'What is it?' I asked.

'Look for yourself, sir,' he said. 'I think you'll find it most interesting.'

I opened it and peeked inside. It contained a dream of a clue – the kind of thing that a private eye would not expect to come up with more than two or three times in a lifetime of snooping. A charred fragment of a letter. It was on a par with the single strand of blonde hair on a suspect's sleeve, the lipstick smeared fag end and the image of the murderer reflected in a dead man's eyes.

I took the little treasure over to the bedside table and looked at it under the light. The bit that had survived the flames, seemed to be a PS at the end of the letter. It said: 'Please, please, if you love and trust me, burn this letter, and be at the gate by ten o'clock.' It was signed with the initials LL.

'What does it mean?' I asked excitedly.

'I'm not at all sure, sir,' John replied. 'But I rather think it may throw some light on how Sir Charles came to be in the yew alley on the night of his death. The gate mentioned in the letter can only be the wicket gate at the end of the yew alley, sir.'

'That sounds reasonable,' I agreed. 'How did you come by this slip of paper?'

'My wife was cleaning the master's study – two or three days ago, sir,' he explained. 'It hadn't been touched since Sir Charles' death and she found it at the back of the fire-grate. I remembered that a letter, addressed to Sir Charles, had been delivered to the Hall that morning by hand – the fragment you have there is very probably all that remains of it.'

'Good thinking, John,' I enthused. 'Who do you know locally with the initials LL?'

'I have already thought about that, sir,' he replied. 'But I cannot think of anyone.'

'Never mind,' I said cheerily. 'You've done very well as it is – it's definitely from a girl and it shouldn't take me too long to track her down.'

'I'm sure it won't, sir,' he smiled. 'Good night.'

'Good night, John,' I said. 'And thanks a lot.'

He said: 'One good turn deserves another, Mr Nelson,' gave me a dignified bow and went out.

CHAPTER TWENTY TWO

The day was half over when I woke, with the usual start and the usual monumental hangover. There was a load of broken glass behind my eyes and I lacked the energy to lift my eyelashes. I stretched out a feeble and trembling hand to the bedside table and groped for my fags and matches.

I lit up, gulped down a lungful of smoke and nearly threw up all over the patchwork quilt. A forty a day man shouldn't start burning snout until he's at least had a cup of tea. But the spasm passed after a bit and I began to feel more or less human. I lay back in the exquisite comfort of my mountainous four-poster and began to chain-smoke while a civil war started up in my nut about the unlikely developments of the night before.

It struck me as double dodgy that I'd actually seen a flying saucer when I hadn't even had enough to drink to give me the taste. Hankey Bannister's can make you see all kinds of things that aren't there if you drink enough of it – mostly pink elephants – but not until now had I seen any flying saucers buzzing around. It crossed my mind that maybe I ought to drop a note to the distillers about it – I reckoned dear old Hankey Bannister would be well pleased to hear from a devoted punter who saw a flying saucer instead of pink elephants. If I turned out to be the first he'd more'n likely send me a lovely case of the stuff free of charge. Then gradually the message filtered through that it hadn't been a mirage at all – I'd actually seen the sodding thing. Looking back, it occurred to me that the humming noise that it was making sounded very much like an electric motor. Which, in its turn, implied that what I'd seen was some kind of mechanical fake-up of a flying saucer.

It had been good enough to scare the pants off me in the middle of the moor in the middle of the night – but almost anything would do that. I cursed myself for a fool. If only I'd kept my head and gone and looked the thing over, I might have discovered how it worked, solved my case, and been able to push off back to London.

I lit yet another cigarette from the butt of the last one, squashed the stub out in the overflowing ashtray, and came to the startling conclusion that if the saucer was a fake someone must have been operating it from nearby. Perhaps Axeman Selden was in on the plot and had tempted us out on to the moor in order to stick the frighteners on us.

The saucer had been a whopper. It would be very difficult to cart that around without someone noticing what you were up to. Which should mean – if it was a fake – that all the sightings had to be around the same place.

There was one obvious way of checking that out. Frankland had them marked on that map of his beside his telescope. I hadn't looked closely last time. Best thing seemed to be to have another shufty.

It was about three o'clock when I turned the nose of the Hillman through Frankland's park gates and started up the drive to Lafter Hall. About halfway up I heard the rattle and clank of a large vehicle coming down towards me at a fair old lick. I swerved into a rhododendron bush, gave a succession of blasts on my hooter and waited for it.

Stapleton's tomato van came round the corner lickety split and whistled by me with about an inch to spare. Crouched over the wheel was the lovely Margaret. She gave me a jolly thumbs up sign as she went by and shouted something which I couldn't hear.

'Ah, Mr Nelson,' Ivor Frankland greeted me. 'I had not expected to see you again so soon.'

His man-eating housekeeper must have been out or locked up in her cage. Frankland had come to the front door himself.

'Yeah,' I said. 'Sorry to trouble you, but there are one or two loose ends about the UFOs you might be able to clear up for me.'

'I think I have alweady told you evwething I know, Mr Nelson.' There was just a trace of impatience in his voice.

'Been buying a few tomatoes, have you?' I asked as I followed him into the hall.

'No,' he snapped. 'What gave you that idea?'

'Natural deduction for a private eye to make when he sees the Stapleton tomato van rattling down your drive,' I apologized.

'Oh, that,' he said. 'I was lucky enough to persuade the wavishing Margawet to lunch with me. I've been showing her wound the house – she's twemendously interwested in art and antiques, you know. But it's put me fwightfully behind with the day's work. What did you want to ask about the UFOs?'

'I have been wondering if there is any pattern to the sightings?' I said.

'Pattern?'

'Yes,' I said. 'You will have noticed if they pop up more frequently in some places than in others – I wonder if I could have a quick look at that ordnance survey map on your attic wall with the little red flags pinned all over it?'

'I have no objection to that,' he clipped. 'But I weally must ask you to be quick about it – I am twying to wite my weekly article for the *Spectator*. I have to have it finished by the afternoon post and I am still wacking my bwains for a suitable topic.'

'How about giving those snotty-nosed lower orders down at the Great Sourton caravan site a going over?' I suggested.

'Splendid idea, Mr Nelson,' he beamed. 'Splendid. It's at least a month since I hauled them over the coals. I'm sure the time is wipe for another salvo.'

The cluster of red flags on the ordnance map did reveal, as I'd hoped it would, that there had been a lot more sightings of UFOs around Grimpen Mire than any other part of the moor. But I was still baffled. If, as I now reckoned, the flying saucers were phoney, why had there been sightings anywhere other than Grimpen Mire? Without revealing my suspicions I put the question to Frankland.

'Gwimpen Mire is situated in the most inaccessible part of the moor, few people ever go there. It is verwy pwobable that visitors fwom outer space are well aware of this and turn it to their own advantage,' was his explanation.

'Know anyone who lives around here with the initials LL?' I asked as he showed me out.

He stopped in his tracks and turned to eye me suspiciously.

'Why should it be of the wemotest interwest to you if I do?' he asked.

'It could shed important light on whether Sir Charles Baskerville was murdered,' I told him.

'Serves him jolly well wight if he was murdered,' Frankland replied. 'But I fail to see what that would have to do with my sister.'

It was my turn to be surprised. 'Your *sister*?'

'Yes, my younger sister, Lauwa Lyons. She has a cottage over at Muddicoombe.'

'Laura Lyons – does that mean she's married?'

'It does.' He didn't appear very happy at the thought of it.

'She mawwied a fwightful television pwoducer she met at Oxford. Like all television pwoducers he was an utter waster and a cwashing bore. Lauwa saw thwough him in thwee months or so and pushed off. After the appwopwiate pewiod of sepawation they got divorced.'

'I see. So she now lives alone?' I said.

He nodded.

'She has a dog to keep her company and wites novels – though I can't say it's much of a way to earn a living. She's had one published and is working on the second. Last time I saw her she was wather bogged down by her plot. Don't go pesterwing her with questions and discouwage her work, will you?'

169

'I'll take it easy with her, Mr Frankland,' I promised and tried out a reassuring smile. 'You never know, a lighthearted chat about the recent death of a neighbour might give her the inspiration she needs to sort her plot out.'

The reassuring smile seemed to have done its stuff.

'Thank you,' he said. 'You may be wight. Lauwa killed off almost all the chawacters in her first novel and a conversation with you will vewy pwobably induce her to slaughter evwebody in her second.'

'I see,' I grinned. 'Wholesome entertainment for all the family.'

'Acquired taste,' he sighed. 'Her male chawacters usually have an Oedipus complex – "Young man happily married to his mother discovers she is not his mother, and shoots himself" – you know the kind of thing, Mr Nelson?'

I didn't much like the way he said that, but I let it go, climbed into the Hillman and waved goodbye.

Muddicoombe-in-the-Moor had about as much claim to call itself a village as Princetown has calling itself a town. It was situated a couple of miles west of Baskerville Hall at the end of the narrowest, death-trap Devon lane I'd chanced my arm in. Tufts of grass had forced their way through the crumbling asphalt in the centre of the road. The hedgerows were ablaze with autumn tints and unpicked wild flowers. The ancient road sign that announced the entrance to the village was tumbledown, crawling with brambles and scarcely legible. I changed down to third gear in case I overshot.

There was no pub, post office or shop, only the red telephone box I'd used with Frankland a few days before. As well as a C of E church and a Methodist chapel there were five or six tiny thatched cottages spaced out, here and there, along the roadside.

I'd just about convinced myself that nothing had changed in this place, except the seasons, since the last time I bought a National Insurance stamp when a terrible monstrosity loomed into view. It was the kind of eyesore that would have made John Betjeman reach for his quill pen – if the first sight of it didn't kill him stone dead.

Some vandalising idiot had knocked two fairy-tale cottages into one, replaced the thatch with slates, planted a modern chimney on the roof, bashed out the old window frames and put in new, painted the front door daffodil-yellow and decorated the porch with hanging baskets of plastic flowers. I wouldn't let myself visualize the interior. There was plenty of modern garden furniture scattered around and garishly coloured plaster gnomes.

It didn't seem likely that a nicely brought up young lady like Laura Lyons lived there. If she did I hoped she'd turn out to be the murderess.

I snailed on, averting my eyes, and was just wondering whether to stop and ask the way when an enormous dog cleared a nearby hedge and completely filled the road ahead. I jerked the car to a halt and waited for him to get out of my light, but he wasn't in any hurry – he waved me a friendly welcome with his big brown tail, then lay down in the middle of the road, stuck his left hind leg in the air and contentedly licked his balls.

Unless the whole of Dartmoor was teeming with gigantic hounds I reckoned that he must have been the friendly fellow I'd met in Coombe Tracey. I wound down the window an inch or two, honked the horn and yelled: 'Get out of my way you great softy ninnny!'

It was a mistake – he thought I wanted to play. He leapt up and lumbered towards me, wagging his tail so hard it looked like he might shake his rear end off any minute. When he came abreast of the car there was a tinkle of glass as his tail sliced off the nearside wing mirror as neatly as the head of a flower.

'Bang goes my hundred quid deposit you clumsy sod,' I shouted out of the window. 'Go on and piss off out of it.'

Further damage was averted by a shrill little voice shouting: 'Heel, Tiny, heel!'

The dog looked around as the girl I'd seen with him the last time we met came around a bend in the lane. She was wearing gum boots, a head scarf and a raincoat at least five sizes too large for her.

'Come away from there, Tiny,' she scolded. 'Come away this instant.'

The massive brute cowered away from the car with his tail between his legs and seemed close to tears.

'Bad dog,' she said as she approached. 'You ought to be ashamed of yourself.'

That was more than he could take – he slunk off down the lane with his head bowed.

'So sorry, Mr Nelson,' said the girl. 'Tiny doesn't mean any harm but he just doesn't know his own strength – I'll pay for the damage, of course.'

'You know my name?' I asked without surprise.

'Yes, you are becoming quite a celebrity in these parts,' she smiled. 'I'm Laura Lyons – I've been expecting you.'

I got out of the car and offered her my hand.

'Can I talk to you?' I asked. 'I take it that your brother phoned to say I might turn up?'

'Good Lord no,' she said. 'I'm not on the telephone – that's why I live in this remote spot. Peace and quiet, you know?'

'City slicker myself,' I quipped. 'Too much peace and quiet makes me edgy. I'm expecting the intake of fresh air I've had since I arrived down here to give me cancer.'

'I wouldn't be surprised, Mr Nelson.' She pointed down the lane the way I'd come. 'My cottage is down that way about a hundred yards – you'll have to back up I'm afraid. There's nowhere you can turn unless you want to drive two miles up the lane to Maitland's farm.'

'It's okay,' I said. 'I'll back up but do me a favour will you?'

'What?'

'Go ahead and give me a yell if you see a milk tanker coming.'

'Yes, of course,' she said and hurried away.

Laura Lyons' cottage was a snug little place, one up, one down and a little kitchen out the back. A slow burning,

Scandinavian stove stood in the big, old world fireplace. There wasn't room for more than bare essentials – two armchairs, a table, a walnut bookcase, a couple of lamps with drum shades and a small side table near the stove. There were thick, rust-coloured velvet curtains hanging from brass rings above the one small window. The carpet looked as though it was worth a few quid and so did the oil painting over the fireplace. My guess was that she'd furnished the cottage from odds and ends that her brother had kicking around in the basement of Lafter Hall.

'Do sit down, Mr Nelson,' she said. 'Would you like some tea?'

'Love some,' I replied. 'But do call me Ed.'

She nodded, smiled and went out into the little kitchen.

'Milk or sugar?' she asked as she poured the tea.

'Both,' I said. 'Three spoons of sugar, please.'

'Gosh,' she said, 'you have got a sweet tooth.'

I stirred my tea and said: 'Do you know why I've come to see you?'

'Yes.'

'Why?'

'You want to ask me if I've seen any UFOs hovering over the moor.'

'Try again.'

She paused with her cup of tea halfway to her lips and gave me a searching look.

'I think you'd better tell me,' she said.

'I want to ask you about the letter you had delivered by hand to Sir Charles Baskerville on the day he died.'

She sipped her tea daintily and looked me over with vaguely amused eyes.

'So the bounder didn't burn it?' she inquired softly.

It's always unwise to show your hand, but I decided to risk it.

'He did,' I told her, 'but part of it survived the flames – the PS with your initials at the bottom.'

'I see,' she smiled. 'I suppose you think that proves something?'

'It did make me wonder if you had something to hide,' I suggested hopefully.

'Only half-wits and one or two Trappist monks have nothing to hide,' she pointed out.

'I expect you're right,' I replied. 'But how am I going to eliminate you from my inquiries if you won't cooperate?'

She shrieked with laughter and almost dropped her teacup.

'You sound like a police sergeant in a third rate crime novel.'

'I picked the line up in the movies,' I said, aggrieved. 'It usually scares the pants off people.'

'Well, I'm obviously not people,' she laughed, then leant forward in her chair seriously.

'Before I talk to you, Ed,' she said, 'I want to see the fragment of the letter you say survived the flames.'

'Fair enough, Laura,' I said, and reaching into my inside pocket I came up with the envelope. I fumbled the slip of paper out of the envelope and held it up to her between a forefinger and thumb.

I was ready for what happened next, but only just. A dainty little hand flashed through the air and snatched the end of it. There was a tiny zip as the slip of paper divided in two. She had more than half of it and I had the rest. She jumped up and backed away from me, screwing the paper into the palm of her hand. I made no effort to stop her and just sat there watching.

'What evidence have you got against me now?' she jeered, then tossed the pellet into her mouth and chewed ravenously.

I glanced down at my depleted fragment and said: 'I've got the bit with your initials on it.'

She brushed her hair out of her eyes and snorted: 'That won't do you any good.'

'Might come in handy as a bookmark,' I said. 'But are you sure you ought to be eating burnt paper? – very bad for the digestion, I'd've thought.'

'I can face a tummy pain for the sake of destroying the

174

evidence,' she told me with a glinting smile.

'It's your tummy,' I shrugged. 'Both the Barrymores saw it before they gave it to me, so I can't see that eating it is going to help you much.'

'That's my affair,' she replied tartly.

'Did you go to meet him that night?' I asked, changing the subject.

'No,' she returned flatly.

I was tempted to point out that she had to be lying, since Tiny had left his unmistakable foot prints in the yew alley. But I decided to keep that card up my sleeve to scare her with later. All the same, I found it difficult to see her as a murderess. She was too pretty, for a start. I tried a little gentle probing.

'Do you make much money out of writing novels?' I asked.

'No one makes any money out of writing novels,' she laughed.

I waved a hand limply around the room.

'But you seem to make out all right?' I commented. 'And that dog of yours must cost a hundred quid a week to feed.'

'My income is no concern of yours,' she said.

'Did Sir Charles help you out financially?' I quavered. 'A lot of self-made men who have made their lolly out of boring stuff like property development or tinned cat food like to put themselves about as patrons of the arts – makes 'em feel good, know what I mean?'

'You're barking up the wrong tree,' she told me kindly. 'Sir Charles never gave me a penny.'

'Were you in love with him?' I asked.

'Christ, no,' she exploded.

'Then what was up between you that made for midnight assignations?'

'It wasn't midnight, it was ten o'clock,' she pointed out. 'I'm not going to tell you anything, you know – so it's no use your going on asking questions.'

I kept going for a while but in the end I got the message

that she meant what she said. There seemed nothing for it but to keep her high on the list of suspects and accept defeat for the time being. I pushed my empty teacup towards her and stood up.

'Thanks for the tea,' I said. 'Do you mind if I use your bog before I push off?'

'Not at all,' she smiled prettily. 'I'm afraid it's only an Elsan round the back of the house. I like having it out of doors myself. It makes me feel close to nature.'

The very idea of having to conduct the simple daily pleasure of my bowel movements in an ivy-covered Elsan was no less appetising than the possibility of having to piddle in a pot or behind a convenient hedge, like a dog.

'You can stuff nature, as far as I'm concerned,' I told her. 'But I'll look in there as I go if you don't mind.'

Tiny met me at the front door with a friendly yap and escorted me to the convenience. It was just as I feared, an ivy covered lean-to, so I got on with the job with no mucking about.

As I played the jet of water into the bucket, it came to me that the hut had a kind of funny smell. It was a very familiar smell, but one that I connected with hot London cellars, rather than outdoor loos. Someone had been smoking hash in there.

CHAPTER TWENTY THREE

Poncing about in the West Country was seriously getting on my wick. The local boozer was always full of horny-handed sons of toil who banged on endlessly about the turbulent weather and the adverse effect it was liable to have on the mangel-wurzel crop. My meal-time conversations with the little baronet weren't all that rewarding either. He banged on a lot but he hardly ever said anything that made me laugh. A wisecracking private eye from up the Smoke only really feels at home in the company of flighty blondes, diabolical tearaways and bent cops.

Since Axeman Selden was billed to be around the manor, it seemed like a good idea to look him up and have a rabbit about old times over a jar or two. A man on the trot from the nick is liable to get rather lonely out on that green splotched bog, and for me it would at least provide a little light relief from the grinding tedium.

As the old retainer was sloshing my regulation black coffee into my gaily decorated, French *faience* breakfast cup, I dived in the deep end.

'Axeman Selden is holed up somewhere around this neck of the woods then, is he?' I inquired casually.

He glanced over his shoulder, went to the door and peeked out into the hall, then came back and looked under the table.

'That's right, sir,' he whispered, having made absolutely certain that the coast was clear.

'Whereabouts?'

Barrymore drew himself up to his remarkably full height and eyed me suspiciously.

'I'm not sure if I should tell you, sir,' he replied at last. 'You may be tempted to turn him in.'

'Do me a favour, Barrymore,' I chuckled. 'I never turn anyone in. Old Axeman is a mate of mine anyway. Many's the time we've had a drink together down the Hide Away club in Soho. I won't snitch on him, you have my word on that.'

This information seemed to melt the heart of the old ham. He dropped his guard and said: 'Nice chap really, isn't he? Didn't realize that you'd actually met him. The wife dotes on him, of course.'

'Can't blame her,' I grinned. 'He's a master craftsman when it comes to blowing a peter. They don't make 'em like that any more – born tea-leaf, know what I mean?'

Barrymore nodded gravely and poured himself some coffee in Sir Henry's dirty cup.

'He's staying down at the Great Sourton caravan park,' he told me, pulling up a chair. 'Peter's got quite a cosy caravan. Nice gas stove, lace curtains and a good supply of tinned food.'

'Nice change for him after a prison cell,' I commented. 'What does he do with himself all day?'

'Keeping his head down, sir, I should think,' Barrymore shook his head sadly. 'I haven't dared ask him about his future plans.'

'Funny he should still be hanging around here though, isn't it?' I asked. 'I mean to say, the moor is crawling with armed filth searching high and low for him. Any con who managed to have it away out of Dartmoor nick would make tracks on the hurry up unless, of course, he had some special reason for hanging about, right?'

'The thought has occurred to me that someone helped him escape for some particular purpose,' Barrymore conceded.

'Mmmm,' I mused.

'There is one thing he did tell me though.'

'What?'

'There's another big time villain from London just turned up there with his caravan.'

'Really?' I said in amazement. 'At Great Sourton? I'd

have thought that tearaways from the Smoke would have better taste than to hang around a slimy dump like that. I suppose there is always the possibility that some firm is starting up a caravan site protection racket – Not a bad idea come to think about it. It's high time them middle class hooray Henrys got the arm put on them for cluttering up the place with their rotten trailers.'

'Quite agree, sir,' Barrymore enthused. 'Quite agree.'

Nothing ventured, nothing gained. I reckoned I'd better creep over there and see what was buzzing. At best, I might run into a Soho mate to have a bit of a booze up with; at worst, I might bump into a few clues to further my investigations. There was also a chance that I might get duffed up by the bad guys Barrymore had put me in about, but I've never met a tearaway yet who enjoys having a .38 shoved up his hooter.

I drove over to Great Sourton in the Hillman, armed with my shooter and the knowledge that Selden had registered under the name of Peter Moffat. Also that the new brigand, whoever he might be, had a dirty great de luxe caravan with blue roses painted on the side and central heating.

My old pal the strawberry-nosed superintendent pointed out where Moffat was parked and held out a hand for some dropsy. I stalked off with my nose in the air and left him standing.

Selden's caravan was locked up and the car was gone. Its wheel tracks were cut deeply into the soft mud of the field.

Disappointed, I set out to see if I could find the de luxe model. It didn't take long. Three down to the right and one row further up the hill was a low slung, spanking new caravan about twice the size of all the others. The sides were decorated with a frieze of twining blue roses. It was the kind of hideous monstrosity that would one day end up in a museum as a monument to the bad taste of the '8os.

A sleek grey Jaguar XJS was parked beside it and new

steps, glistening with vinyl gloss, were propped below the door which stood invitingly open.

'Anyone home?' I called, as I reached the bottom of the steps. There was no reply.

I climbed the steps and rapped on the door, but from there I could see that there was no one inside. It was furnished like a model home advert in a tarty colour magazine, only in miniature. A gust of hot air belched out at me from the central heating system and I stepped over the threshold, my feet sinking ankle deep into lush carpeting.

I made a half-hearted attempt to turn the gaff over for clues which might have put me in about the identity of the occupant. But everything was in apple-pie order and all I came up with was: he was a man who sometimes wore size ten brogues and he'd had eggs for breakfast.

I opened a cupboard above the diminutive fridge and came face to face with a bottle of Bell's whisky. It was not my brand, but it seemed to say to me. 'Help yourself, sucker, someone'll show up to share me with you any minute.'

I found a tumbler on the draining-board, clinked some ice in it from the fridge, added a mammoth slug of whisky and looked around for the soda. It was hiding, along with several tins of soup and a double-barrel sawn-off shotgun, in a store cupboard under the sink. I yanked the gun out and broke the barrel open – there were two orange scatter-shot cartridges in the chamber. I plucked them out with a forefinger and thumb and slipped them into my pocket. Then I put the gun back where I found it and closed the cupboard.

With the tumbler clutched reassuringly in my hand I subsided into the deep well-sprung sofa in the sun lounge. I pulled a spotless ashtray towards me and settled down to wait.

Two large ones later, I heard the squelch of approaching footsteps. I shifted the glass to my left hand and pulled my gun out of my armpit holster with my right. The footfalls paused a moment as they reached the caravan, then mounted the steps. I had my gunsight trained on the doorway.

A hole as big and black as a workhouse oven appeared under Drummer Bill's broken nose when he caught sight of the gun, then he roared with laugher and slapped his knee.

'Better drop the shooter, Ed,' he bawled. 'Or I might be forced ter make yah eat it.'

'Stone me, Drummer,' I gulped. 'What are you doing here?'

Willy Paradis' right hand man blocked the doorway with his massive bulk and shut out the sun like a big black cloud.

'Never mind abaht that, son,' he snarled, edging past me towards the cupboard under the sink. 'Fortcha was snoopin' arahnd 'ere somewhere on account of I seen the 'Illman parked up by the office.'

I reached into my pocket and took out the two scatter-shells and said: 'Don't make no daring moves like diving for the popgun in there – it ain't loaded.'

'Yah learnin', Ed,' he chuckled. 'There ain't no doubt abaht that wotever. Fact is it's double 'andy runnin' inter yah coz the guv'nor told me ter pick yah up for a meet over Princetown.'

'Christ,' I groaned. 'Don't tell me Willy's down here too.'

'Just did, didn't I?' said Drummer aggrieved. 'Yah gotta meet wiv 'im dahn the Old Police Station Caff, four o'clock. Nar put the shooter away and stop larkin' abaht.'

It was downright insulting the way people always thought I was larking about when I pointed my gun at them, but I let it go and returned it to its snug little holster. Then I polished off the remains of the whisky and asked Drummer to give me the low down on what was going on.

That didn't get me anywhere, of course. Willy knows that his first lieutenant is as dim as a Toc H lamp and doesn't bother to tell him what he won't understand –

which means just about everything. To find out the full strength of this top level delegation from the Smoke, I'd have to wait for my four o'clock appointment with Willy himself at the Princetown café.

The stories that old lags had spun me, over the years, about the dreaded Dartmoor Prison were frightening enough to chill the heart of Vincent Price. There wasn't a tearaway in the underworld who wouldn't lose control of his bottle at the prospect of being sent there.

But my first glimpse of it didn't strike me as all that much to write home about. I'd expected to see a dirty great gothic fortress, shrouded in mist and surrounded by green-scummed pits and foul quagmires. Instead it was just a sprawl of buildings, mostly new looking, with corrugated iron rooves. It looked more like some big commercial enterprise than it did a nick. The approach road into Princetown from the moor was festooned with police notices saying: 'NO ADMITTANCE', 'IT IS FORBIDDEN TO PHOTOGRAPH THE PRISONERS', 'KEEP OUT', 'TRESPASSERS WILL BE PROSECUTED' and 'PRISONPROPERTY' – one word, for some reason. It'd probably been knocked up in the nick workshop by an illiterate. There were double yellow, no parking, lines down both sides of the road.

I left the car in the centre of town, outside the Prison Officers' mess. Two screws eyeballed me as I got out. One of them scribbled something on a slip of paper – probably my licence number – then both disappeared from sight.

I had a quick butchers at the goodies on display in the window of the Porrij Gift Corner and wondered if the proprietor was an old lag who couldn't bear to leave the place, or a shrewd entrepreneur who'd sussed out the easy pickings to be lifted off tourists.

A sign outside the Old Police Station Café said: 'Cakes, Scones, Pies and Pasties. Devon cream teas'.

'Yuck!' I muttered and went inside.

There they were slouched around a corner table, nice as you please – Willy Paradis, his henchman Drummer Bill

and two lesser lights of the Soho mob called Salvatore
Gizzo, a one-time Italian waiter who had gone to the bad,
and Joe Clayton, a bloke I didn't know much about except
that he had more form that Red Rum, the three-time
Grand National winner.

'Wotcha, chaps,' I hailed them from the door. 'You're a
bit close to home aren't you?'

Willy looked around at me and grinned his welcome.

'Right comical geezer Ed is,' he laughed. 'Sharp as a
razor-blade – ain't that right, Drummer?'

The knuckle-man glanced at me and said: 'Yeah, boss,
sharp as a raza-blade – only fing is 'e needs to watch out 'e
don't cut 'is own ears orf.'

That tickled everyone pink and they fell about laughing.

'Pull up a chair, Ed,' said Willy, 'and 'ave a cream tea.'

I said: 'Not bloody likely, mate,' and sat down at the
table.

'Suitcha self, Ed.' Willy spooned half a gallon of clotted
cream on to a scone, topped it off with a dollop of straw-
berry jam and raised the whole thing towards his mouth.
'Yer don't know wotcha missing, son.'

'This is a pretty conspicuous place for us to make a
meet, isn't it?' I remarked under my breath. 'I mean to say
right opposite the flaming nick.'

'In the caff opposite the nick is the last place the law'd
fink of lookin' fer a geezer wot could 'elp 'em wiv their
inquiries, ain't it?' Willy assured me.

I shrugged my reluctant agreement and said: 'Right,
lads, what's the full strength? – Did you spring Axeman
Selden? Are you gonna sort out Reg Mortimer? And what
are you going to do to get me out of the jam you've
lumbered me with down here?'

'Don't arf wonna know a lot, don't 'e?' grinned Willy.

'Yer wonna know wot I fink, boss?' Joe Clayton asked.

Willy game him a fatherly smile.

'No fanks, Joe,' he said. 'I wonna little rabbit wiv Ed in
private. You and Salvatore 'ad better sod orf an' wait in
the jam jar.'

They got up complaining and pocketed a couple of dung-coloured Cornish pasties to keep them going. As the door closed behind them, I turned to the Soho gang boss.

'Let's get down to cases, Willy,' I said. 'What's buzzing?'

He looked at Drummer, then around the deserted café and finally at me, and said: 'I reckon yah entitled, son. If I 'adn't offered to fill yah in if yah didn't keep an eye on Reg Mortimer I don't reckon yah would a touched this caper wiv fire tongs.'

'You read me like an open racing form book, Willy,' I said. 'The sooner I get back to a few safe and peaceful back alleys the better.'

'Me an' all,' grunted Drummer. 'I done a laggin' in that slammer across the bleedin' road an' I don't like bein' so near it, guv.'

I said: 'They tell me they do it hard by the yard in that place, Drummer.'

'Ain't so bad,' he came back at me. 'Yah cry yahself ter sleep the first few nights, then yah find yahself a screw ter 'ate an' yah can do the rest of yah time larfin'.'

'Yah don't get no cream teas up in the Smoke,' commented Willy licking his fingers. Then he explained the set up. 'Wot brung me an' the lads dahn 'ere, Ed, was readin' in the linens as 'ow Axeman Selden 'ad 'ad it away on 'is toes outa the nick.' He nodded his head across the road.

'So it wasn't you who sprung him?' I said with interest.

'Nah,' Willy shook his head. 'An' if I ain't done it, 'oo did? That's wot I asked meself – no one don't get aht of the moor wivaht outside 'elp, am I right or wrong?'

'Yah right, boss,' said Drummer enthusiastically. 'Ain't no one ever scarpered aht of there wivaht ahtside 'elp, an' if we ain't given Axeman a bit of a 'and 'oo 'as?'

Apparently he was following the gist so far. I looked at Willing inquiringly.

'What's the answer?' I said.

Willy did not reply directly.

'Axeman's a specialist, right?' he said. Drummer and I

nodded. 'So 'oover wanted 'im ahta there 'ad a job for 'im, stands ter reason.'

We nodded again.

'So 'oo 'as a job fer 'im, 'an might be living 'andy ter the nick for bunging a few screws an' cutting some wire?'

I pondered, but couldn't see the answer. Willy sighed at my slowness.

'Only the geezer wot 'as bin fixin' the West Country stately 'ome jobs, an' the export froo Plymouth, wouldn'tcha say?'

'I see,' I said slowly, as the light began to dawn. 'So you came down to have a bunny with Axeman and fill in the mug that got him out of the nick. That's the story, is it?'

'Nah yah getting' it, son,' Willy congratulated me.

'And you snuck your dirty great caravan into the park at Great Sourton, so's to be nice and handy for chatting up Selden and seeing who he's working for?'

'Right agin,' Willy beamed. 'Always fort you was a genius, Ed.'

'And who is it?' I asked.

Willy looked from me to Drummer and back again, then let out a raucous peal of laughter.

'If I was to tell yah,' he told me. 'First fing wot would 'appen is yah'd be runnin' orf and lettin' the cat ahta the bag. I don't reckon yah'll rumble 'oo it is on yah own, so stick arahnd and let me tell yah wot ter do.'

'But my life may be in danger,' I wailed. 'If he murdered Sir Charles, you never know, I may be the next on the list.'

'Yah are, me ole sunshine,' grinned Willy. 'No doubt abaht that wotever.'

CHAPTER TWENTY FOUR

Getting told that I'm liable to get bumped off at any minute never fails to put the frighteners on me. Up till now such warnings had been laid on me in the convivial atmosphere of sleazy Soho dives in which threats of sudden death are bandied about as casually as tennis balls at Wimbledon. But the ignominious prospect of getting murdered out here in the sticks, more than two hundred and fifty miles away from my square mile of vice, was more than my ragged nerve ends could take. I fell apart at the seams and was so shaky on my pins, as we left the Old Police Station Café, that I couldn't even open the door of my car let alone drive it.

'Yah awright, son?' asked Willy as I leaned against the Hillman, fumbling in my pocket for cigarettes.

I gave him a watery smile and said: 'Nothing wrong with me that a bullet proof waistcoat and a bottle of Hankey Bannister's wouldn't cure.'

''E ain't so tough,' Drummer put in. 'All mouf and trousers, like most geezers wot ain't got no real villainy under their belt, know wot I mean, guv?'

'Shutcha face, Drummer,' growled Willy. 'Cummon, Ed, we'll give yah a lift in the Jag.' He glanced over his shoulder at Joe Clayton and Salvatore. 'Yah two follow us in the 'Illman.'

I tumbled into the back seat of the Jag and Willy got in after me while Drummer took the wheel. A couple of hefty belts from the brandy flask that Willy carried around in the motor for medicinal purposes brought the colour back to my cheeks and I began to feel as well as I was going to feel that day.

It was dusk as we climbed the hill out of Coombe

Tracey. As usual the spectacular sunset wasn't making it. It was locked behind an iron grey sky that had been keeping a thin drizzle going all day. Buggered if I knew how generation after generation of hill farmers and tin miners had managed to survive in this remote and cheerless landscape. A view that tourists take snaps of spread out before us as we crested the hill, looking grey, dreary and windswept. I gave Grimpen Mire a dirty look as we coasted towards it, and thanked my lucky stars that I wasn't decomposing in its murky depths.

Then out of nowhere something glowing appeared. I tried to gee myself up that there'd been a break in the clouds and a beam of watery sunlight was filtering through. But that wasn't it. Something very nasty happened in the pit of my stomach and I clutched at Willy's arm.

'For Christ's sake look over there,' I yelled at him. 'It's the flying saucer!'

'Leave go of me arm, yah berk,' snapped Willy, trying to shake himself free of my clutching hands. 'Wotcha on abaht?'

'You gone blind or something,' I shrilled. 'Over there, hovering over Grimpen Mire. It's the UFO I told you about, the sodding saucer.'

Willy leaned forward and tapped Drummer on the shoulder.

'Pull in, will yah,' he said, 'and let's take a butchers at wotever it is Ed's doin' 'is nut abaht.'

Drummer slammed his foot on the brakes and we slithered to a tyre-burning halt at the side of the road. Joe and Salvatore were coming up fast on our tail – and skidded to a stop behind us with the nose of the Hillman an inch and a half from the Jag's rear bumper.

We rolled down the left-hand side windows and peered out across the forbidding moorland at the glowing object that hovered in the distance. It was quiet except for the sighing of the wind. Then a spine-chilling scream echoed from tor to tor across the wasteland and even after it had died away the stain of fear still hung menacingly in the air.

'Some berk's runnin' dahn that path next to the bog,' cried Drummer excitedly. 'D'yah see 'im?'

I narrowed my eyes and put up a hand to shade them from the cutting wind. He was dead right. A small figure was scuttling and tumbling down the cart track that ran beside Grimpen Mire.

'Poor sod's gorn bananas,' commented Willy, leaning across me to stare intently out of the window. ''E must fink the stupid fing's from ahta space. Wot a con!'

As we watched, the hurrying figure let out another pitiful scream, tripped and fell forward on his face. He didn't get up again.

'Better shoot over there and take a butchers at 'im,' said Willy, after a minute had passed.

'D' yah reckon that's all that much of a good idea, guv?' asked Drummer nervously.

It was the first time in all the years that I'd been acquainted with Willy's right hand man that I'd ever seen him show the slightest glimmer of human emotion or good sense. If I'd been able to speak, I'd've agreed with him. The wisest thing to do would have been to have it away a bit lively, down the M4 at 70 mph and not stop until we had reached the safety of the Hide Away club.

'Do like I say,' Willy grunted, 'and fast!'

Drummer let out the clutch and belted off down the road hell-for-leather. It was more than half a mile to the point where the cart track joined the main road. We made it in under thirty seconds. Drummer slammed on the brakes and nearly turned the flipping car over as he swung us round on to the track. We bumped and skidded from side to side like a drunken stumble bum in a Soho alley on a rainy Saturday night. The Hillman was not far behind and having an even tougher time of it than we were.

The terrain was very steep, very rocky and even Drummer, who had out-stripped more police cars in his time than you could shake your fist at, had to take it easy. He kept to the low gears most of the time and it was ten minutes or more before we topped the ridge and Grimpen Mire came into view. There was no sign of the glowing saucer from outer space, but a body was spreadeagled on the path ahead of us. Both cars stopped dead.

The doors of the Jag sprang open like flick-knives, we tumbled out and dashed up the track. Joe and Salvatore were close on our heels.

Drummer Bill dropped down on one knee, turned the man over and shone a flashlight on his waxen face.

'It's Axeman Selden.' There was no trace of emotion in Drummer's voice as he stated the obvious. "E's dead.'

I bent forward to get a closer look. The eyes of the corpse were wide with terror and the corners of his mouth were twisted into a frightening grimace.

'Stone the crows,' I gasped. 'The poor bleeder looks like he had the living daylights frightened out of him.'

"E always did 'ave a dodgy ticker,' Willy said sadly. 'Back in the old days I done a spot of porridge wiv 'im in Wandsworth nick. Double jumpy 'e was, frightened of 'is own shadow, let alone anyone else's – never could do 'is bit in the prison riots and 'e did a lot of 'is bird in the 'orspital wing.'

I was standing there staring down at him feeling nothing. Later, full of Hankey Bannister's whisky, I'd probably lament the passing of a great peterman, the like of whom we were unlikely to ever see again. But for now I just wondered idly how come he was wearing *my* trench-coat? I did a double take and saw that he also had on my trousers, jacket, shirt and tie.

Willy gave me a sidelong glance, saw a dodgy expression on my face and said: 'You awright, kid, yah ain't gonna pass aht at the sight of a stiff are yah?'

'What I want to know,' I replied, keeping a tight grip on myself, 'is what the bleeding hell he's doing wearing my bloody clothes?'

It was Willy's turn to do a bit of reacting.

'Gotcha clobber on 'as 'e?' he said with interest. 'Well,

that's one up for the book, I've gotta admit - any idea 'ow come?'

'Maybe,' I faltered. 'It's the gear I was wearing the night I took a dip in Grimpen Mire. I gave it to Barrymore to get rid of – it stank to high heaven.'

'The crafty old devil musta 'ad it cleaned and 'anded it over to 'is bruvva-in-law,' Willy commented with a chuckle. 'Looks like 'ooever was operatin' that saucer fing was trying to 'ave a right go at yah, Ed.'

'Me?' I screeched.

'Recognized that trench-coat of yours and fort it was you, geddit?'

'You reckon they were trying to bump me off, right?' I stuttered.

'Yah smart as pink paint, Ed,' he nodded without taking his eyes off the body. 'All we gotta do nah is put the arm on the face behind all this monkeyin' abaht.'

'Wot are we gonna do wiv 'im, guv?' Joe Clayton asked nervously.

'Leave 'im for someone else ter find,' said Willy, shaking his head sadly. 'It's the only fing we can do.'

'We could make an anonymous phone call to the law,' I suggested.

'Yeah, awright,' sighed the tzar of Soho. 'It's the least we can do for one of our own.'

'I think I could do with a drink,' I quavered.

A couple of hefty doubles down at the Devil's Stone Inn failed to raise my spirits. I asked myself for the umpteenth time what a fun loving, carefree and happy-go-lucky divorce snooper was doing tits-up in a lousy situation like this. I sank a couple more and felt only a trifle better, then I got a handful of small change off Molly the barmaid and tottered off to the telephone cabin next to the gents. I remembered to take another double whisky with me.

After I'd rung the law at Tavistock and told them about the sad demise of poor old Axeman Selden on the moor, I gave Sir Henry a bell. He sounded surprised to hear my voice and stunned by the small earthquake in Chile, not many dead, news I laid on him.

'You'd better break it to the Barrymores,' I advised him. 'I daresay Eliza's going to be pretty cut up. And don't forget nobody knows I found him. Keep your trap shut, okay?'

'Where are you, Ed?' stammered the baronet.

'The American bar at the Savoy hotel,' I told him and hung up.

Once you get a taste for making telephone calls it's difficult to stop. I've known a lot of birds who go telephone crazy especially at three o'clock in the morning – I dialled the *Western Morning News* in Plymouth and asked for Fletcher Robinson.

''E'm just gone 'ome, zur,' said the friendly girl on the switchboard.

'How about giving me his home number?' I suggested.

'Us can't do that, zur. It be agin regulations,' she replied apologetically.

'Okay, okay,' I sighed. 'Perhaps you can give him a message?'

'Us'll take it down, zur,' she said.

'Escaped convict has just been frightened to death by flying saucer over Grimpen Mire,' I enunciated slowly. 'Be sure to tell him that, there's a good girl.'

'Us'll be telling the news editor,' she whispered in a shaken tone.

I rang off rather pleased with myself and rejoined Willy at the bar.

I found him in deep, but barely audible, conversation with Reg Mortimer. Giles Stapleton was loitering nearby nursing a pint of ale and listening in. Drummer, Salvatore and Joe were holding up the other end of the bar and keeping a discreet eye on the boss from a distance.

I thumped my empty glass on the counter and called out: 'A man could die of thirst in this pub. Come along, Molly, drinks all round.'

'Double or single, zur?' she inquired eyeing me measuringly.

I told her and fell into inconsequential chit chat with Willy and Co. It was heavy going. It's never easy to stay shtoom about a cold blooded murder you have just been an eye witness to, especially when the murder weapon was a flying saucer. But Willy was an old hand at the murder game. I wasn't sure how many he'd actually committed himself, but I was in no doubt about two or three that he'd got members of his firm to do for him. He carried the whole thing off with great aplomb, as though nothing had happened on the moor that day worse than a steady downpour of rain.

'Take it easy on the juice, Ed,' he had growled at me out of the corner of his mouth, during one lull in the conversation, but apart from that all was sweetness and light.

Something over an hour later Sir Henry came striding into the pub as though he owned the place – which of course he did since it stood on his land. Ashen-faced, he pushed his way through a knot of yokels to reach where we were standing.

'There's been a death on the moor,' he announced as he came abreast of us. 'The moorland road is crawling with police. They stopped my car as I was driving over.'

'Who is it?' and 'How did he die?' chorused Reg and Giles in horrified excitement.

I wondered why they took it for granted that it was a *man*, but didn't ask.

'I have no idea,' lied Sir Henry. 'Not a local, as far as I could make out from the police.'

'Whereabouts did it happen?' asked Giles.

Sir Henry told him.

'Good grief, that's where the UFO sightings have been,' Reg chimed in excitedly. 'Do you think he was scared to death like Sir Charles?'

'Wouldn't be surprised,' I murmured. 'Fear is a lovely murder weapon – you can't leave your finger prints on it.'

The baronet looked daggers at me and I thought, for a moment, he was going to take me to task. But he turned his eyes away from me and locked them on Willy in a puzzled kind of way. Reg and I both realized that they hadn't met before. But Reg got in first with the introductions.

'You don't know Willy Paradis, Sir Henry,' he said. 'Willy is down here on a brief visit. He is the proprietor of a night club in the West End of London.'

I put my hand to my mouth to muffle a snigger.

The gangster and the baronet exchanged a firm handshake.

'Taking a late holiday to avoid the tourists?' Sir Henry suggested mildly.

'Yah got it in one, Sir 'Enry,' grinned Willy. 'Nevva go a tuppeny bus ride off me patch in the 'oliday season. 'Course, most years I nip over ter the Souf of France or the Balearics, but all that foreign grub gives me the gip and I can't do the lingo, so I reckoned it might be favourite ter give the West Country a try, know wot I mean, Sir 'Enry.'

'Yes, yes, of course,' he agreed. 'Dartmoor can be quite breathtaking in the autumn.'

Willy tipped me a cheeky wink and said: 'Yeah, in more ways than one from what you've been tellin' us.'

It is company policy at the Ed Nelson detective agency that the firm's clients should never be permitted to meet each other, let alone compare notes. The condition is specifically stipulated in the fine print of the firm's unwritten contracts: 'Don't talk to no one about the case, especially anyone involved in it directly or indirectly, on account of blabbing stuff out is liable to fuck up the investigation'. A second reason for the clause was that if the firm's clients got around to discussing the success rate of the firm's services, discontent was likely to break out and the company chairman might end up with a sackful of letters of complaint.

In spite of the chairman's sound and far-sighted thinking there didn't seem to be any way of keeping Willy and Sir Henry apart. They took a shine to each other right from the off and started rabbiting away nineteen to the dozen. Then, of course, the dodgy mental processes of the aristocracy and big time hoodlums have so much in common.

At five minutes to closing time Molly rang a quaint old cow bell and shrilled: 'Last orders!'

'Plenty to drink at Baskerville Hall,' Sir Henry informed us hospitably. 'Why don't you come back for a nightcap or two?'

'Don't mind if I do,' grinned Willy.

Giles Stapleton shook his head sadly.

'I've got to take the tomatoes in to Tavistock market tomorrow,' he said. 'And that means a five o'clock start. Better get some beauty sleep.'

'You workers!' Sir Henry exclaimed goodnaturedly. 'But you're bringing Margaret over to dinner tomorrow night, aren't you?'

'It's a date!' cried Giles and saluted the baronet in a manner he no doubt considered humorous.

'How about you, Reg? On for a spot of serious drinking?' Sir Henry inquired.

'I've got a bit of a day tomorrow too,' simpered the pusillanimous antique dealer. 'Furniture auction over at Buckfastleigh and I'm hoping to pick up a few really good bargains.'

'I say,' the baronet cried excitedly, 'I'm on the look out for a really nice mahogany wardrobe, Georgian, if possible. Not more than six feet in height. Do keep an eye out for me, there's a good chap, I'm terribly short of cupboard space in my bedroom.'

'Yes, of course,' Reg replied. 'But I don't think there'll be anything of that quality at the Buckfastleigh auction, Henry.'

'I can getcha one dirt cheap,' Willy volunteered. 'Stuff like that is always fallin' orf the backs of lorries.'

Reg gave Willy a glare and flung out of the pub in a huff. So it turned out that just me and the Soho gubernator were going back with Sir Henry.

'Pick me up abaht one,' Willy yelled to Drummer before following us out to Sir Henry's Rolls.

There was only one police car left, standing sentinel, as we passed the beginning of the cart track that led to Grimpen Mire. Back at the Hall, a light was burning in an upstairs window. Sir Henry glanced up at it.

'I don't think we ought to disturb the Barrymores at this hour,' he said. 'But if either of you feel peckish I'd be only too delighted to knock up a little snack myself. I'm a dab hand with the frying pan when the need arises.'

We rolled into the house and Sir Henry ushered us across the imposing hall to the drawingroom.

'Whisky all round, I take it?' he said, heading for the drinks table.

'Do me, guv,' said Willy.

'And me,' I added.

Sir Henry was no slouch when it came to giving away his whisky. He handed us a couple of hefty tumblers of it.

We chatted about this, that and the other for a bit and then our host shoved off to the kitchen saying he'd fix some eggs.

'Where's the soddin' dinin' room in this dump?' Willy demanded to know as soon as Sir Henry had departed.

'Across the hall,' I said. 'Why?'

Willy tapped the side of his nose with a forefinger and said: 'Never mind abaht why, son, just lead the bloody way.'

It crossed my mind that he was thinking about half-inching the silver candlesticks – tearaways very seldom visit anyone's house without pocketing a few knick-knacks that take their fancy – but I didn't feel like getting my nose broken so I showed him the way.

'Cor, Ed, look at all them Sexton Blakes,' Willy gasped, when I snapped on the dining-room lights.

'What?'

'Them pitchers,' he chortled, indicating the portraits of Sir Henry's forefathers that decked the walls. 'Musta bin some right bright spark wot run 'em up for 'im.'

'What the hell you on about, Willy?' I asked, looking

around the dreary row of paintings in their heavy gold frames.

'They're all pitchers of the same geezer,' he pointed out. 'Same geezer togged up in different kinds of old world clobber, if yah get me meanin'?'

'The faces of people in ancestral portraits are supposed to have certain facial characteristics in common,' I told him in a superior voice. 'It's called a family likeness.'

'Betcha a 'undred quid to a penny they're all of the same bloke and was all painted yesterday,' he came back at me.

'No thanks,' I said and took a closer look at them. Then I got excited. 'You could be right, mate. They all look like Giles Stapleton in drag.'

'Well done, son,' he congratulated me. 'I fort it was gonna take from nah 'til Christmas for yah ter tumble it.'

'What does it all mean?' I asked, momentarily sobered by the strange discovery.

Willy shook his head and let his eyes wander down the whole gallery wonderingly.

'Can't say, Ed,' he said at last. 'Ain't even got a sneekin' sus, but I'll tell yah one fing for nuffink.'

'What's that?'

'There's sumink pretty niffy in the state of Denmark, mate,' he chuckled. 'There ain't no doubt abaht that wotever.'

Then he reached forward and tipped up the Tudor Baskerville he'd been gawking at. He produced a small plastic looking button thing from his coat pocket and pressed it carefully against the back of the picture with a clubbed thumb.

'Now what are you up to?' I asked in surprise. 'What is that thing?'

'Silicon fish 'n' chips, Ed,' he laughed. 'A posh bird took me ter the National Gallery once and she reckoned all these ole time geezers was always lousy wiv bugs. So I don't fink this bloke is even gonna notice 'e's got anuvva one – 'specially if it don't even itch.'

'Supper's up,' cooed Sir Henry, suddenly appearing in the doorway with three plates of rashers and eggs balanced precariously between two hands.

CHAPTER TWENTY FIVE

Sudden death makes stunning copy for the linens and Fletcher Robinson's scoop in the morning paper was a knockout. It was the kind of story that makes Fleet Street hacks go bananas and it crossed my mind that old Fletch was not going to have it to himself for long. Before the day was much older platoons of reporters from the nationals would be pouring into the West Country to get in on the act. If the locals played their cards right they'd almost certainly end up with a bundle of folding money and their faces on the TV news.

I propped the slim regional newspaper against Sir Henry's marmalade pot and swallowed a mouthful of lukewarm instant coffee. Barrymore hadn't put in an appearance this morning to do his usual butler-hovering act and I'd been forced to fend for myself in the kitchen. I wasn't surprised by his absence. His grief-stricken old lady had flooded the place out with her tears the night before. The whole house had echoed with her sobs till sparrow's fart.

There was a banner headline right across page one *MYSTERY MOORLAND DEATH OF 'AXEMAN' SELDEN*. Below this, in letters just a little smaller, it said: *'Cunning Dartmoor convict's bid for freedom ends in tragedy'*. There was a stark flashlight photo of police humping a bulky, blanket covered stretcher into an ambulance. Fletcher Robinson's by-line was also prominently displayed.

I lit a fag and settled down to read his rattling flow of words. It was excitable stuff. About halfway down he tackled the UFO business and it was easy to tell that he was into his favourite topic, 'Unconfirmed reports', he said, suggested that the escaped prisoner had died crazed with fear after being pursued across the moor by a flying saucer. What he didn't say was that he only had my anonymous phone call to go on for that bit, but it was too juicy to leave out and the age old newshound's axiom, 'check it or chuck it', had gone out of the window. He slung in a resumé of the saucer sightings over Grimpen Mire for good measure.

As I got to the end of it, my eyes suddenly bulged with amazement. In a big, black outlined box across two columns they advertised the scoop of the century starting in the *Western Morning News* tomorrow. *FAMOUS CRIMINAL TELLS ALL* they announced, then explained: '*Fletcher Robinson talks to Axeman Selden – EXCLUSIVE*'.

'Well I'm blowed,' I said aloud. 'How the Hell did he manage to pull that off?' There were plenty of people about, not excluding me and the screws of Princetown nick, who had been longing to have a cosy little bunny with Axeman, but Fletch had beaten the lot of us to the punch. I didn't believe that the *Morning News* had been putting their cheque book about, like they do in the Street of Shame. So it had to be down to the old pals act or maybe Fletch had promised to put a word in for him with the prison governor when Axeman got captured.

I shook my head in puzzled admiration and decided I'd better pull myself together and drive over to Plymouth to have a little rabbit with the dazzling journalist in person.

I'd just reached this momentous decision and laid the paper aside when Sir Henry came striding into the room with a brow as black as thunder.

'Like a cup of cold instant?' I asked. 'I made a whole jug of the muck while I was about it.'

'No thanks,' he snapped. 'I want to have a word with you.'

'Sure thing,' I said. 'Fire away.'

He sat down and began to draw lines across the highly polished surface of the table with a stubby forefinger. He went right on frowning and I got the feeling that he had something pretty objectionable to say but didn't quite know how to get started.

'The Barrymores have given in their notice,' he told me finally. Then he lamped me with the eyes of a man who was in no mood for an argument. 'I can't manage visitors staying here without them, so I'll have to ask you to leave.'

I am a man who is used to getting the elbow. I shrugged slightly, gave him a sympathetic smile and said: 'Tough titty, guv. But don't worry about me. I'm sure I can get a room at the Devil's Stone Inn. I'll move out right away if you like.'

'I don't want you at the Devil's Stone Inn either,' he rasped.

'Why not?' I asked in surprise. 'I wouldn't wonder if it wasn't a better base for my investigations than Baskerville Hall, anyway. Maybe I should've stayed there from the off – pub licencing laws don't apply to bona fida travellers who are actually staying on the premises, you know.'

'What I'm saying to you,' he replied icily, glowering at me from beneath beetling brows, 'is get out of my house and get out of the county.'

'Come, come,' I gasped. 'Devonshire is not Dodge City, it is a very big county and I'm sure there is enough room in it for the both of us.'

Sir Henry did his nut.

'I have put up with you hanging about my house, half cut most of the time, eating my food and drinking my drink and making smart-Aleck wisecracks *for long enough*!'

His boatrace had turned fire-engine red and it looked for a bit like the blood was going to come boiling out of his ears.

'Get out of my house,' he wailed. 'You are absolutely bloody useless. You don't know any more about Sir Charles' death now than when you came down here.'

That kind of fighting talk was right up my street.

'Now that wasn't a very nice thing to say, Sir Henry,' I countered as casually as passing the time of day with a policeman. 'I've slaved my guts out on this case, hacking my way inch by inch through a quagmire of red herrings and old cobblers. Most of the time I've felt like a blind man walking barefoot on a mile of broken bottles - but I've tumbled a lot more than you think I have, guv, I'll tell you that for nothing.'

'What do you know then?' he sneered.

I gave him a crafty smile and tapped my temple with a forefinger.

'What's in there is going to cost you, Sir Henry,' I drawled. 'Cough up the lolly you owe me for services rendered or I tell you nothing.'

His eyes bulged with fury.

'Clear off and get back to the sleazy streets of London where you belong,' he yelled. 'You won't get another penny out of me, do you hear, not another penny.'

'I'm sure you're going to thoroughly enjoy the lively correspondence you'll be having with my solicitor, Theordore Socolofsky,' I remarked, getting up. 'He's the greatest fiddler since Paganini and a dab hand at squeezing welchers.'

I hurried out of the room, before he could box my ears and went upstairs to pack.

There are few things more satisfying to me than getting chucked off a case I never wanted to take on in the first place. I was as chuffed as a horse punter on a winning streak as I buzzed along the twisting lanes towards Coombe Tracey with my battered old suitcase in the back of the Hillman. I was free at last. A cosy lunch-time Pullman from Exeter, and I'd swim back to town in an ocean of booze in the buffet car. Tonight I'd be right back in my beloved Soho, pickling my liver in back street dives and puking my ring up in the gutter – maybe, if I played my cards right or even if I didn't, I'd get my leg over Black Satin Hotpants before the crack of dawn. Thank God this sodding case was over.

I didn't see what further use I could be to Willy now that Sir Henry had given me the slingers. But it seemed like a mistake to ask him. I might miss my train.

I was absent-mindedly whistling *Why Should we Quarrel for Riches* under my breath when two figures suddenly hove into view walking along the lane ahead of me. One was a slim young girl in a headscarf. She had a bigger chap with her; the bigger chap was a gigantic hound. I didn't have any difficulty recognizing Laura Lyons and Tiny.

I slowed down, pulled up beside them and wound down the window.

'Hello,' I cried beaming from ear to ear. 'Fancy a lift into Coombe Tracey? I reckon I can fit the big fella in the back at a pinch.'

'Woof! Woof!' went Tiny in friendly recognition. In one great bound he leapt over to the car and licked the top layer of skin off the hand I was resting on the window.

Laura floated up to the window behind him, looking pale and worried.

'Heel, Tiny,' she called mechanically. The dog gave me a parting smile and padded off to sit down behind her and thump the road with his tail.

'Hello, Ed,' said Laura with a wan ghost of a smile. 'What on earth have you got to be so cheerful about?'

'Just lost two bob and found half a crown,' I quipped. 'How about the lift?'

'Thank you so much for the offer,' she replied sadly. 'Actually we're on our way over the moor to Lafter Hall. The house has been burgled.'

'You don't say,' I cried. 'When did it happen?'

'Yesterday apparently,' she said. 'I've only just had a message to go over there. Poor Ivor was up in London for the day and his housekeeper had gone to visit her daughter in Launchester. They had the place to themselves and made a thorough job of it by all accounts.'

The alarming revelation that Mrs Reynolds, the man-eating housekeeper, had at some time in her life given birth to a daughter was too ghastly to contemplate, let alone comment upon.

'How big was the haul?' I asked with professional interest.

'The best of the antiques and all the clocks have gone,' replied Laura. 'Plus the contents of the safe.'

'I didn't notice a peter in the house,' I commented.

'It's hidden behind a Dutch landscape in the drawing-room,' she told me with a nod. 'You wouldn't notice it unless it was pointed out. Ivor keeps a hoard of Kruger-rands and gold sovereigns in it. He says they're the best hedge against inflation. But they weren't insured, of course, so they'll be no use to him now.'

Every cat burglar knows that the first place to look for a wall safe is behind the first Dutch landscape painting they come upon in a drawingroom and only a right mug punter keeps his valuables in such a vulnerable place. Surely everybody knew that the safest place to hide gold coins is in a metal box buried in the garden? It didn't seem like the right moment to go into all that so I just mustered a sympathetic smile and said: 'How frightful.'

'Ivor asked me to go over and see if I can help remember what's disappeared. It's such a big house and almost everything has been there for generations – I don't expect I'll be able to remember stuff that isn't obvious. But apparently the police need a complete list if there's going to be any hope of getting things back.'

'The CID have to go through the motions,' I told her and added with conviction: 'You won't get anything back.'

'What do you mean?' she asked in surprise.

'Antiques are as negotiable as gold bullion,' I explained. 'Hot goods will fetch their price anywhere, particularly on the Continent. Most professional tea-leaves have got a tie-in with a Common Market fence in France or Germany nowadays. A good haul from a stately home anywhere in Blighty will find its way across the Channel within twenty-four hours.'

'I say,' gasped Laura. 'Are you sure?'

I lit a cigarette and beamed at her through a cloud of smoke.

'Big time burglars don't pussy foot around these days,' I assured her. 'No stately home is safe any more, no matter

203

how tight the security – it's only because most tearaways are very patriotic that Buckingham Palace and Windsor Castle haven't been turned over, you can take my word for that.'

Laura gave me a pretty little smile.

'You're pulling my leg.'

'No I'm not,' I laughed. 'I think it's because most crooks have spent a fair amount of time as Her Majesty's guests. Whatever else you can say about the underworld they seldom rob anyone who has given them hospitality – that goes double for the Queen.'

'Honestly, Ed,' she chided me good-naturedly, 'you're impossible. But Ivor badly needs some professional advice – will you come over to Lafter Hall with me?'

'Sorry, love,' I apologized. 'I've got an urgent appointment in London. I'm on my way to catch the train at Exeter now.'

'You aren't leaving?' she cried in alarm. 'What about the investigation you've been doing for Sir Henry?'

'Got the push this morning,' I smirked. 'So you can stop worrying about your involvement in this little caper ever coming out. Now I'm off the payroll, I will take the truth to my grave.'

'Don't be silly,' she huffed. 'I wasn't really involved. I'll tell you the whole story sometime. But right now it's Ivor that needs your help. You've simply got to come over to Lafter Hall with me.'

'Oh no I haven't,' I said. 'Not unless you happen to have a gun in your pocket and you're prepared to use it on me.'

'Please, Ed!' she said pleadingly. 'If you only got the sack this morning, you can't have got anything fixed up for the day.'

'I've already told you my presence is urgently required up the Smoke,' I told her condescendingly.

She mustered a sweet watery smile and said: 'I don't believe you. You just want to get back to London, don't you?'

The girl was uncannily perceptive. I racked my brain for a new and unshakable excuse. But she got in ahead of me, laying her cool white hand impetuously on mine and soothing the raw flesh where Tiny had licked the skin off. Then she did all that soft dewy stuff that girls do with their eyes when they want a bloke to do something he wouldn't dream of doing in his right mind.

'Please, Ed. I'm appealing to you. We need your help.'

I should have stuck to my guns and said no. But what can a private eye do when a bird brings that kind of artillery into action, except come over quixotic? The rule was on page one of the private eye's handbook, so there was no way I could get out of it without being shitty.

'Okay, kid,' I sighed, leaning over to open the back door of the car. 'Pile in, both of you, and I'll run you over to Lafter and see what's buzzing.'

To my surprise, Laura hung back and the worried frown she'd been wearing earlier returned to her brow.

'I'm fearfully sorry, Ed,' she said all in a rush, 'but the thing is that Tiny won't go in cars – it sounds ridiculous, I know, but he's actually petrified of them. There is simply no way of persuading him and if one tries to force him he just bursts into tears and might even bite one of us.'

I looked over at the big soft nelly. He was sitting there behind her laughing his stupid great head off with about three yards of wet tongue lolling out of the side of his mouth. He looked a lot bloody bigger than me and I didn't fancy a trial of strength.

'What do you suggest we do then?' I asked Laura.

At least she had the common decency to flush before making the suggestion.

'Walk over the moor,' she whispered. 'It doesn't take much more than half an hour if one takes the short cut along the cart track past Grimpen Mire and over the top. Lafter Hall is just over the side of the ridge, you know.'

'I didn't know,' I told her sternly. 'And I have no wish to find out. Apart from the fact that tramping across moors is my least favourite pastime, especially in suede shoes, that path is double dangerous. Axeman Selden was killed there only yesterday in case you haven't heard.'

'Was he really?' she breathed excitedly. 'Then perhaps we'll find some clues. Tiny's fantastic at nosing things out.'

The dear little doggie woofed his loud agreement, jumped up in excitement and started chasing his tail. I actually found myself liking the silly bugger.

CHAPTER TWENTY SIX

Beautiful men in distress can stew in their own juice as far as I'm concerned. I don't give a monkey's what happens to beautiful men in distress and at this late date I don't expect I ever will. But beautiful girls in distress are a very different kettle of fish – the more beautiful they are and the greater their distress the more likely I am to allow myself to be suckered into giving my life for them. It's pretty sloppy thinking, of course, because it's a well known fact that the more beautiful a girl is and the more acute her distress the more likely it is that she'll turn out to be the murderess.

On the other hand there are the perks. If, like now, I happen to run into a very beautiful girl who turns out to be suffering from a heavy dose of distress there is always the chance, if I get her out of it, that she will reward me with at least one thrilling night of love – maybe two if I lose an arm and a leg fighting off the bad guys responsible for her distress.

But Laura Lyons was pushing it a bit. She'd dragged me bodily out of my cosy Hillman and forced me to abandon it at the side of the road. Then she led me up a lonely path on to the moorland with this dirty great dog, gambolling and woofing around us, obedient to her slightest command.

It idly crossed my mind, as I followed her gasping for breath up the side of a tor, that it was all a sinister plot. Once we got out of view of the road she was going to turn Tiny on me and instruct him to tear a tasty hunk of flesh out of my neck like the hell hound in the Baskerville legend. My corpse would be left to rot hidden by the soggy bracken. I reckoned it could do no harm to give her a warning.

'Just in case you've got any gruesome ideas in that pretty little head of yours,' I panted. 'You may as well know I'm packing a rod.'

She turned back to look at me, her puzzled face attractively framed by the damp headscarf.

'What kind of rod?' she asked whimsically. 'And where have you packed it?'

'A Smith and Wesson .38 special, lady,' I told her. 'I pack it in a shoulder holster.'

Her brow cleared and she smiled at me demurely.

'How exciting,' she squeaked. 'I always thought that private eyes went unarmed like the police.'

'You're a bit out of date, gal,' I replied. 'Shooters are all the rage nowadays. In any case, I've based my style on James Cagney and he wouldn't be seen dead without a gun in his hand.'

'A girl always feels a lot safer when she knows that she has the protection of a real *He* man,' she confided. 'I was getting a nasty little feeling in the pit of my tummy that Selden's murderers might still be around.'

'Don't say things like that,' I groaned. 'Tangling with murderers is my least favourite pastime.'

She pouted a little and said: 'I thought private detectives were supposed to be tough and fearless?'

'Not this one,' I snapped. 'I'm not the kind of private eye who goes around in the guise of a quasi-policeman. I keep a low profile, drink a lot more Hankey Bannister's whisky than my clapped out pancreas can comfortably cope with and chain-smoke Rothmans King Size. I used to chain-smoke Senior Service, but they don't have a filter tip and they gave me chest pains after about twenty years, so I gave them up.'

'Do go on,' she prompted. 'I've never met a private eye before and I'm absolutely fascinated.'

'I spend most of my time lounging about in the battered old swivel chair in my London office,' I told her. 'Cogitating about where my next wad of drinking money is going to come from and waiting for the phone to ring.

From time to time people ask me to do things for them. Usually it's a bit of keyhole work in dingy hotels, for some sordid divorce action. I don't much like that kind of work, it gives me housemaid's knee and watery eyeballs. Occasionally, when I'm flat skint, I slap writs on people who get behind in their weekly payments to loan sharks. And once, purely by accident, I reunited a kidnapped heiress with her distraught parents. That little caper got me a bit of publicity on the front pages of a couple of tabloids and a thumbnail mention in *The Times*. But it was a once in a lifetime fluke and my mind is still clogged with conjecture about how I pulled it off. I have a sneaking sus that the girl's parents coughing up the ransom money so promptly had a good deal to do with it.' I paused to light a cigarette.

'Murder cases,' I went on, 'are not up my street at all. They unfailingly end badly and clients who turn up in my office with tales of woe about a relative or friend who has just met a grisly end get kicked out of the door on their ear.'

We were standing below a jagged outcrop of rocks that sheltered us from the cutting wind and Laura was eyeing my fag impatiently.

'I think we'd better get a move on when you've finished your cigarette,' she said. 'If we go on loitering at this sort of pace it will be hours before we reach Lafter.'

'It is undignified to walk fast,' I pointed out. 'Unless, of course, someone happens to be chasing you.'

I looked down the track ahead of us. We were approaching a Y-shaped division of footpaths; one snaked up over the steep hill while another plunged down into a deep valley and disappeared from sight.

'How much further have we got to go?' I asked wearily.

'Once we get to the top of the tor,' Laura replied, indicating the upward track with a slight nod of her head, 'it's only about half a mile to Lafter Hall and it's all downhill.'

Tiny snuffled about in the undergrowth beside us and barked several times. Then he trotted off a short distance, whimpering plaintively. A moment or two later he retraced his steps, nuzzled his mistress's hand and padded off again in the same direction. He seemed to be finding the overgrown track down into the valley strangely attractive.

'I think he wants us to follow him,' I said, after he had returned a second time and gone through a similar routine.

'You're right, Ed,' Laura was suddenly alert and excited. 'Let's see what it is he's got the scent of?'

I said: 'Right behind you,' and the pair of us took off after the big dog.

With his massive black boot of a nose skimming along, not more than an inch or two above the ground, Tiny led the way at a brisk pace for a quarter of a mile or so with Laura and me close behind.

'Should have brought the car,' I puffed, and pointed down at tyre tracks clearly imprinted in the mud. 'Someone's been down here in a motor pretty recently.'

'Mmmm,' said Laura non-commitally. 'I wonder what Tiny makes of it – maybe a hill farmer has been down here in his Land-Rover looking for lost sheep.'

The dog looked over his shoulder at us impatiently, and with a series of short excited barks he followed the track around a corner and out of sight.

Turning the corner behind him a great expanse of mouldering disused quarry opened before us. There were humps of gravel dotted about and green stagnant pools. Brambles and wilting nettles fought to obtain a foothold amongst the unfriendly stones. While the craggy and scarred rock face that had been quarried away (probably by generations of lifers from Princetown jail) rose to a height of some three hundred feet, towering over us, and threatening to drop loose boulders on our nuts at any moment. Some kind of junk-yard crane or hoisting mechanism stood rusting against the sheer rock face in one corner.

It was towards this that Tiny bounded across the length of the quarry, snarling like a police dog about to taste blood. Laura paused watching him anxiously.

'Tiny,' she called to him. 'Come away from that thing. Heel, Tiny, heel.'

He looked around at her apologetically for a moment, but his hackles had risen and he was eager for the kill. I just hoped to Christ that it was only a rabbit he was after. He leapt elegantly up on to the hoist, paused for a moment, then disappeared from sight behind it. He began barking and whining, as if some tough old alley cat had hold of his tail.

'Sounds like he's found somebody nice to eat,' I remarked.

'A dead badger, most likely,' snapped Laura tartly. 'I'd better go and drag him away before he gives himself a tummy upset.'

She sprang after the dog, dodging from one hump of solidified gravel to another and somehow avoiding the temptation of a slippery slide into a nasty pea-green pool. She climbed aboard the hoist in her turn and stood clinging to a tall rusted shaft. Then she turned back towards me and her face was glowing with excitement.

I would never have expended so much energy all in one go – and I found myself wondering, not for the first time, what the younger generation of lissom country girls were coming to. The depressing thought made me homesick for the heavily scented B-girls down the Hide Away club in darkest Soho, whose daily exertions consisted of nothing more strenuous than conning the punters out of their pocket money, drinking sweet drinks and turning a few tricks.

Laura jerked me back to reality with shrill cries of:

'Ed! Ed! Quick! Come here! He's really found something. Come and see!'

'What is it?' I called back without moving. I hadn't liked her passing reference to a dead badger either.

'It looks like a removals truck, a fairly new one.'

The answer was so surprising that I started across the quarry on the hurry up, but only just fractionally faster than a tortoise. There had once been a track across and I followed this until it submerged itself in a deep scummy pool. Cursing a blue streak I skirted the pool and picked up the track again on the far side.

I climbed up to where Laura stood impatiently waiting for me. Then I saw what she'd seen.

CHAPTER TWENTY SEVEN

Completely obscured by the bulk of the old crane, a cave opened into the rock face. Jammed into its entrance, like a fat old cow in a milking stall, was a tall pantechnicon, built on the lines of a Pickford's van. Crouched beside it was Tiny, barking his head off.

'How the bloody hell did they get a sodding great thing like that in there?' I muttered in amazement.

'I suppose this crane thing must be easier to move than it looks,' Laura returned sensibly.

'Let's have a closer butchers at it,' I said.

The number plate, when we came up with it, indicated that the van was about ten years old. It looked in good working order. I squeezed my way into the cave and stood back to get a view of it from the side.

'There's something painted on the side,' I called to Laura. 'But it's as black as Newgate's knocker in here and I can't see what it says – looks like the name of a firm or something.'

'Can't you strike a match and read it?' she replied impatiently.

I fumbled in my pocket and came up with my Zippo petrol lighter, flicked it open and scraped my thumb on the flint wheel several times until the wick caught fire. The flame dispersed the gloom and I raised my arm until I could read the sign writing.

'Well if that don't beat all,' I exclaimed and in my astonishment dropped the light.

'What does it say?' shouted Laura in a voice trembling a little at the edges.

I was down on my knees feeling around for my lighter on the soggy ground.

'It says: "The Barrymore Travelling Theatre Company",' I told her. 'And I've lost my flipping lighter.'

Laura scrambled down to join me with a bump.

'Oops! I think I've trodden on it,' she said. 'Aren't the Barrymores that couple who "do" at Baskerville Hall?'

'Got it in one,' I returned. 'And if you've busted my faithful old Zippo lighter, I'll give you such a kiss you'll never forget it as long as you live.'

'Promises, promises,' she sniggered and put the lighter into my hand.

It still worked, but I gave her the kiss anyway – hard on the mouth like hotshot private eyes do in the movies. But she didn't melt in my arms like Lauren Bacall did in Humphrey Bogart's arms in *The Big Sleep*. Maybe it was because I didn't have a nancy boy name like Humphrey or maybe it was because of my bad breath. She squirmed away from me and shrieked:

'What on earth do you think you're doing, Ed?'

'When a private eye gets a beautiful girl trapped in a dark cave in the middle of Dartmoor,' I drawled, 'he's supposed to kiss her.'

'Well you can keep your bloody kisses,' she told me straight. 'Don't you think we ought to break into this van and see what's inside?'

'Yeah,' I sighed, 'I think we ought to do that.'

With the Zippo lighting my way I groped along the side of it to the driver's cab and tried the door handle. To my surprise it wasn't locked. I jerked it open and clambered inside. There were no keys in the ignition but I did find a powerful flash light on the dashboard shelf.

'That's double handy,' I muttered and beamed it around to see what else I could find.

There was a metal tool-box on the floor, full of spanners and things that might come in handy for throwing at people if we got caught. There was also a jemmy that ought to make short work of the big padlock that secured the back doors.

Armed with the jemmy and the flashlight I climbed out

and rejoined Laura, who was waiting for me at the back of the van.

'What luck,' she cried gleefully when she saw what I'd come up with. 'Ed, you're a genius.'

I was still pretty put out by the way she'd rejected my passionate advances, but a fulsome compliment can be confidence building to a private eye quaking in his shoes. I wrenched the padlock off the door with the jemmy in a trice and swung the big doors open.

In the beam of the torch a bright silvery glow met our eyes and just for a moment I thought something might be on fire, but there was no crackle or smell of burning.

We were looking at a large object smothered with phosphorescent paint. It was ten or so feet across, about three feet thick and completely circular.

'Blimey O'Reilly,' I gasped. 'It's the bloody flying saucer!'

'Ivor will never get over it,' sniggered Laura.

'This certainly puts the kibosh on his theory about an invasion of the moor by the Martian hordes,' I agreed.

'I wonder how it works,' she said, gazing at it inquisitively.

'Hang on a sec,' I said and clambered up into the back of the pantechnicon. By the light of the torch I inspected the contraption more closely. I jabbed it gingerly with an extended forefinger and found that it gave under the slight pressure like a balloon. On the under side of it there was a low powered motor with small propellers attached.

'Seems to be made on the old airship principle, light as a feather,' I told Laura. 'Probably full of helium gas and a small motor to power its flight. Buggered if I know how they guide it, though.'

'The Archimedean precept,' she instructed me, bringing her expensive boarding-school education into play. 'Airships lighter than the air they displace experience a buoyant force tending to make them rise.'

'Thanks a lot,' I sneered. 'Any ideas on the steering?'

'All that's needed is an electrically operated remote

control box,' she went on bossily. 'They sell them in toy shops with aeroplane kits. A child of ten can easily operate it.'

'You're a real mine of information,' I congratulated her grudgingly. 'Perhaps you can tell me where they actually got hold of a thing like this?'

'The Barrymores were in show business, weren't they?' said Laura. 'I expect it's a prop from some space fiction saga, like *Doctor Who.*'

'You could be right,' I conceded. 'It certainly looks realistic enough from a distance.'

I stood looking at the object, amazed by our discovery. I gave it a hefty squeeze; some of the phosphorescent paint came off on my fingers and scattered like fireflies in the air.

'So it was the Barrymores all along who have been operating the spectral UFO, and scaring people to *death*,' I muttered, a prickle of fear creeping over me at the dangerous company I'd been keeping. 'I realize that actors are prepared to go to extremes to draw attention to themselves, but mass murder does seem a bit excessive. They might have bumped me off in my sleep any night during the past ten days.'

'They wouldn't have done that,' Laura said, as I clambered to the ground. 'The way they've been playing it, it's got to look like an accident.' She paused and then continued reflectively. 'I imagine they must have driven the whole contraption up to Baskerville Hall the night they frightened Sir Charles to death.'

'What makes you so sure it was the saucer that did for the old boy?' I asked. 'I haven't been able to dredge up any real proof.'

'In the first place the remote control system will only work effectively over a very short distance,' she explained quietly. 'And in the second place I saw it.'

'You what?' I shouted.

'I said I saw it with my own two eyes,' she repeated.

'Phew!' I sighed. 'I don't think I can take many more

216

shocks today. Let's get the hell out of here and you can tell me all about it somewhere cosy, like bed.'

'I don't want to get boring about it,' she replied pertly. 'But I'm afraid you're going to have to learn to take *no* for an answer.'

We clambered out and settled on a granite spur that commanded a fine view of the quarry. Laura pointed up the sheer cliff face to an outcrop of rocks perched precariously at the summit.

'That's Grimpen Tor,' she said. 'Grimpen Mire is just over the other side. I imagine they must have been able to fly the thing from down here and make it hover over the mire. Nobody would have been able to get close enough to see what it really was without falling into the bog themselves.'

'Pretty good thinking, Laura,' I said with a shiver. 'But I think it's about time that you levelled with me about Sir Charles' death.'

'Very well,' she agreed easily. 'But there isn't much to tell. We were to meet that night at ten o'clock at the wicket gate. I walked up with Tiny. From about a mile away across the moor I saw this saucer-shaped thing glowing in the night sky somewhere close to Baskerville Hall.'

'Here we go again,' I muttered.

'We hurried as fast as we could but by the time we got there it had disappeared. There was no sign of Sir Charles either, so I slipped into the yew alley to look for him. It was Tiny who found him – but it was too late. I felt his pulse and he was already dead.'

'Why didn't you raise the alarm?' I asked.

'The police would have asked me what I was doing there, stupid,' she came back at me.

'Very likely they would,' I agreed. 'What *were* you doing there?'

'Actually, it was perfectly innocent, though I'd rather not tell the cops. I was taking him a quarter pound of finest Moroccan grass. I'd just got hold of some lovely stuff and he'd begged me to sell him some.'

'Perfectly innocent, child of five fun and games,' I chuckled. 'Just peddling dope. The CID would've loved that angle.'

'I expect they would have taken a fairly dim view of it,' she said, swinging her legs to and fro and infuriating Tiny who was trying to nuzzle her knee.

'So who's your supplier?' I asked.

'Who do I get it from you mean?'

I nodded.

'Giles Stapleton,' she said. 'His prices are a bit of a rip off. But hash can get very scarce in the West Country.'

'Why didn't Sir Charles buy his directly from Giles, then?' I was getting off my mark at the right time for a change, and asking proper private eye type questions.

'Giles is very secretive about it, of course,' she explained. 'People in the country always show a keen interest in everyone else's business and the slightest hint of scandal spreads like wildfire. I only discovered about it by chance. Margaret was high one day, really out of her skull, and told me about how Giles was a pusher. I asked him if he'd sell me some the next time I bumped into him in the village and he absolutely did his nut. Swore me to secrecy and all that before he agreed to let me have any.'

'How does he do such a roaring trade in the stuff if no one knows he has it?' I asked puzzled.

'Don't ask me,' she shrugged. 'All I know is he wouldn't let me tell Sir Charles, so I used to buy it from him and take some over there at the dead of night.'

'The PS to that letter read more like a lover's assignation,' I pointed out.

'That was the code we used as a cover,' she explained. 'It let him know that I was coming over with his supply.'

I didn't like it much, but it sounded so daft it had to be true.

'Muddicoombe is a den of iniquity,' I told her with a smile. 'I'm scarpering back to the cosy confines of my London patch as soon as I've put my old friend Willy wise to the Barrymores.'

Suddenly she slid off the rock and stamped her feet impatiently on the muddy ground.

'Hey! We're supposed to be on our way to Lafter Hall to help poor old Ivor,' she reminded me.

'So we were,' I groaned. 'I'd forgotten about that. But I think I'd better get things moving on the flying saucer front. You go to Lafter with Tiny and I'll go back and pick up the car. Willy gets the dead needle if I keep things from him that he feels he ought to know.'

'Who on earth is Willy?' she inquired curiously.

'He's only the tzar of Soho,' I snapped. 'The most powerful man on my manor.'

'But what about Ivor? You promised to help.'

She tried out a repeat performance of her little girl lost routine. But it got her nowhere – I can get pretty unbending when it comes to doing favours for beautiful girls who refuse to melt in my arms like Lauren Bacall melted into Humphrey Bogart's arms in *The Big Sleep*.

I said that I might try to get over later, but made no promises.

CHAPTER TWENTY EIGHT

'I don't rightly know where 'e'm to, zur,' the strawberry-nosed superintendent of the Great Sourton caravan park scratched his stubbled chin pensively.

'Of course you don't,' I groaned, pulled a crumpled quid out of my trouser pocket and passed it out of the car window.

A slow smile rippled over his face as he plucked the note out of my hand.

'Reckon you'm might find un over to Coombe Tracey,' he told me.

'Thanks a bunch,' I sneered and backed the Hillman out on to the road again.

As I crunched into the car park of the Devil's Stone Inn, Willy's sleek grey Jag was the first thing to catch my eye. How he could besport himself along the highways and byways of the West Country in a car like that without quickening the interest of the traffic cops was a bit of a mystery until I gave the matter two seconds' thought. The guv'nor rarely took chances – if he was more or less advertising his presence in Devon it could only mean that there was no chance of getting his collar felt. And if there was no chance of him getting his collar felt it could only mean that he had straightened out some high ranking rozzer in the Devonshire Constabulary. Nothing unusual about that, of course, Willy was the most accomplished straightener out of high ranking filth the criminal fraternity had ever produced.

I parked the Hillman next to the Jag and got out. I glanced idly at the big expensive job standing next to it. It was a white Mercedes – it was a racing certainty what the licence plate number would be, but that didn't stop my blood from running cold when I actually saw it. PHY 64 Q. I was getting pretty sick of my blood running cold three or four times a day.

The boys were congregated at the far end of the bar and sounding like they'd already enjoyed more than their usual intake of lunch-time drinks.

'Listen, darlin',' Drummer Bill was slurring at Molly. 'I wonna light ale, brown ale, pint of mild and bitter, a large vodka an' tonic and a bit of the uvva.' The team laughed heartily at Drummer's witty punch line.

'And a large gold watch,' I added approaching the firm from behind.

Drummer gave me his warm-hearted gangster glare and tacked a large whisky on to the round.

Willy was standing apart from his torpedoes deep in conversation with a geezer I knew by sight only too well. He had a bushy black beard and went with the Mercedes out in the car park.

When he heard my voice, Willy turned round and gave me the once over.

'Wotcha, Ed,' he rasped, grinning at me fondly. 'Where the 'ell yah bin? I fort yah'd be 'ere before us.'

'I took a fit in my head this morning and went for a hike over the moor,' I admitted.

'I 'spose the next fing yah gonna tell me is yah gone on the wagon and packed up chain-smokin',' he quipped good-naturedly.

I was sizing up his bearded companion.

'You going to introduce us?' I asked.

'Don 'tcha know each uvva?' Willy said in amazement. 'This 'ere's Fletcher Robinson, the bloke wot writes in the linens – Ed Nelson.'

I looked the bearded fellow up and down some more and said: 'No you're bloody well not.'

He said: 'Not what?'

I said: 'Fletcher Robinson.'

He said: 'Yes, I am.'

Willy said: ''Course'e is, Ed. 'oo the bleedin' 'ell is 'e if 'e ain't?'

I shrugged and passed a weary hand over my face.

'He can't be Fletcher Robinson,' I told Willy. 'Fletcher Robinson hasn't got a beard. I asked the girl on the switchboard at the *Western Morning News* only last week and she reckoned Robinson was clean shaven.' I pointed an accusing finger at the bushy beard. 'That fungus would take a month of Sundays to grow. So he must be an impostor, right?'

Willy looked him right in the eyes and said: 'Wotcha got to say abaht that, mate?'

'For God's sake keep your voices down,' the man whispered. 'There's a perfectly simple explanation.'

Salvatore handed us some drinks and we retired discreetly to a corner table.

'The thing is,' the bearded man began, in a slightly tremulous voice. 'I didn't want anyone around here to recognize me – I do come to Coombe Tracey and Muddicoombe from time to time to cover weddings and the local flower show for the paper, so there was a very good chance of my being spotted. I was doing this series of in-depth interviews with Selden, you see. He made it a condition of his co-operation that no one would be able to trace his whereabouts through me. It was a real scoop and no newspaper man worth his salt would pass up the opportunity of getting it. What he told me about his life of crime and his life in Dartmoor prison is going to make *Western Morning News* readers' hair stand on end.'

'So it's a false beard?' I put in.

'Yes, of course, it is,' he smiled. 'I stuck it on with cow gum.'

I reached across the table in a flash and plucked a handful of the fuzzy fun-fur out by the roots. He hardly even winced as it came away in my hand.

'Going around in a fake beard, when you're high on the list as a murder suspect is a bloody barmy thing to do,' I complained. 'If I'd run into you on any one of the dark and foggy nights I've been down here, I'd've filled you full of hot lead and asked questions after.'

'I'm sorry about that, Mr Nelson,' he simpered. 'I really am, but it was the only way I could think of to conceal my identity effectively.'

'Okay, okay,' I blustered. 'But if you were going around incognito how come you told the caravan park superintendent your real name?'

The geezer gazed at me in open-mouthed horror.

'He didn't tell you my name, did he?' he cried. 'I slipped him a fiver and swore him to secrecy.'

'Probably wasn't enough,' I grinned. 'That bloke charges people half a quid to tell them the time. All the same you haven't done too badly as an impostor.' But deep down I still wasn't satisfied, so I worked him a crafty one he might not have been expecting. 'How comes you're driving around in a dirty great Mercedes that you've reported got nicked?'

The puzzled look that came into his eyes seemed genuine enough.

'What do you mean?' he asked.

I said: 'Come off it, chum, the police have got it on their list of stolen vehicles.'

'When was that?'

'Months ago,' I came back at him sharply. 'I got the information from a mate of mine at the Yard.'

'Oh, yes,' he agreed. 'Now that you come to mention it my car was stolen from an Exeter car park some time back, but the police got it back within a week. Some youngsters had pinched it to go joy riding, I was told.'

'Not the kind of tool that'd interest a tearaway ter do any villainy in,' Willy opined. 'I fort that from the off when yah told me it'd gorn on the missin' list, Ed. Too conspicuous, know wot I mean?'

'Bloody typical,' I blurted out. 'The bird-brain bogey in charge of the police computer forgot to programme the sodding thing with the good news that you'd got it back.'

'Stands ter reason that's wot musta 'appened,' Willy agreed, and the geezer nodded.

'All right,' I said slowly, 'I suppose I'm going to have to take your word for it that you are Fletcher Robinson after all.'

As if to clinch matters he reached into his inside pocket and flashed his NUJ card.

'Sorry to disappoint you, Mr Nelson,' he chuckled.

Now that I'd got it straight who he really was there were a whole bunch of things I wanted to ask him. But the first drink had slipped down a treat and it seemed like a good idea to get in another round before I got down to the nitty-gritty.

I plodded back from the bar, trying to balance two glasses and a tankard of mild and bitter. Mild and bitter, as any drinking man will tell you, is the most ignorant beverage in the world and the fact that it seemed to be Fletcher Robinson's favourite tipple would have set me dead against him even if he hadn't caused me so much aggravation.

'So you were hiding out at Great Sourton to get your interviews with Axeman Selden?' I asked, as he sipped his disgusting beer.

He nodded and spoke in sad solemn tones.

'Peter was a wonderful person. There was a great deal more good in him than bad – I think he was far more a victim of society than an enemy of it and I have said so in my forthcoming series of articles on him.'

'Glad you've given 'im a decent write up,' Willy shook his head regretfully. ''E was the top peterman in the country. And I'm double pissed orf that in the last days of 'is life 'e was tryin' ter go bent on me.'

'What kind of fiddle are you on?' I asked Fletch casually. 'I mean to say, you can't make enough on a provincial rag to run a big beautiful Mercedes.'

'My father gave it to me, actually, as a twenty-first birthday present,' Fletch replied hotly. 'He's quite well off.'

'He'd need to be.'

The young journalist gave me a quelling glare.

'You needn't try to patronize me just because I've been working for the *Western Morning News*,' he snapped. 'I'll have you know that both the *Telegraph* and the *Mirror* have offered me jobs in the last week.'

'What else is new, kid?' I smirked. 'You're a great journalist, *okay*. I sussed you had your minces on Fleet Street when I first read your UFO guff. But take a tip from me, mate, you'd be wasted on the *Telegraph*. I'd go for the *Mirror*, if I was you.'

'That's just what I've decided,' Fletch informed me.

'You want to watch what you say, guv,' I warned Willy. 'Or this whipper snapper is gonna have your entire Soho set up blasted across the linens in four-inch headlines.'

It was only when the hack had scarpered that Willy told me the full strength of the situation. He reckoned the underworld weren't getting a fair shake in the national press. By setting up a special relationship with an enterprising young bloke like Fletcher Robinson, he was hoping to redress the balance. It was my secret belief he just wanted to get his picture in the papers – which is the kiss of death for gangsters – but just you try telling them.

With Robinson safely out of the light, I settled down to tell Willy about what a busy morning I'd had. How Sir Henry had given me my cards, and how Tiny had hunted down the saucer. He didn't seem as impressed as I'd hoped.

'Yeah, yeah,' he said. 'Axeman told me 'ow the Barrymores worked that fing before 'e snuffed it.'

'Then why was he frightened to death by it?' I asked in astonishment.

'Double dodgy, that is, ain't it?' mused Willy. 'All I can come up wiv is 'e nevva seen it workin' before. And when they got it goin', finkin' it was you they was 'avin' a right go at, poor ole Axeman got a terrible fright stuck on 'im. Fing is, Ed, that soddin' moorland is liable ter make anyone a bit jumpy, 'especially a geezer who is on the run from the nick. So when a dirty great flyin' saucer starts buzzin' arahnd on yah *Daily Mail*, yah liable ter go bonkers, which ain't all that tasty if yah raspberry tart is on the blink, anyway, see?'

'I see,' I nodded. 'That certainly makes a lot of sense. I fell to pieces the first time I saw it too. Nearly slid into a silent grave in Grimpen Mire and all.'

Willy turned his attention to the other part of my story.

'So 'Enry's finally tumbled wot a loser yah are, eh?' His mouth twisted into an ugly grin. '' Avin' yah clutterin' up 'is 'ouse all this time I'd a fort 'e'd a tumbled yah a lot sooner.'

'That,' I snorted, 'is not a very nice thing to say. I've busted a gut trying to put two and two together on the case and what thanks do I get for it? – bloody none!'

'Don't do yah nut, son,' Willy chortled. 'But yah can't exactly claim ter be the world's greatest private eye, nah can yah?'

'I may hide my light under a bushel,' I told him indignantly. 'But when the chips are down, I always come up with something. You sodding well know that as well as anyone. Now if it's all the same to you, Willy, I'll shove off up the Smoke and see how many new clients have been beating down my door this past fortnight.'

It was almost two o'clock already and I reckoned I'd have to get my skates on if I hoped to catch a train from Exeter that would pull into Paddington Station by opening time. I stood up to go.

'Sorry, son,' Willy drawled. 'I've gotta ask yah ter stick arahnd till termorrer. I've got a little job for yah to do ternight.'

'There's nothing to keep me here, Willy,' I assured him. 'I may have been able to do a spot of useful snooping for you while I was on Sir Henry's payroll, but I'm all washed up at Baskerville Hall, like I already told you.'

'I'm the best judge of that, Ed.' That all too familiar menacing glint came into his eyes. 'Wotcha gotta do nah is give yah friend Lestrade a bell at the Yard and tell 'im ter make a meet wiv us dahn 'ere ternight.'

'Lestrade,' I croaked, gazing at him in amazement. 'What on earth do you want a Scotland Yard detective inspector sticking his hooter into your affairs for?'

'I'll tell yah when I'm good an' ready,' snapped Willy, letting those steely blue eyes of his hold mine with a nasty threat of physical violence lurking in their depths.

'Oh, all right,' I groaned wearily. 'I'll do whatever you say. But I can't see Lestrade sirening all the way down the M4 just because you want to stand him a drink.'

'You can tell 'im we've got a nice little collar all stitched up for 'im,' Willy said evenly. 'We'll hand 'im the finger wots bin 'andling all the stately 'ome jobs and frow in the cold blooded killer inter the bargain. That oughta be enough ter bring 'im darhn 'ere a bit lively.'

'You've really rumbled the whole thing?' I asked in disbelief.

Willy nodded.

'Barrymore?'

The big tearaway tapped a finger against his nose in a familiar gesture, and a slow smile of real pleasure spread across his meaty face.

'That'd be tellin',' he said.

'And you can prove it?' I probed.

'Do me a favour and stop rabbitin',' he growled. 'Just get on the blower to the filth like I told yah, son.'

CHAPTER TWENTY NINE

'Just the bloke I'm looking for,' Bill Lestrade chuckled down the wire, before I'd hardly passed the time of day with him. 'Where've you been holed up, Ed? My lads have been wearing out a lot of shoe leather looking for you.'

'How come?' I groaned. 'What are you trying to stitch me up with this time?'

'Just want to have a little rabbit with you about the reward lolly you got off Bert Fagley for the return of Lady Leach's tomfoolery, that's all,' he told me in that friendly tone of voice the cops use when they are about to put the arm on you. 'We lifted poor old Second Thoughts Steegmuller, bang to rights, papering the town with his whack. Barclays sent us a list of the serial numbers of the two grand in new twenties – I didn't reckon even a twit like you would accept freshly minted reward money.'

I knew that if Lestrade had managed to squeeze a statement out of Second Thoughts, he would have changed his mind in it so often, it would have as much chance of standing up in court as a drunken Irishman. I made a mental note about handing that poxy shyster, Bert Fagley, a knuckle-sandwich the next time I bumped into him –but played it cunning with Lestrade.

'Someone's having a right go at you, Bill,' I said into the phone. 'I never heard of no Lady Leach let alone a whisper about her having her tomfoolery half-inched.'

'I've got the goods on you this time, Ed,' the inspector replied aimably. 'Fagley has agreed to go into the witness box.'

That was a whopper, if ever I heard one. Acme Alliance would never allow him to give evidence – despite their toffee-nosed aura of respectability they needed layabout private eyes like me to do their dirty work for them. Without layabout private eyes like me around to do their dirty work for them their balance sheet would go on the blink.

'See you in court then,' I sneered. 'But you'll have to feel my collar first.'

Lestrade chuckled, but he'd been around long enough to know when he was on a sticky wicket.

'See, the thing is, Ed.' There was a strong element of climb down in his tone now. 'I wouldn't give a sod normally. Them insurance companies are right con artists and they deserve everything they've got coming to them. But the proper conditions for collecting the reward dough on the emeralds weren't stuck to. We got to have a face behind bars before an insurance company can pay out. You know that as well as I do, old mate.'

It was my turn to chuckle.

'I hear you, Bill,' I said. 'You're not saying anything that interests me much. But I've got something for you that's gonna interest you a lot.'

'What?'

'Deal?' I said.

'What kind of deal?'

'Forget about the hot reward lolly for Lady Leach's emeralds and let Second Thoughts go,' I told him straight. 'And I'll hand you a murderer on a silver plate.'

'I don't like it,' he replied after a short pause. 'Who is it?'

'That'd be telling,' I said. 'But he's running a profitable little sideline in stately home burglaries as well as bumping off people he doesn't like. We got a deal about dropping the reward money nonsense or haven't we?'

'Maybe.'

'No "maybes" inspector – yes or no, or I'll hang up and come to some cosy little arrangement with the local Chief Constable down here.'

There was an even longer pause, before he came up with the goods.

'All right, Ed, but if you bugger me about . . .'

'Take out an open warrant and get down here with a sergeant,' I interrupted him. 'Just a sergeant, got it? – Not the entire heavy mob, okay?'

'All right, all right,' Lestrade snapped testily. 'Do you mind telling me where exactly it is you want me to come?'

'Devonshire,' I replied airily. 'Village called Coombe Tracey. I'll meet you in the local pub. It's called the Devil's Stone Inn.'

'Where?' he shouted.

I told him again.

'Blimey,' he gasped. 'That's a bit of a shlap, isn't it?'

I said: 'Think big, Bill, there's probably a promotion in it,' and hung up

With the possible exception of stitching up tea-leaves with a lagging for some tickle they didn't do, there are few pastimes the CID enjoy more than fraternizing with tearaways in boozers. Bill Lestrade had stitched up more than his fair share of tea-leaves and had bent his elbow in the company of some of the biggest villains the British Isles have thrown up in the post-war years. It was Lestrade who busted up the Sabini racecourse razor gang in the '40s and put the block on them wheedling protection money out of bookies; he captured the London airport gold bullion robbers in the early '50s and was largely responsible for wiping out an international firm of Maltese ponces who had been engaged in the white slave traffic for three generations. His word was his bond and he was the only Detective Inspector at Scotland Yard that tearaways tipped their hats to.

I found him where I expected to find him, at six o'clock that evening, standing shoulder to shoulder with Willy Paradis, Drummer Bill and the two pilot fish in the Devil's Stone Inn at Coombe Tracey.

'You must have got your skates on, Bill,' I said loudly as I bore down on them.

All heads turned and lips smiled, but the eyes remained

ice cold.

'Hello there, Ed,' Lestrade blustered jovially. 'I flew down to Exeter, actually. Only way to get here on time. Pleasant surprise running into so many old friends off our patch.'

'Yeah,' laughed Willy. 'Just goes ter show wot a small world it is, when yah come right dahn ter it. Me an' the lads fort we'd pop dahn 'ere for a bit of trout fishin' an' who should we run inter but me ole mate, Ed.'

Lestrade gave him a sidelong glance but let it go and ordered another round of drinks.

Half an hour later Willy glanced at his bejewelled gold watch, and signalled down the bar to Drummer, Salvatore and Joe. They drained their glasses and slipped silently out of the pub.

'I fink it's abaht time we was movin' along,' he said, turning to Lestrade and me.

'Where to?' I asked.

Lestrade let out a throaty chuckle.

'So it's you who's master-minding this little collar, is it, Willy?' he asked.

'Not so's you'd notice, Bill,' replied Willy. 'It's Ed's caper from start ter finish. I'm just along for the ride.'

'I suppose it would be churlish of me to ask what's in it for you?' Lestrade murmured pleasantly.

'Yah know me motto, Inspector,' Willy winked. 'Justice 'as gotta be done and seen ter be done, right?'

'You're a comical fella,' laughed Lestrade. 'Nearly as comical as our mate Ed, here. Lead the way, it promises to be an interesting evening.'

'You still haven't told me where we're going,' I complained to Willy as we went out into the car park.

'We're gonna shoot over ter me caravan,' said Willy.

'What? Great Stourton?' I exclaimed incredulously. 'I reckon it might be favourite if I pop back in the pub and lash out on a bottle of Scotch.' I turned on my heel and was about to dive back into the saloon bar when Willy's voice stopped me in my tracks.

'There's plenty of booze laid on, Ed,' he laughed. 'Yah don't need to worry abaht that.'

'I polished off most of your bottle of Bell's the other day,' I pointed out anxiously. 'And I haven't got a single drop of Hankey Bannister's left.'

'I got stocked up,' he rasped. 'Nah stop muckin' abaht an' let's get this soddin' show on the road.'

I'd've given a lot not to be there, but I was there and there was no way I could odds seeing the thing out. Lestrade's sergeant, a big beefy flat foot, whose name turned out to be Tom Oakshott, cruised over in an ordinary looking Rover. It had a hopped up Corvette Sting Ray engine under its smug middle class bonnet, if I knew anything about Lestrade's tactics.

'Who's going with who?' asked Lestrade.

'I'm not all that stuck on police cars as yah know, Bill,' chuckled Willy. 'But I'll come wiv yah in the Rover and Ed can get on our *Daily Mail*.'

'Be a nice change to be following a police car,' I ventured half-heartedly. 'But I've been to Great Sourton so often, I'd know my way blindfolded.'

'But me caravan ain't at Great Sourton no more, yah berk,' Willy explained, beginning to lose patience with me. 'Just belt up and do wot I say, right?'

'Okay,' I grunted and climbed into the Hillman.

Willy's hounds were long gone in the Jag. It wasn't a lengthy or difficult drive. The two car convoy took the main drag out of Coombe Tracey towards Baskerville Hall. Just past Sir Henry's driveway, the car in front of me started to slow down and began winking its indicator for a left turn. I knew there wasn't a crossroads, but had a vague memory of a track that led into a spooky wood. The police car turned down it and I bumped cautiously along behind.

About a hundred yards down the track, the vast ghostly bulk of Willy's fibreglass caravan sprang into view in our headlights. The sleek XJS was parked beside it and friendly orange lights were winking in the windows.

It may have been a monster as caravans go, but when four tearaways, two burly cops and little me were all squeezed in there, it was a case of elbows in and don't try any sudden moves. I wasn't sure what Willy had in mind, but if Lestrade had alerted the local nick and we found ourselves surrounded we'd be caught in there like stoats in a sack. I didn't reckon he had, but you can never be sure about such things.

The tzar of Soho enthroned himself in the best chair and waved Lestrade to the second best. The rest of us crammed ourselves on to the sofa as best we could. Drummer did the honours with the whisky bottle.

'I've brung yah dahn 'ere a bit early as it 'appens,' Willy apologized. 'Sir 'Enry's invite to the Stapletons is for seven, but I didn't want ter miss anyfing if they showed up early, see.'

'Clear as Guinness to me,' I remarked mystified.

'We're gonna 'ave a bit of a ear'ole in on their dinner party chit-chat, that's wot,' Willy announced with a twinkle in his eyes. 'Don'tcha remember that little bug I slipped Sir 'Enry's ancestor?'

'Modern technology is a wonderful thing,' I sighed. 'Where's your receiver?'

'Out in the kitchen,' he said and glanced at Salvatore. 'Nip out and get it, son. We'd better get tuned in.'

'Okay, boss,' piped the little Italian waiter who had gone to the bad and stepped gingerly over the mass of legs extended across the floor. He returned in a moment with a small, hand-held receiver and gave it to Willy. There was an aerial sticking out of the top of it and a thin wire with a two pronged plug dangling out of the bottom.

'Right,' said Willy, pointing at a small tape recorder resting on a side-table. 'All we gotta do is stick this little plug in this 'ole 'ere and press this button 'ere and the next fing yah know we'll be in business.' He suited the actions to his words and then winked at Lestrade. 'I reckon you're gonna be 'avin' a bitta company on yah journey back ter the Yard, Bill – all we gotta do is wait.'

'I reckon I ought to get myself one of those contraptions sometime,' I said. 'It wouldn't half save me a lot of keyhole work.'

We sat around boozing for about three-quarters of an hour. Then suddenly voices started to come out of the receiver. Willy leaned over quickly and pressed a button on the tape recorder. Cathedral silence descended upon us as we leaned forward to listen.

Sir Henry's voice came over the receiver with bell like clarity – so clearly could we make out his words that he might just as well have been right there in the caravan with us.

He sounded angry. 'Are you trying to blackmail me?' he snarled.

CHAPTER THIRTY

Nobody moved a muscle in the caravan, not even to carry a glass to their lips. We sat there frozen, like a waxwork tableau in Madame Tussaud's chamber of horrors, listening in jaw-sagging bewilderment to the showdown Willy had sussed would take place up at the Baskerville corral that night. How he'd worked it out was, like everything else, beyond the wit of my addled brain. But it probably had a lot to do with the profound ability that Willy had for putting two and two together when it came to anything to do with skullduggery. He had a better understanding of the criminal mind than any prison shrink and was living proof of the old adage about setting a tea-leaf to catch a tea-leaf.

Giles Stapleton pooh-poohed the suggestion that he was sticking the black on the young baronet.

'I am merely suggesting a mutually beneficial arrangement.' His voice came over the receiver heavy with menace. 'It might interest you to know that I took a number of flashlight snaps of the van and its contents when I drove down to the quarry last week. The police would, I believe, find the evidence quite conclusive.'

'Conclusive of what, you fool?' barked Sir Henry.

'You know very well *what*,' Giles foxed. 'A plot to scare the neighbourhood – and finish off one or two of the neighbours.'

Barrymore's rich baritone cut in lamely saying: 'He can't have seen inside. It was locked.'

'My dear man,' Giles came back at him. 'Picking a common or garden six-lever Chubb padlock presents no problem to a man of my experience.'

'A jemmy is quicker than a hairpin,' I muttered.

Willy gave me a quelling glare and put a finger to his lips.

Eliza came over the air with an over-emotional: 'I warned you we should have been more careful, John. I knew that we'd been found out when we saw those tyre marks on the track down to the quarry.'

'Well, it's too late now,' her husband responded gloomily.

'Lovely stuff,' commented Lestrade. 'Better than that whispering grass Shaw Taylor on TV.'

'Ssssh!' everybody went at him at once.

'It's awright,' chortled Willy. 'We can 'ear every dicky bird they say, but they can't 'ear us, see? But I reckon we'd better keep shtoom or we might miss the juicy bits.'

Sir Henry piped up again, still apparently seething with anger.

'You won't get away with this, old boy,' he sneered. 'If you think the police will take the word of a bounder, like you, against that of a member of the aristocracy you have another think coming. You would be well advised to leave my house this minute, otherwise you may force me to take desperate measures.'

Margaret's dulcet tones were heard for the first time.

'Don't be so pompous, Henry,' she purred. 'Do you seriously believe that your position and title give you a licence to commit cold-blooded *murder*?'

'That girl has got a lot to learn,' I laughed. 'The upper crust are very adept at bumping off the lower orders and getting away with it. They have enjoyed the sport of shooting peasants for centuries and the cops have been turning a blind eye to it for just as long.'

'Shutcha face, Ed,' snapped Willy. 'The real goods are comin' up any minute.'

I slugged some whisky, lit a fag and listened.

'How exactly do you propose to tie me in with the death of Sir Charles or even Selden, come to that?' Sir Henry inquired.

'Easily,' scoffed Giles. 'The Barrymores are not going to

cover up for you if it means incriminating themselves.' He added as an afterthought: 'But I must admit that there is one thing that puzzles me.'

'What, may I ask, is that?'

'What in the world induced you to invite a private detective down here?'

'It wasn't my idea,' growled the baronet. 'Mortimer had fixed it up by the time I flew in from Kuwait. I checked up on Nelson and discovered that he had a serious drinking problem and a poor reputation as an investigator, so I decided to bluff it out. I even sent myself an anonymous threatening letter to make it appear that I was in danger too – quite an ingenious ruse, wouldn't you agree?'

'Thanks a lot, chum,' I clipped. 'I'll get you for that.'

Lestrade roared with laughter and slapped his thigh.

'Clear case of malicious slander, Ed,' he bellowed.

'Yeah,' agreed Willy, 'the greater the troof the greater the libel. Butcha can rely on me and the lads ter stand up for yah in court, son.'

Sir Henry went on to complain about the botched job the Barrymores had made of scaring me away with the UFO. My mates in the caravan sniggered.

'He thinks himself so high and mighty,' snarled Barrymore down the intercom. 'He wouldn't think of soiling his hands with his own dirty work.'

His wife backed him up.

'He hired us to work that machine when he was last on leave. But he didn't talk about killing anyone with it – just frightening a few people.'

'Thank you!' laughed Giles. 'Very interesting.'

That gave Eliza Barrymore the dead needle.

'But you won't get away with it either,' she shrilled. 'Peter told us how you were the biggest thief in Devonshire. You helped his escape from Princetown, didn't you? You have master-minded all the big stately home burglaries in the county and you needed him to blow the safes for you.'

''Ad ter 'ave 'im out to blow the peter dahn Lafter 'All,'
Willy nodded. 'After Frankland told that skin and blister
of 'is abaht 'ow much gold 'e'd got stashed away in it.'

'The beautiful Margaret is in on it too, is she?' I asked
with interest. The same thing seemed to have occurred to
Sir Henry.

'You were just after my money, were you, Margaret?' he
said.

'I wouldn't have minded your body thrown in,' she
returned saucily.

'She made up to all the stately home owners,' Barrymore informed him, 'and cased the joints for her brother.'

Then the baronet got all riled up and started yelling the
roof off.

'You're not getting away with this!'

Suddenly a wild hullabaloo came over the receiver. It
sounded like a scuffle and a lot of panicky voices were
talking at once.

'Watch out, for Christ's sake.' . . . 'He's got a gun.'

'You're not getting a brass farthing out of me,' howled
Sir Henry. 'I'm quite prepared to put a bullet right between your eyes instead.'

'He won't pull the trigger,' grated Giles. 'He hasn't got
the guts.'

He got his reply loud and clear – Bang! Bang! – two
pistol shots rang out of Willy's portable receiver.

Lestrade sprang to his feet, snatched the cassette out
of the tape recorder and was out of the caravan like a dose
of salts, belting hell-for-leather down the path towards
Baskerville Hall with his burly sergeant hard on his
heels.

'That's it, lads,' snapped Willy. 'The jig is up. Get the
motor hooked on the front of this bloody fing – we're goin'
'ome!'

'Do me a favour, Willy,' I bleated. 'Surely you're not
going to leave me stranded out here, in the middle of
nowhere, all on my tod?'

'Sorry, son,' he said, almost apologetically. 'When

shooters start goin' orf all over the place, I 'ave it away on me toes a bit lively, right?'

'Thanks a lot, mate,' I groaned. 'You're a real pal.'

'Pop dahn the 'Ide Away soon as yah get back on the manor and I'll lay a 'ole bottle of 'Ankey Bannister's on yah on the 'ouse, son.'

The tzar of Soho climbed into the front passenger seat of the Jaguar XJS and his henchman, Drummer Bill, settled himself behind the steering wheel, as though squeezing his massive body into a tight shoe. Then the engine roared and the whole kit and caboodle went careering off down the cart track in a shower of mud and small stones. I stood there watching until it disappeared from sight, then I got into the Hillman and drove slowly round to Baskerville Hall, feeling as downcast and lumbered as a pissed Liverpool soccer fan in a four-ale bar at closing time on cup final night when his team has lost the match away from home.

It turned out that the first shot that Sir Henry got off only winged Giles in his right shoulder and the second had knocked a few quid off the value of a portrait of Admiral Sir Auberon Baskerville, whose ancestral mug shot was second along the rogue's gallery that festooned the dining-room wall.

Everybody looked at me as I strolled into the room, but nobody said anything. Eliza was sobbing her heart out in a corner and Margaret sat ashen-faced in an armchair, with a nerve end twitching uncontrollably in her left cheek. Her brother, Giles, sat bolt upright in the chair opposite her clutching his bullet wound. Lestrade was shouting down the blower at some poor copper at the local nick.

'I want an ambulance and a Black Maria up here at Baskerville Hall immediately!' he bellowed. 'Who am I? I am Lestrade of the Yard, that's who!'

The only person in the room who seemed to be having a good time was the hammy old butler. He was shaking handcuffed fists at the burly sergeant and protesting his innocence with the vehement eloquence of a seasoned advocate. It was a performance of which he could be justly proud, even if the flow of words added up to a load of old cobblers.

My eyes scanned the room for Sir Henry. He was conspicuous by his absence.

Lestrade issued one final dire threat into the blower, then slammed the receiver down and rounded on me.

'Where is he, Ed?' he demanded to know. 'Come on out with it, or you'll regret the day you were born!'

'I've already been regretting that for some years now, Bill,' I replied amiably. 'What are you on about?'

'Sir Henry,' he rasped. 'You know where he'd go and it's no good denying it.'

It was unusual for Lestrade to use that old copper's ploy of threatening innocent by-standers with terrible consequences if they failed to cough up information they didn't have.

'What's up?' I grinned. 'Flown the coop, has he?'

'That's right,' he snapped. 'And you've been around here long enough to know where he would hide out.'

'Don't ask me, Bill,' I said. 'Dartmoor is a big place – he could be anywhere.'

The inspector frowned thoughtfully and gave me a slightly apologetic smile.

'The little bugger did a bunk out of the French windows just as we came through the door,' he explained. 'He still had the gun in his hand and he disappeared into the night before we could nab him. I've put out his description and an all points alarm, but I don't think there's much we can do before daybreak.'

'You're right there, Bill,' I agreed. 'The Moor is a treacherous place even in the daytime, but at night it's a death trap.'

A little later the meat wagon pulled up outside the front door with an ambulance and for five or ten minutes the house was full of policemen.

Lestrade ordered them about like an army drill-sergeant.

'Take him, her and her down to the station and hold

them overnight,' he snapped, jabbing a forefinger at Margaret, Eliza and the butler.

'Wot be the charges, zur?' asked a weedy little constable, who looked not much more than fifteen years old.

'Don't ask questions, you snotty-nosed little squit,' blazed the man in charge of everyone's destiny, including mine. 'Just hold them for questioning, pending further inquiries. I'll be around to charge them with something in the morning.'

Two little peak-capped ambulance men appeared in the doorway. Lestrade's deadly forefinger bore down on Giles like the sword of Damocles.

'Get him to Tavistock hospital and dig that bullet out of his shoulder.' He glared at the uniformed sergeant from the local lock-up. 'I want a guard put on him day and night till the quack says he's fit to be discharged.'

He glanced around at the gawking policemen. 'Now get a bloody move on, will you? I want this place cleared of bodies in double-quick time, I've work to do, even if you haven't.'

Strong young hands grasped the haul of malefactors and escorted them out of the room. John Barrymore continued to protest his innocence all the way across the hall, out of the front door and into the meat wagon. Eliza kept up her sobs the same distance. Margaret shook a fresh-faced constable's hand off her arm and glided ahead of him across the hall with her nose in the air in haughty disdain.

The ambulance men strapped Giles to a stretcher and humped him out of the room. A moment or two later the lot of them went sirening off down the drive.

'Phew!' sighed Lestrade, mopping his brow with a pocket handkerchief. 'It's all go in this game, Ed, I can tell you. And I'm getting too flipping old for it.'

'I know how you feel,' I sympathized. 'So what's your next move going to be?'

Lestrade sat down at the dining-table and rested his chin wearily on a clenched fist.

'What I could do with is a good kip, Ed,' he said. 'But I

suppose there'll be no sleep for me tonight – even though, as you say, there is no point in mounting a search party to hunt down Sir Henry till sunrise.'

'There isn't any sunrise in the West Country,' I told him bleakly. 'The sky is always slate grey and it pisses down with rain, day and night, from the middle of August until late April. The only way you can actually tell day from night is a very slight lightening of the sky and the postman delivers the morning mail.'

He stood up abruptly and said: 'Do you think a man who is on the run from a possible murder charge would mind if we had a swig of his whisky?'

'Tricky question, that,' I beamed. 'But I reckon we could just about risk it.'

'Good lad,' he beamed back at me. 'Lead the way – I imagine you know where he keeps it.'

I led the way out of the room – the inspector paused for a whispered conversation with his sergeant at the door – then followed me into the drawingroom. The dying embers of a fire were still glowing in the grate and shortly after I'd stoked it up with logs a merry blaze was licking flames up the chimney. Bill Lestrade and I lounged in the fireside easy-chairs with whisky tumblers clenched in our fists and our legs stretched out before us like a pair of Old Bailey judges at the Athenæum club.

'This is the life,' the inspector mused cheerfully, casting a beady eye over our surroundings. 'Beats me why a bloke who's got all this has to go around murdering people.'

I swallowed a mouthful of whisky and puffed at my cigarette.

'He had to bump off Sir Charles to get it,' I replied thoughtfully. 'The upper classes are a bunch of loonies, anyway. Did I ever tell you about the old Indian army Brigadier I did a little work for once?'

Lestrade sipped his whisky appreciatively and sank even deeper into his luxurious armchair and said: 'No, Ed, I don't think you ever did.'

'Right silly old bugger he was,' I said. 'But he reckoned

that when he was out in Calcutta, or some place like that, when the British Raj was still going strong, he was put in charge of the officers' mess, see? Well, anyway, according to him the young subalterns used to get pissed and take potshots out of the officers' mess window at the natives as they took their evening dip in the Ganges. The old Brigadier told me he tried to stamp the unwholesome practice out – but they just laughed in his face and went right on doing it. Some nights the river ran red with blood and floating bodies clogged up the shipping lanes, apparently. Right bunch of loonies, like I said, sons of dukes and earls, most of 'em, according to the Brigadier.'

'Still,' Lestrade sighed contentedly, 'Baskerville stocks a decent brand of whisky – a man who stocks a decent brand of whisky can't be all bad.'

'You've got a point there, Bill,' I agreed. 'It isn't Hankey Bannister's, but it's slipping down a treat – let's have a spot more?'

'Just a drop,' he said and handed me his glass. 'Did I ever tell you about the time I went around to Tools Gunstone's gaff to sort him out for beating up his old woman?' he asked when I returned with our replenished tumblers.

'No, Bill,' I said, 'I don't think you ever did.'

'Well, I went round there on account of the neighbours had phoned the station to complain about her screams. Sounded like he was half killing her – but when I barged into the house and tried to restrain him, she only beaned me with a rolling-pin for interfering.'

'Jush goesh t'show yah,' I slurred. 'There'sh no doin' shum people any favoursh.'

And so an extremely pleasant hour or four was spent guzzling whisky and swapping corny old anecdotes about days long past when fun loving tearaways carved each other up with open razors, and little old ladies seldom got mugged on their way home from the Post Office with their old age pension allowance.

'Robbery with violence merchants got the cat, and kill-

243

ers got topped,' Lestrade pointed out nostalgically. 'Everyone knew where they stood, right?'

'Shtandards are fallin' off,' I agreed. 'If yah bump anyone off nowadaysh yah gotta good chansh of windin' up with two yearsh probashion.'

For reasons best known to himself the crafty old bleeder never once got around to the hairy topic that was upper-most in both our minds. But if he didn't want to talk about the shady goings on around Baskerville Hall, neither did I.

The good whisky overcame us eventually, as good whisky can when you drink enough of it in front of a blazing log fire, and we both passed out.

CHAPTER THIRTY ONE

The first thing I saw when my eyelids flickered open a few hours later was a dried soup stain, shaped like the map of Burmah, on a grey waistcoat. I nearly threw up.

A heavy hand was roughing up my shoulder and a rasping voice was bawling. 'Rise and shine, me lucky lad. Hands off cocks and on socks!'

I averted my eyes from the soup stain and looked up into the ugly mug of Lestrade's detective sergeant.

'Be gentle with me, mate,' I pleaded. 'My head is made of glass.'

'Got to get cracking, Ed,' he shouted. 'Reinforcements from Tavistock are already scouring the Moor for Sir Henry and the inspector says we've got to look sharp – it wouldn't look good if they captured him before we got on the scene.'

'What time is it?' I groaned.

'Five-thirty,' he said. 'Now, come on, look lively.'

I eased myself gingerly out of the chair and walked unsteadily towards the door. Lestrade was hanging about in the hall in a pair of Sir Henry's wellington boots and a heavy duty weatherproof.

'Hello there, Ed,' he greeted me briskly. 'Ready for the fray?'

'No,' I told him bluntly, 'I need some black coffee.'

'No time for that,' he chuckled. 'Grab a pair of them wellies by the coat rack and let's be on our way.'

'Do you mind if I have a piss first?' I asked.

'Okay,' he snapped, 'but if you're not ready in two minutes I'm going without you.'

I dashed into the downstairs lavatory, had a nice long pee, splashed some cold water on my face at the corner

245

wash-basin, dabbed myself dry with a hand towel and then rejoined Lestrade in the hall still needing a shit.

A thin veil of drizzle was weeping from the leaden sky as we left the house. It was the kind of soggy stuff that soaks right through to the marrow of your bones. But for these parts you couldn't really say it was raining – locals would've called it a fine day. A white woolly mist was rolling across the Moor as far as the eye could see. It wasn't like those cosy banks of pea-soup that blanket London from time to time – it was thin and wispy and only waist high, almost like shifting snow drifts swirling about in a light but turbulent wind.

Armed with a stout knobbly walking-stick that he'd borrowed, together with the rest of his kit, from the hall stand, Lestrade strode resolutely off along the yew alley towards the wicket gate that gave on to the Moor. The sergeant and I trotted along at his heels like obedient Jack Russell terriers.

We paused for a moment at the edge of the Moor and scanned the horizon. Far off in the distance a long string of black uniformed figures were edging their way like giant ants through thigh deep mist.

'That'll be the Tavistock heavy mob,' said Lestrade, pointing his walking-stick at them. 'Any notions about where we should start our own search, Ed?'

'Only a right berk would stay out in the open in this rotten weather,' I replied gloomily. 'If Sir Henry was using his loaf he'd be long gone from here. Probably hitched a lift to Exeter and caught the London train – fast akip in a nice warm bed in the Savoy hotel by now I expect.'

'I don't think so,' Lestrade replied. 'I found his wallet on his bedside-table, so I doubt if he has enough money on him to get far.'

'The rich don't need readies,' I snapped. 'Their tick is good anywhere in the world.'

'He's still around here somewhere,' the inspector persisted. 'We had road blocks on all the routes away from here last night.'

'Have it your way,' I shrugged. 'I suppose we could try old Barrymore's pantechnicon – it's hidden in a cave at the bottom of Grimpen tor.'

'Where's that?' the sergeant put in.

'Bloody miles,' I told him. 'Follow me and for Christ's sake keep to the bridle-path, if you fall in the mire it's curtains.'

The drizzle was letting up a bit and by the time we'd picked our way about half a mile along the track the sky had lightened a little and a ray of watery sunshine suddenly peeped out of the clouds. The mist cleared a little and we were able to see our way more clearly.

Then suddenly, some way off to our right, came the sound of someone approaching. I yanked my trusty .38 out of my armpit holster and Lestrade pulled an even bigger gun out of his raincoat pocket.

'Quick, lads,' he whispered. 'Hit the deck.'

We fanned out from the path and fell forward as one man, face first into the bog.

I glanced up at the heavens and muttered: 'Thanks a lot, pal.'

The dull footsteps grew closer and closer through the bracken and each of us looked one to the other pale with fear but also exultant at the prospect of capturing Sir Henry, without the Tavistock heavy mob getting so much as a look in. I cocked my shooter and held it at the ready. There came the sharp click of Lestrade doing the same.

Then suddenly out of a bank of fog sprang a gigantic hound. He landed just a few feet away from us, and stood there wagging his tail furiously and barking.

'Don't shoot, Bill,' I called to Lestrade. 'It's only my old friend, Tiny. He's as harmless as a kitten.'

'Well, he don't bloody look it,' growled the inspector, getting to his knees and still pointing his gun at the dog.

'He's okay,' I insisted. 'Belongs to a friend of mine.'

My friend now put in her appearance, out of the mist, shrilling her familiar orders at the dog.

'Heel, Tiny, heel. Bad dog, come here when I tell you!'

I introduced Laura Lyons to Lestrade and his sergeant, then asked her what she was doing out on the Moor at such an unearthly hour of the morning.

'Oh, Tiny and I often go for a long walk at first light,' she replied breezily. 'It gives me inspiration for my writing.'

'That a fact?' I drawled.

'My God, Ed,' she said, taking in my appearance. 'You look terrible.'

'Sticking your face in the bog when you've got a raging hangover doesn't make you feel good,' I assured her.

She let that go and asked us what we were doing on the Moor.

'Hunting down a desperate killer,' snapped Lestrade.

'Good heavens,' she screeched. 'Who?'

'Sir Henry Baskerville,' he told her. 'He has murdered two people already. He is armed and will kill again if he is not apprehended.'

Tiny came over wagging a warm greeting and I gave Laura a sly look which I hoped she interpreted as meaning she should say as little as possible. She seemed to get the message.

'How dreadful,' she gasped. 'Is there anything I can do to help?'

'Very probably, miss,' Lestrade replied stiffly. 'You obviously know your way over the Moor far better than we do – I would be very much obliged if you would take us to the cave where the Barrymores have hidden their van. I am pretty sure that that is where we will find Sir Henry holed-up.'

'If Sir Henry is anywhere on the Moor I'm sure I can lead you to him,' she said.

'You mean you know where he is?' the sergeant asked gruffly.

'Well, no, I wouldn't say that,' she smiled. 'But if Tiny can pick up his scent we'll track him down in no time.'

'Clever girl,' I congratulated her. 'Let's get cracking.'

'But we need something of Sir Henry's before Tiny

knows which scent he's supposed to be following,' she pointed out wisely. 'An article of clothing or something. We'd better pop back to the Hall and dig something out.'

We all looked at each other disconsolately, not fancying the long walk back to the base, and then out of the blue I came up with the answer.

'Bill,' I cried, 'you're wearing his weather proof raincoat. That still ought to have some of Sir Henry's sniff left on it.'

'By George, you're right, Ed,' he came back at me excitedly. 'Better still there's an old cloth cap here in the pocket. That ought to smell of Sir Henry to high heaven.'

Laura plucked the cap from his outstretched hand and wafted it under Tiny's outsized hooter.

'Follow, boy,' she commanded him. 'Follow!'

The hound sniffed the cloth cap as appreciatively as a beautiful girl sniffs a red rose from her lover and then he sniffed around on the ground for a bit before taking off ahead of us along the narrow path. We followed close behind him in single file at a jog trot. The exhilaration of the chase threw off my hangover and I was no longer worried about having skipped my morning shit. Even a face full of bog seemed a small price to pay if Tiny's fat nose tracked down our quarry.

We made good progress for about a mile, then suddenly Tiny stopped dead in his tracks and started sniffing this way and that, obviously puzzled about which way to go.

'Grimpen Mire,' Laura remarked flatly, pointing a finger a few yards to our left. 'Watch your step, Inspector – if you fall in there you will never set foot on dry land again.'

Tiny trotted over to the edge of the mire and sniffed around in a clump of cotton grass. Then he snapped up something in his huge jaws that I thought at first was a stick. But when he strolled over and dropped it at Laura's feet our eyes bulged like organ stops. It was a big black gun – a Luger automatic. I had never seen Sir Henry's shooter, but this had to be it. Who else's could it possibly be?

Lestrade reached into his breast pocket and produced a pencil and from another pocket he produced a transparent polythene bag.

'Forensic will tell us a lot about this little tool,' he said, dropping to his knees.

'He must have thrown it away when he fell in the mire,' I suggested. 'He'd need both hands to save himself – I know, mate. I've taken a mud-bath in there.'

Lestrade shoved the pencil up the barrel of the gun and lifted it from the ground. 'Perhaps you're right, Ed,' he said as he placed the gun carefully into the polythene bag.

'On the other hand, sir,' the sergeant volunteered. 'He may have just thrown it away in his flight, thinking that it would sink into the mire, never to be found again.'

'Good thinking, Sergeant,' Lestrade complimented him.

Something was still bothering Tiny. He bounded around to the far side of the stretch of slimy mire we stood beside and started barking frantically. Laura went round to see what he'd found and called to us to come and look. Just below the surface of the green, quivering bog there was a dark shape that looked like the shoulders and outstretched arms of a man.

Lestrade was a tough old Cockney cop, who seldom showed his emotions, but he let out a gasp of horror and took several steps back from the edge of the mire. The sergeant did the same – I just stood there frozen with fear. Young Laura, who was used to the ways of the Moor and knew all too well the terrible fate that awaited those foolhardy enough to stray from the bridle-path, stood her ground and gazed at the dark outline inquisitively.

'I don't think it's a body,' she ventured at last. 'If it was it would have sunk without trace. Find me a stick and I'll fish it out.'

Without speaking Lestrade handed the sergeant Sir Henry's knobbly walking-stick that he'd borrowed. Under Laura's guidance he fished about in the slime and at last came up with a muddy rag that might have been a man's hacking jacket. A dip in a nearby moorland stream washed a little of the mud off it and revealed that it was indeed a jacket. It was one that I had seen Sir Henry wearing.

'That clinches it,' I said. 'The poor sod has sunk in the mire. What a muddy way to go.'

'Not so fast,' said Lestrade. 'How do we know that he didn't throw his jacket into the mire just so that it would look as though he'd gone under?'

'Because,' explained Laura bossily, 'the jacket wouldn't have sunk at all unless there was a man in it – it would simply have floated on the surface, for several days anyway. He must, somehow, have struggled out of it in a vain attempt to save himself.'

Lestrade let out a long heavy sigh, but he wasn't happy. The CID never are happy unless they've got the corpse of the victim on a slab in the morgue and the face that did it behind bars – or at a pinch the murderer laid out on a slab alongside his victim. All other permutations are looked upon as highly sus and the file remains open for ever and ever.

But the hundred-strong heavy mob from the Tavistock Constabulary hadn't come up with anything either - so that, as they say, was that.

It had been a bloody awful caper and I was glad to be shot of it at last. I might still be able to get my fee out of Sir Henry's executors, if I kicked up a fuss about it. But I vowed as I raised the first double Scotch to my lips in the buffet car of the express to Paddington, that never again would I take on a case that was likely to involve me in more travel than a quid on the meter of a black London cab.